Copyright 2017

All rights reserved. No part (reproduced in any form or by an) written permission of the author.

All characters in this publication are fictitious and any resemblance to real persons, living or dead is purely coincidental.

Any electrical activities described in these books are also fictitious and should never be attempted in real life.

Second edition July 2020

Dear Venetia
Hope you enjoy reading!
Roney xx

For Karim, Xav, Alex and Lucy.
Thank you for putting up with all my mad ideas.

Preface

The metal hulk nose-dived and fell like a stone, taking the side of the roof with it. Then, as it hit the floor, its fuel tank exploded on the road below. A shockwave pulsed the air and then hollowed out in a ghastly, empty silence.

My reason for living had gone. My fragile house of cards collapsed. I was so paper thin that I nearly floated off the edge, diving hopelessly into the devastation below, but one thing remained...

Alice.

Chapter 1

"You bought me a hairdryer?"

"I've been meaning to do it for years, You never put the heating on and towel-dried hair in that damp bedsit will make you ill, especially now that you're getting older."

"I'm turning twenty-five not eighty!" I wedged the phone against my shoulder as I bent to pick up my backpack, "Besides, you know I can't use one."

"This is special, I got Dennis in the hardware store to make a rubber casing and you can press the on and off switch through it."

"Phyl it's still mixing electricity and water."

"Trust me, Dennis knows what to do. Now what time will you be here?"

"I'll try and get across by seven." I glanced at the clock, "Oh God, I'm late. I've got to go Phyl, I'll catch you this evening."

I downed a last glug of coffee, tugged on the string to turn off my light and headed for the front door where my downstairs neighbour, Paul, was waiting for me in the corridor.

He held out a large envelope that had just been pushed through the brass letterbox and then revealed an oblong package that he had been hiding behind his back. It was wrapped in superhero wrapping paper.

"Happy birthday Alice!"

"Paul, you remembered!" I dodged an attempted kiss on my cheek.

"Of course I did. I hope you like it, it's a limited edition."

"That's so thoughtful. Can I open this at the office though? I'm running really late."

"Of course," he pulled the door open, "What time are you coming home?"

"I'm not. Didn't I tell you? I'm going across to visit my aunt this weekend."

"Oh," Paul looked crestfallen.

"Did I say something wrong?"

"No, nothing, I can always eat the cake by myself."

"You brought me a cake?"

"Yes, but it got a bit squashed while I was wrapping your present."

I put a mortified hand on my chest.

"Paul, I'm so sorry. I didn't realize."

"It's fine, the sponge looks more like a pancake now and most of the icing is smeared across my trousers." He showed me a sticky pink patch under his bottom. "Plus, I haven't got anything for supper and I need something sugary to boost my energy."

"Why?"

Paul's eyes gleamed with excitement, "Because I'm planning a rebellion,"

"You are?"

"Shh, I can't tell you anything else, it's a secret." He tapped his nose mysteriously, "I'll reveal all when you get back."

As I speed-walked down Stratford Broadway, I wondered how Paul, my flaccid, geeky neighbour could ever muster a rebellion and noticed the 135 bus stop.

Leaning against its grubby, plastic shelter was a young, fresh faced man. He had his eyes shut and was wearing big red headphones that cocooned his ears. I passed by with a tinge of envy and kept walking.

I would love to be a normal commuter, would love to queue up in an orderly line and get driven to work by a steamy London bus, but I have to avoid the densely packed, rush-hour crowds.

I have to stick to the pavement and choose the long walk to work every day because I am hiding a very unusual problem.

And, when it comes to unusual problems, this one is a whopper.

For some unknown reason, I have developed a severe case of static shocks.

I'm not talking ordinary static build up here. Think of the static that fires into your fingertips when you walk along a nylon carpet and touch a metal stair rail. Then multiply the power of that spark by one hundred and you'll begin to understand what I feel every time I touch anyone or anything metal.

You might think that, having had this problem for my entire adult life, I would have grown used to these static outbursts and learnt to avoid them. However, at the experienced age of 25, I still find myself flinching away from human contact and hitting new hazards at every turn.

Even speed-walking to work has its pitfalls, by the time I reached Piras, the Greek newspaper vendor outside Billingsgate Market, my hands were more charged up than normal and my first disaster of the day was about to strike.

Piras was depressed about his job.
For the two minutes that I saw him every day, he moaned about his customers, the government, the traffic and even the rubbish from the restaurant down the road, so I was ready for a misery download as I walked up to his kiosk and asked how his morning was going.
"It's good today."
"Really?"
"Yes, the sun, it is shining all day long."
Well that was unexpected.
I smiled in surprise and reached out to pick up a newspaper, but, as I brushed his metal stand, I felt a sharp shock fire off and jerked backwards.

I don't normally react to small shocks, but this jolt was bigger than normal, and it made my elbow ram into his display of 'I love London' mugs. The whole stand shook and the cheap porcelain tumbled like a house of cards, breaking into fragments as they hit the floor.

I put my hands on my cheeks and bent down, trying to fit the pieces back together.

"Piras, I've broken all your lovely mugs."

"It's no worry," he reassured me in broken English, rushing around to help.

Three were completely shattered and a fourth had a chipped handle. I rested it on my lap.

"I'll buy the ones that are broken."

"Not today."

"Piras, you have to make a living."

I grappled for my bag.

"No, put your purse away, you don't have to pay me nothing."

"But I could still use this one."

"No." Piras snatched it and retreated behind his stall, "It's my fault. I put them in a place where they get knocked. Look I have plenty more."

He produced a cardboard box and lifted another mug from it.

"If I don't pay you then I'll feel bad all day."

"You can't feel bad today," he said dramatically, "It's your birthday!"

"How did you know that?"

"I was told the news by a secret admirer of yours."

I looked at the empty street around us, "I think you're mistaken; I don't have any admirers."

"You may say that, but I know when a man makes eyes at a beautiful woman."

He placed his expressive, Greek hand over his heart, and I looked around me in puzzlement, "I haven't noticed any man anywhere, do I know him?"

"I don't know," he lifted his shoulders unhelpfully, "I don't know nobody's names. But he gave me a tip on a horse," Piras patted his pocket, "And the horse won! And, because I am now rich. I even give you a new cup as a present!"

"But..."

"No buts, it's going to be a beautiful, hot day and I am not taking no money."

I was humbled into accepting his kindness and wandered away in shock, cradling the new mug. Something or someone had made the glum Piras unusually chipper this morning.

After fifteen minutes of rapid walking, I felt mildly pleased with myself, I had almost made up for my delayed start. In fact I even had time to sit on the low brick wall opposite my office and change into my work shoes.

Drawing a pair of heels out of my backpack, I bent down to pull off one trainer and wriggled a foot into the back of my stiletto. Then I looked up and frowned.

A shadow had fallen across my legs.

"That's a wewy risky thing to do you know?"

A wrinkled, grubby tramp in a torn overcoat was staring down at me.

"What?"

"Sitting like that. In a place like this."

"Why?"

"Because it leabes you wulnerable." Having barely any teeth was seriously impacting on his Vs.

"I have more defences than you think," I warned and scooted across the brickwork to pull my bag towards me.

He shook his head, "Forget about the dosh, I don't want your money."

"Oh?"

"You see. I habe other wices." He smiled showing two revolting brown teeth and then shoved his hands deep into his pockets, flapping his coat.

I opened my eyes wide, "Oh my god, are you a flasher?"

He made a low croaking sound which might have been a chuckle and let out a puff of foul odour. "Naaa, I take a simpler path to happiness. Hab you seen my dog?"

I peered around me and said a cautious, "No..."

"Only he has a bit of a penchant for ladies' shoes."

I scowled as he shot me a gummy grin and bent down to grab my loose stiletto and trainer.

"I'm talking about these babies."

He braced himself to run and I caught his eye.

"You wouldn't."

"I would."

"No, not my shoes, please!"

"Catch me if you can!" he taunted, clutching them to his chest and scampered off, whooping down the street.

I tried to follow him but after five stumbling steps forwards, I realised it was hopeless and shouted.

"Well at least take a pair!"

He held my stiletto up and wiggled it back as he turned the corner and disappeared.

"Great, another crap day," I huffed, dumping all my earlier joys of summer.

Bad luck seemed to follow me everywhere. In fact, I'd had so many 'crap' days recently that I was beginning to lose count. I now had to face a morning of ridicule and stroll into the office wearing odd shoes.

Scooping up my newspaper and backpack, I strengthened my resolve and limped towards the thirty seventh floor of Colbert Tower.

After several sarcastic comments I reached my desk, gave a forlorn sigh, and flopped down on my swivel chair, taking another jolt of static as my leg wrapped around its metal base.

Then, to cheer myself up, I rummaged in my backpack and tugged out Paul's present. Keeping it on my lap, so that big ears Megan on the desk next to me couldn't see, I pulled off the colourful wrapping and discovered a plastic, articulated model of Jill Valentine from Resident Evil.

I rolled my eyes. This was the character Paul thought I looked like and, even worse, he said that he imagined me every time he played the game, and he played the game a lot.

The envelope that I had shoved in beneath it caught my eye. This was the large card that had been pushed through the door as I left my flat.

Slightly bent from its journey, I drew out the red oblong and juddered my finger along its top edge, revealing a large, cut out '25' embossed with gold leaf.

I flipped it open.

One day you will choose to find me, but, until then, I wish you all the happiness that distance can bring.
Happy birthday my darling Alice.

This was the fourth communication that I had received in the last six months. All of them had been anonymous, all nudging me towards contact and all wishing me some form of paternal affection.

I rested it on my lap and bit my bottom lip as dread iced the base of my lungs. Why had he begun to contact me now?

"Something interesting?" Lola Rose asked as she perched her rear end on my desk.

"This thing? No." I folded the card and wedged it back into my bag, "It's just a birthday card from an old friend."

"Not a mystery admirer?"

"Yeh, like that's likely!" I laughed as Lola pointed under the desk and asked, "What's with the shoes?"

"A tramp took one of them."

"It's a bummer when something like that happens," she said without surprise and picked up Jill Valentine, "Is this your new role model?"

I grinned, "I wish."

"She's smoking hot. If you dressed like her, you'd have hundreds of men running after you. Especially if you came out with me to a nightclub."

"Perhaps, but quiet evenings in are far safer."

Lola shook her head, "You won't win, you're not allowed to curl up like a dormouse on your birthday, you have to at least come out with us for a drink."

Lola was one of my best friends at work. She was strikingly beautiful with voluptuous curves, shining chestnut hair and a peachy smooth skin. She also loved roses, always wore one in her hair and smelled overpoweringly of rose perfume.

She plonked another package beside my keyboard.

"I brought this for you."

"For me?"

She nodded and I opened it, pulling out a blue silk scarf with tiny pink flowers stitched through the hem.

"It's beautiful, Lola you shouldn't have."

"Vinny helped me to choose it," she explained, smiling with delight.

I twisted it around my neck and asked, "Do you think it will draw attention away from my mismatched shoes?"

"No, Gavin's already got a video of you limping in on his phone. He's threatening to post it on Facebook if you don't go out with him."

Gavin leant back grinning on his swivel chair, flicking his pen up and down and I mouthed, "No chance."

He looked crestfallen and then stretched, saying to the entire room, "I don't see any doughnuts anywhere. Isn't it someone's birthday today?"

He had a point, everyone brought in a box of doughnuts on their birthday, and I would be letting the entire office down if I didn't. I'd have to go and buy a packet later.

I ignored him and said, "I stopped to pick up your newspaper, Lola."

"Oh, thanks," she said as I handed over the Daily Speculator, "How was Piras?"

"Unusually happy, he told me he'd won on the horses and gave me a free mug."

I showed her my 'I Love London' mug and she scowled in distaste.

"Are you going to use it?"

Most of Lola's mugs were strewn with dainty, noisette roses or damask patterns. I looked inside the shiny porcelain and nodded, "Why not? I've only got two others and one of them has a dodgy handle."

Lola shrugged and unfolded the paper, eagerly scanning its front page.

The lead title read, "Woman with two uteruses has Sextuplets three days apart."

I drew my eyebrows together.

"What do you see in that rag? It doesn't have any real news in it."

She had turned to another page and read, "My inferno hell. How I survived in an incinerator for six hours."

"Really?"

She clicked her tongue, "It may not be the Financial Times, but it does give me all the latest goss. Look, 'Third husband disappears on green widow's honeymoon.' Very suspicious if you ask me. I wouldn't like to be husband number four."

I shook my head. "It will be telling us that aliens have invaded next."

She pulled an appalled face, "Get real Alice."

Then, tucking the paper under her arm, she returned to her favourite subject, "So about celebrating, are you going to join us tonight?"

"I can't tonight, I'm going back to my aunt's for the weekend, but I'm free next week."

"Great, I'll arrange a big night out for everyone next Friday then."

"You always do a big night out, every Friday."

"But this will be just for you."

I rolled my eyes. Lola's existence was almost the exact opposite of mine, mainly because she embraced her sociable and gregarious life, whereas I tried to hide from it.

"Where will you take me?"

"Kinley's?"

"Are you clubbing afterwards?"

Lola sighed. "No, strictly drinks, if that's what you want."

I couldn't see the harm in it, so I nodded and said, "It's a deal then, drinks next Friday. What did you do yesterday in the end?"

Lola beamed. "Oh, Vinny was feeling down because he had broken up with Emmanuel, so Donna and I took him out to a club and…"

"And?" I could tell by the smile there was more to come, there always was with Lola.

"And I met this really fit bloke."

"Lola...," I warned. Lola landed a new man every week.

"No, he was drop dead gorgeous. He's coming around again this evening."

"What happened to the farmer?"

"Milk man," she corrected and screwed up her nose, "He was just odd, plus he had a weird fetish about milk bottles."

"How can you have a fetish about...?"

"Shh," Lola cut me off and jumped off my desk, "I'll tell you in a minute."

Stephanie, the no-nonsense manager of our division, was on the prowl for late starters.

She was tall and thin, always wore black and had very sharp eyes that could pinpoint any slackers within seconds.

I work as a data inputter which means I have to use computers and keeping them safe is a bit of a tightrope.

I can use a keyboard because I lock my feet around my metal chair-leg while I type. However, portable tablets are more of a challenge, if I'm not grounded by something metal, the electricity in my fingers will simply blitz my screen.

The same applies to mobile phones. I've tried several, fused them all, and have had to resort to an old-fashioned pink dial up phone that Lola lent me, a remnant from the eighties which makes my desk look like a homage to Barbie.

I looked up and gave an innocent smile. "Good morning Stephanie."

"Those are not regulation shoes."

I wiggled the foot with the stiletto on and said hopefully, "One of them is."

She glared back at me and I sighed, "Ok, I'll buy a new pair at lunch time."

"You had better. Type quickly and I'll give you an extra five minutes off, as it's your birthday."

My computer pinged as she walked away and I read, "He used to make me stick my fingers in them."

It was Lola.

"Stick your fingers in what?"

"Milk bottles. He got a kick out of the way the tin foil gave way under the pressure of my thumb."

"I'm seriously concerned about the people you date Lola."

"Don't worry, it got boring after about forty lids. Plus, I've moved on already. Did you know my new man thinks I have exquisite shoulder blades?"

I didn't even want to ask.

Chapter 2

On the proviso that I made up the work later, Stephanie let me have a whole ten minutes extra at lunch, just enough time to buy doughnuts and a new pair of shoes.

I lolloped out of my office, bobbed through the revolving doors, emerged into sumptuous heat and sighed. Today I wanted to enjoy a Mediterranean alfresco lunch with Lola, not a humiliating stagger to a cheesy shoe shop.

I haven't always had a problem with static shocks. They didn't appear until I turned ten and then they were only tiny, like little splinters catching the ends of my fingers.

To begin with I thought the needle like sensations were caused by my clothes, my shoes, the lino flooring at school, my washing powder, my diet and even my hormones. Everything in fact, apart from the blunt reality that I was becoming a static disaster zone.

I took a wide berth around a woman walking her dog and waited for someone to press the button for the traffic lights.

Over time my shocks worsened and cost me my friends, my confidence, my social life and even my pets. Mootie, my hamster, developed a tremor in its back legs after a sweaty trampoline session one lunch time, and my cat, Coco, started to jump like a popcorn every time I went near him.

I stopped at a Tesco's Metro and picked up a variety pack of Crispy Creams.

Boyfriends have also been completely out of the question. Dating me would be like playing Russian roulette with a set of spark plugs, a shock in the wrong place and you'd be crippled for life. That's if I ever got that far. Most men would probably run in horror after feeling my first static, lip zapping snog.

This fear of contact has grown to dominate my life and now, having reached the ripe old age of 25, I face the depressing reality that I'm going to grow old as an isolated spinster, never daring to touch, kiss or go on a date with anyone.

Two women sitting outside the Canary Café sipping cappuccinos stared witheringly at me and I wondered whether to take my shoes off completely. Several wet lumps of chewing gum put me off the idea and I continued down the Marsh Wall Road in a muscle aching, lopsided limp.

The front of my bank had one of those secure foyers where you can get out of the rain. Most people would use the machines in here to withdraw their money, but, as I've broken two cash point machines in the last year, I had to push through a double set of doors and stand in a long queue to get mine.

"You do know that you aren't wearing matching shoes?"

"Er...yes," I tried to smile pleasantly as the teller looked over the counter. "Is that a problem?"

"Oh no, I thought you might not have noticed." The woman had green slanted eyes and too much make up on.

"It's a running shoe and a stiletto. It would be hard not to notice," I said dryly, and then added, "If it makes you feel any better, I am going to buy some new shoes once I've got some money out."

I put my cheque on the counter and her shiny forehead wrinkled.

"You can use one of our bank machines to do this, you know?"

"I know."

"Or I could scan your card in my reader."

"I know. But I like cheques." I kept my voice light and ignored her growing frustration.

"Also, you can talk to one of our staff if you have a problem."

I was used to the patronising spiel. "No, I'll just take the cash."

Sat 6th May.
4th Teo + 1 = Walter

424 ⎱ every
425 ⎰ 20
        30 mns

P.O. BOX 40741   CY-6306   LARNACA CYPRUS
TEL: 24 645 444   FAX: 24 645 451,   24 644 644

She blinked her green eyes and spoke slowly, as if I was an imbecile.

"You won't be able to use cheques soon."

"I know," I replied equally slowly. "I'll cope with that when we get there. Can I have it in tens and twenties please?"

She shrugged, said, "Technology makes everyone's life easier, that's all," and pushed the money through the counter.

Just as I turned away from her and began to walk to the door, two things happened: Firstly I slipped, nearly did the splits and hurtled head first towards the wall, dropping my doughnuts everywhere; and secondly the main doors of the building slammed open as three masked men burst into the room.

The reaction inside the bank was not one of frantic escape and mad screaming but body paralysing shock and utter silence as the gunmen dominated the scene.

One of them fired off four sharp rounds at each of the security cameras mounted high on the ceiling, then he took out the camera by the back door, causing the security bolts to lock down and trigger an incessant alarm bell.

Another man grabbed an old woman around the neck and held his gun to her head, shouting orders at us to lie down on the floor.

Everyone followed obediently, except for me as I was already flat on my stomach. Then he turned his attention to the tellers, ordering them to stand away from the glass panel.

The teller I had spoken to backed off from her window and the third, thinnest, robber walked up to it. I thought he was going to try and shoot out the glass but instead he threw himself at the narrow slit that the money was passed through.

I could have sworn this gap was only about fifteen centimetres wide and far too small for a person to fit into but, with a strange twisting and bending of bones, the thin man's body dislocated and posted itself through the security glass.

I blinked with amazement as he emerged and reformed into his original shape on its far side.

Perhaps he was one of those double-jointed circus performers who can fit themselves in a jar, I reflected. Perhaps the circus didn't pay him enough and he had to top up his pension with a brutal bank robbery every now and again.

"Quick," the first man barked, "We've only got two minutes." The circus performer nodded, levelled his gun and shot out an inner lock.

Every teller was then ordered back against the far wall and I watched in silence as the criminals invaded their space, snatching and grabbing wads of money from all of the tills, shoving it into the deep pockets of their black biker jackets.

It was during this minute of pillaging that I turned my attention to the room around me and began to think like a woman with a useful and potentially powerful secret.

I had landed close to the exit that led to the cashpoint foyer. I couldn't escape or try to crawl to it because the gunman holding the old woman was watching the floor for any movement. Besides, with just one running shoe on, what kind of opponent was I going to make? I had to think about the building and how it worked.

It was obvious that the men had taken out the inner security systems and knew how much time they had before the police arrived. But I had the ability to scupper their plans.

I scanned the room and spotted a panel halfway up a wall not far from me. A panel that probably controlled the entrance and exit to the foyer.

I had to get to it.

I edged myself closer to the wall and, snakelike, began to wiggle through all the squashed Krispy

Kreams, advancing every time the gunman glanced away.

The two looters finished stuffing their pockets and emerged as the most aggressive man released the pale old woman from his grip.

She stepped back and warned him, "You'll never get away with this you know."

He grunted and lifted the butt of his gun, ramming it into her nose, "Get out of my face, you old hag."

She collapsed in a heap, her nose gushing blood down her shirt and I seized the distraction to edge right up to the wall, bringing my feet close in to my chest and preparing to spring upright when the time came.

Then, as the three of them backed out of the main hall, crossing into the foyer, I uncoiled like a snake, leaped up and shoved my fingers into the wall panel.

A harsh spasm of electricity jumped across into my hand and paralysed the muscles in my arm. A sharp blue light shot out and a strange humming noise rose up behind the whine of the alarm.

The bank robbers, having barged into the foyer, discovered that, because of a well-timed electrical short out, all the doors had bolted down and locked them in.

They fired angry bullets off at the security windows, but the impacts simply made white dents in the glass.

They were going nowhere.

The three of them span around like frantic goldfish in a tank until men in black SWAT uniforms arrived, ordering the gangsters to disarm and give up all their booty.

I had slumped down against the wall and cradled my painful wrist in my lap, regretting my attempt at bravery and hoping no one in the bank saw me do anything.

Most of them were so caught up in their own trauma that I thought I might have avoided discovery. Until…

"That was a very impressive move back there."

A man crouched down in front of me holding a cup of water. I put out a shaky hand to take it, being careful not to touch his fingers.

"I don't know what you are talking about."

He was dressed in a slim fitting black suit with a crisp white shirt and had one of those handsome, dark eyed, faces seen in fashion magazines.

"Is your hand alright?"

I nodded and tried to drink but my wrist trembled so much that I couldn't control it. He put a hand out to hold the base of the plastic cup to stabilise it enough for me to take a sip.

"Thank you."

"You should get a medic to check it."

I tried to move my numb fingers, "There's no need. I'll be fine in a few minutes."

He shifted to sit beside me and smelt of aftershave and soap. The move seemed to ally him to me and created a strange sense of trust.

Because of this I risked asking, "Can you do me a favour?"

"What?"

"Don't tell anyone what I just did."

"Really?" I nodded and he looked baffled, "I can keep quiet if you want but..."

"I don't want any attention. Plus, I didn't really do anything anyway."

"You did I saw you fuse the box."

I tried to swallow over my desiccated throat and felt sick. If the police or, worse still, the newspapers got hold of this I would never hold onto my anonymity.

"What did you use? Your keys or something?"

I thought about it for a millisecond and then grasped the lifeline. "Of course. I used my keys. How else would I have...?"

"Shorted out the entire building?"

"The whole building?" That was why my hand was so painful.

"Well, whatever you did, I'm very impressed and I can keep quiet if you really want me to." He smiled and revealed beautiful white teeth, "My name's Adam, by the way. I think you work in the same office block as me."

"Oh?"

"I err...saw you walking in this morning."

He gestured down to my feet and I realised that, not only was I wearing odd shoes, but my skirt was now smothered in Krispy Kreams. I gave a huff of laughter and shook my head.

"I'm not having a good day today am I?"

He grinned back and I pushed my hair out of my eyes.

"I'm Alice, Alice Carter, and I don't normally look like this." I tried to brush my skirt off but only made the icing smears worse. "I work for TSI Systems."

"You're a few floors above us then. I am with Warner and Suma, the fuel commodities company. We have just moved into the building."

I managed to take a sip of water, by myself this time and Adam asked, "So what happened to your shoes?"

"A tramp took them on the way to work."

"Them? Did he take one of each?"

I nodded.

"That's unlucky."

I shrugged, "No more than walking into a bank robbery at lunch time."

He shook his head, "And now you have met me. Your stars must be in a really bad alignment today."

"I don't think meeting you would ever count in the same category!"

He said nothing but looked over at the staff who were pulling their bank back into order.

I, meanwhile, began brushing myself down and flicked a lump of icing onto one of his patent leather shoes.

Adam wiped it off and handed me his handkerchief. "You seem to be covered in cake!"

The white, sugary paste had dried like glue to my legs and I swore, wondering what tight-trousered Gavin would say when he saw me wearing his afternoon snack.

There would be some wisecrack about licking it off me, no doubt. I shivered with revulsion at the idea.

"Were you celebrating something?"

"It's my birthday," I sighed. "All day, unfortunately."

"Well perhaps I can make up for your bad karma by buying you a drink some time."

"A drink?"

He laughed and added, "Don't look so worried, it wouldn't involve banks, tramps or doughnuts." His eyes held humour and a hint of enquiry behind them.

I was saved from answering by a stout policewoman who stepped in front of us and said abruptly, "I need to take your statements please. Can one of you come with me?"

Adam stood up to follow her but turned back to me to whisper, "Make sure you put some ice on your hand when you get back to the office."

It only took five minutes of formal questioning about who I was and what I had seen to make me pocket my fantasy conversation. I reassured myself that the tall, dark and handsome stranger would never remember me again but still found myself harboring a smug smile as I wandered back to the office.

That was, of course, until the lift doors opened, and I realised I had returned without a new pair of shoes and covered in Krispy Kreams. I had to face the wrath of Steph, the gibes of Gavin and the unwanted sympathy of big ears Megan.

Chapter 3

The following morning the sun had vanished, and I watched a torrent of rain pour off the gutter as I gazed out of my aunt's kitchen window.

"You know you have to get this fixed, it'll end up ruining you damp course."

"I know, I need to get so much fixed, Alice my darling, I can only cope with one thing at the time."

My Aunt Phyl's marigold gloves flapped towards the rest of the house and went back to snipping with the scissors, her yellow hands jerking backwards as a spark flew off.

I had tried to use my aunt's new hair dryer earlier, without success. Even though she had rubberized its handle, electricity still managed to jump out from my hair and into the nose of the machine.

The resulting short-out had deafened me in one ear, burnt the hairs off Phyl's hand and fused all the electrics in her house.

Fortunately, Phyl was used to my static disasters and laughed it off, lighting several candles and joss sticks to create a calm ambiance and a flickering light source.

Then she perched me on a stool with a tea-towel wrapped around my shoulders and faced a barrage of harsh shocks as she snipped away at my split ends.

This home hair cut had become a tradition with Phyl. She always cut a line straight across my shoulder blades, only ever taking a couple of inches off.
The style was boring and mundane but it meant that I never had to face the nightmare of a salon.
"Gary from down the road said he would fix the washing machine for me if I gave him a couple of free treatments."
I cringed; I had fused it on my last visit by pulling a nylon blanket out of the drum. Phyl's extra treatments cost her time and effort and she should have been stepping back from work now that she was nearing sixty.

My aunt's alternative therapy career had provided a crucial income throughout my childhood. It had dressed and fed me and even funded the mortgage on her semidetached house in Watford.
Every day she would guide odd looking strangers into her 'relaxation' room where they would receive a half hour session of Reiki, Crystal therapy or a hot stones massage. Then, feeling at one with the world, they would all walk out

holding one of the herbal cakes that she loved to make in the kitchen.

There had never been a mum or a dad on the scene. They were, simply never discussed and, if I ever spoke to Phyl about them, she would become tight-lipped and develop a deep frown-line between her eyebrows.

This 'fret line' upset me so much when I was younger that I eventually gave up asking and accepted my improvised family.

But sometimes there are reasons that you need to know about your ancestry and with a weird trait like mine, I had to push her for answers.

Everything came to a head one morning when I was thirteen, just as I finished eating my breakfast.

Phyl was washing up the supper plates from the night before and the tang of lemon washing-up liquid hovered in the air.

I put my breakfast bowl down into the sink and passed her my spoon without thinking, her hand closed on the metal and then sprang backwards.

Aunty Phyl froze and then became so pale I thought she was going to faint.

"Phyl are you alright?"

"I need to sit down."

"Shall I get you a glass of water?"

"Water? No, not water. I just need to…"

I watched her eyes scan the room, as if working something out. Then I said quietly, "I gave you an electric shock, didn't I?"

She nodded.

"I hope it didn't hurt."

Phyl opened her shaking fingers and then bunched them tight as I explained, "These strange little clicks keep getting worse. They're embarrassing more than anything, that's why I've try to hide them."

"How long have you had them?"

"A couple of years I suppose."

"God in heaven! You've been giving out static shocks all this time and I never noticed?"

Phyl lifted her hands to her cheeks and murmured to herself, "He said you wouldn't have it. He warned me about it, but you were so normal. Just an ordinary little girl."

I hadn't told her because I didn't think it was a big deal but now I was worried.

"Does this mean something is wrong with me?"

I touched her arm and she jumped at the crackle, "There it is. You have it."

The accusation sounded like a death sentence and I pleaded, "Aunty Phyl, you have to explain, you're not making sense."

She reached for the cake tin on the table and shoved half a fairy cake into her mouth. I gasped in amazement, Aunty Phyl never ate her own cakes.

"It's something that your father could do."

"My father?"

Phyl never spoke about my father so I stared, stunned, as the fairy cake was swallowed with a dry gulp.

"Yes, your father was always unusual, Alice. Of course, I put all of this down to those strange experiments your grandfather used to do with electric eels."

She stuffed the other half of the cake into her mouth and chewed pensively, "We were second cousins you know. I barely knew you existed until Chris turned up at my door and asked me to look after you."

"Why did he do that?"

"He was a very nice man, Alice and he loved your mother, Sophia very much. But he did something wrong."

"What?"

"Something so bad that he had to leave you here, had to get away from everything. I vowed never to talk about it."

My mouth fell open wide as a thousand horror scenes flashed through my head.

"Did he do something with his static?"

"I shouldn't say, I promised to keep everything a secret from you."

"Phyl what did he do?"

"He…," she took a deep breath, "He…," she hesitated again and then licked her lips, the words rushing out quickly, "He...sort of...killed your mother."

"What?"

"Yes, it doesn't sound good does it."

"My mother?"

"And perhaps a few other people."

She pulled away from me, wringing her hands together as I shrank back on the kitchen floor. "Oh my God, my father is a murderer."

"No...no, no, don't think of it like that, Alice. He was a good man."

Good man? The words murderer and good man didn't fit together in any language.

I asked flatly, "How did he do it?"

"Well..."

"He gave them electric shocks, didn't he?"

"That was the rumour, but I don't know the details."

I dropped my head and groaned. "So I might do the same thing?"

"No, not necessarily. Your static is just like everything else in life, it depends what you do with it."

Aunty Phyl tried to reassure me and patted my shoulder, receiving a sharp zap in return. "Your father's power just grew too strong, he simply lashed out one day and..."

"Killed everyone around him," I finished morosely, viewing my hands as alien weapons.

Phyl knelt down beside me.

"Alice, it's very important that no one ever realises that you can do this. If anyone connects you with him, it would be very bad. For both of you."

I didn't say anything.

"There are people out there, who will come after you for what he did. You must promise me you will keep this thing a secret. Do you want a cake?"

She picked up the tin and shoved another sponge delight in her mouth as I sank into a long and lonely withdrawal.

Welcome to adulthood. Here's your future, here's your inheritance and here are relationships, make sure you don't kill anybody on the way through!

As I grew older, I imagined every possible thing my father might have done to kill my mother.

I longed to hear that it was a giant mistake, that he had simply stepped on the frayed wire of his bedside lamp as he brought her breakfast in bed. But inside I knew that the facts didn't fit. My father's static fury had gone further than that. Aunty Phyl had said he killed other people too.

I also began to wonder whether I might lash out one day, my temper flowing out of my fingers in a catastrophic arc of blue light.

But my wondering got me nowhere, and here I was, still desperate to know more but too terrified to find out, still hiding, still trying to sink into the background and still resenting my father for leaving me with such a huge burden to bear.

I studied aunty Phyl as she assessed her handy work from various angles. Wearing her draping ethnic clothes and soft smile, she seemed so happy and comfortable that I didn't have the heart to tell her about the mysterious letters that had been arriving recently.

Phyl was my rock and my greatest confident but the possibility that my 'lethal' dad was trying to contact me would simply stress her out with no benefit.

Instead I asked brightly, "Are you still doing lots of treatments?"

"Well only for friends these days. My arthritis plays up if I do too much."

"I can send across some money to help out with the house you know."

"No." She flapped me away. "I've started selling my cakes to the hospice down the road."

I choked on my tea.

"Do they know what's in them?"

I had never asked how Phyl bought all the weed that went into her baking miracles but, as most of my life had been punctuated by visits from my 'uncle' Mo, a Rastafarian giant with the longest dreadlocks I have ever seen, it wasn't hard to guess.

My aunt and I adored him, loving the sunshine of the Caribbean in his voice and the happiness he brought into our house. The strong herbal smell that arrived with him was just an extension of his exotic personality.

"Of course they do. My old ladies get quite excited when they hear me coming down the corridor."

"But you can't do that not in a hospice, that makes you a..." I lowered my voice to a whisper, "It makes you a drug dealer."

"You worry too much, Alice. I've been making and selling these cakes for a long time. Besides," she tapped her nose, "Who is ever going to tell on me?"

Chapter 4

When I got back to work the following week, I heard all about Lola's rapid break up.

The latest ex in Lola's life turned out to be a trainee tattoo artist who had his eye on her shoulder blade because he wanted to plant a rose on it.

Lola loved the idea but the artist, having only just begun in his profession, managed to go hideously wrong and ended up inking in something that looked more like…well, a piece of female anatomy, than a rose.

Lola was fuming and kicked him out, the unsightly tattoo lasting far longer than the relationship.

She didn't despair for long, of course, and started dating someone called Zac the very next day.

Zac was a computer whiz kid who was apparently amazing in bed (too much information I know but this was Lola after all). Zac also happened to be my good friend Donna's youngest brother.

Donna is short, apple shaped, gay, loves parties and grew up living in a caravan in Dorset. But I also know she smokes cannabis, muscles up for any fight going and is drawn to trouble like a magnet, meaning that this brother of hers sounded far too good to be true.

    A giant puff of warm wind had gifted London with scorching weather by Wednesday and office workers rejoiced by rolling up their shirtsleeves, taking off their tights and exposing blanched arms and legs to the humid air.

    I was caught up in the sun worship and lounged on a bench by the River Thames, sipping an iced smoothie with Lola and Donna at lunchtime.

    Sunbathers with burnt patches of skin the colour of rhubarb and custard strolled past, oblivious of their pink and white tattoos until they stripped off their layers later that evening.

    I looked at my own arms wondering if I had developed a tan-line in the ten sleepy minutes we had been soaking up the UV light and caught sight of the headline in today's Daily Speculator.

    It had been placed in my lap after being perused by Lola and I shook it out, drawn in by the story on its front cover:

HEROIC PLOD PADDLES IN POOP TO SAVE UNCONSCIOUS WOMAN

A plot using London's sewerage system to transport heroin out of Luton airport has been foiled by police after illegal drugs were flushed down the airport toilet.

The drug dealers escaped and later turned up in a nearby sewage processing plant where they began collecting their dodgy deposit. However sewage security worker, Denise Feck, noticed the strangers and phoned for police support before confronting the two men.

By the time the officers arrived, they found Denise floating unconscious in the primary treatment tank and the two men fleeing the scene. One heroic officer plunged into the dung and saved the day, saying, "I had no option but to jump in and stay with Denise until a support team joined me."

Police have issued photographs of the suspects and are investigating..."

Donna broke in, "What's making you frown Alice?"

"Lola's paper. Not only is it completely crap, it is also full of crap. Look."

I pointed at the headline and Donna raised her eyebrows, "Yeah, it was a seriously revolting act of heroism. Just imagine having all that sewage in your mouth." She yawned, stretched her plump fingers up in the air and asked, "What are you eating Lols?"

"Honey glazed sausages," Lola replied, her nose buried in a magazine.

Honey was like heroin to Lola. If every sandwich, meal or drink wasn't topped off with a hefty slathering of it, she became quite twitchy and had to have an emergency honey hit from a jar in her handbag. Despite the diet's high calorie count, she seemed to be doing pretty well on it and had an amazing figure.

I pulled out the last crust from my sandwich packet and threw it out to a brave duck who had been casing our bench. He waddled forwards but was beaten by a cheeky sparrow who nipped in and left my duck looking at empty ground.

"Poor duck." Donna mused, slurping her milkshake, "It was too slow to get any food."

"But the fast and light birds are vulnerable," I countered, "There's never a perfect solution in life. Every animal has a design flaw."

"Except humans."

"Do you think humans have got it right then?"

Donna shrugged, "We've conquered the earth. What more do we need?"

My duck waddled up to peck around my feet and I tucked them under the bench, afraid of shocking it. I said, "Would you ever design humans differently Donna?"

Donna regarded her pale legs, "I would give everyone legs that would tan up in the summer. I read that it makes you look thinner."

"You don't need to be thinner Donna," Lola reassured, looking up from her magazine, "Thinner is weaker and you barely eat anything anyway."

Lola was right, although Donna was extremely short and round, I had only ever seen her drinking milkshakes, coffee or alcohol. She was either a nighttime hoarder or had one heck of a slow metabolism.

A lazy bee buzzed around us and landed on Lola's sausage, I shouted, "Stop Lola!"

She paused with her mouth hovering open.

"You've got a bee on your sausage!"

Lola drew back to look at the chipolata.

"He's just confused by the honey." She let the insect crawl across her hand, "I would re-create us with pollen sacks so we could all collect our own honey."

I laughed. For Lola's birthday we had all clubbed together to buy her some Royal Jelly which she kept in her desk. She took a tiny teaspoon to cheer herself up after every failed relationship. Interestingly her pot had not been opened in the last week.

Lola asked the bee, "Do you think I would look better in fuchsia or ashes of roses?"

She put the bee on the page of her magazine and studied which way it walked.

"Tell it to go for fuchsia, at least that has some balls behind it," Donna urged, fanning herself.

I asked, "Why are you looking at wedding dresses Lola?"

The bee flew off and Lola flicked over to the next page, saying, "Why not?"

"You aren't exactly engaged to anyone."

She had a mysterious glint in her eyes as she said, "I can plan, Alice. And you should too, it might happen to you one day."

I shook my head, "Believe me, marriage is never going to be on the horizon in my life."

"You should visit my palm reader, she could see something unexpected in your future," Donna suggested, and I wrinkled my nose.

"I'll give it a miss, knowing my history is bad enough."

"What's wrong with your history?"

"My history? Nothing."

"But you said…"

"Is that the time?" I changed the subject and stood up, studying my watch, "I'd better get going, I promised Steph I'd catch up with some extra work from last week."

"You sprint around too much, Alice," Lola said looking lazily up as a button from her tight shirt came undone. A racy red and black bra hemmed in her bulging cleavage and a very happy bee could just be seen wandering down it.

"You've got a bee...," I pointed at her chest.

"I know," she said and shivered as it disappeared, "I love bees."

Donna joined me as I walked back to the office and asked if we could stop outside a small chemists, saying that she needed some hay-fever tablets for her brother, Zac's streaming eyes.

Donna put the irritation down to the hot weather, but I had a feeling that the condition went far deeper than that. After all, if you went out with Lola, pollen was never far away.

I waited in the heat outside and watched a mother stroll past with a shopping laden pushchair. Her young son was trailing behind with a football tucked under one arm looking sulky and refusing to walk next to her.

A whistle sounded out and I spotted a stylish, thin figure across the road. He had a warm, latte glow to his skin and was signaling vigorously, trying to catch my attention. I raised a hand to wave back.

It was Vinny.

Vinny worked in sales on the floor below us, wore his gay-pride badge with a flourish and always dressed in the most expensive, designer clothes on offer.

However, although he looked like a suave, sophisticated film star, he didn't behave like one. Vinny was extremely clumsy and had hands that seemed to stick to almost everything he touched.

Calling across the traffic, I told him that Donna was in the shop.

"Stay there then," Vinny mouthed, waiting for a break in the flow to join me.

Vinny and Donna had a strange relationship that I had always struggled to work out. Vinny permanently put Donna down and she permanently forgave him.

In fact, she went beyond forgiveness, she ran to save him almost every time he got in trouble, and, with blundering, clumsy hands, trouble seemed to follow Vinny wherever he went.

I gave him a double thumbs up as the young boy beside me stamped his foot, refusing to hold his mother's hand. The protest popped the ball out of his arms and, without thinking, he darted forwards to collect it.

The world dropped into slow motion as a large, white van hurtled towards the child, slamming on its breaks as it swerved sharply across the road and then juddered to a stop.

The mother shouted, the pushchair tipped backwards, and the white football bounced lamely out from under the van's wheels.

"Oh Jesus, no! Craig? Craig!" the boy's mother screamed as the driver jumped out of his van.

"I couldn't stop! I couldn't stop! Did I hit him?"

All three of us ran around the bonnet, anticipating a scene of carnage at the front of the van but the road was clear, there was no blood on the bumper and the boy had disappeared.

"Oh my god, he must be right underneath," the mother sobbed as a loud whistle drew our attention from the far side of the wide road.

We all looked up and, to our astonishment, saw Vinny standing on the far pavement, holding the scowling child's hand.

It was a miracle.

"How did the boy get over there?" the van driver asked as the mother ran across, smoothing her hands over the boy's body, soothing and checking, "Did you get hit? Did the van hurt you?"

The boy shook his head and crossed his arms. "No but that man stuck his tongue out at me."

He pointed an accusing finger at Vinny who blushed and bit his lip.

The boy's mother tugged him away, "Don't tell tales Craig, I've told you a hundred times. Thank you so much for saving him, I don't know how you did it but I owe you my entire world."

As the nonplussed driver climbed back in the van and the mother went across to tend to her pushchair, I caught up with Vinny and asked, "You weren't anywhere near the boy, how did you...?"

"I'll tell you how," said a gruff voice behind us, "I recorded the whole thing on my phone and it's gonna go viral. One hundred thousand views, here I come."

A bulky man with a buzz-cut and full body tattoos was standing about ten meters away from us.

Vinny became ashen, murmured a faint, "No!" and darted forwards, trying to snatch the man's phone. "No! Please don't post it."

"You're jokin' mate. This thing will go ballistic."

The beefy man swung his hand up as Vinny tried to grab the phone and was swatted away like a fly.

"No, please..." I heard real distress in Vinny's voice, "Don't post that... please stop...don't. Alice help! He can't..."

Vinny struggled to keep his balance as the man swiped at him again, typing gleefully into his phone.

I was going to have to step in, I had never seen Vinny so distressed. I took a breath and did the riskiest thing that I had ever done in front of a friend.

I sprinted around the man, stood in front of him and reached a finger forwards to touch the back of the phone.

Charge leapt between my skin to the metal casing and a sharp crack made the man startle and jump backwards, dropping the phone.

"Shit. My phone just burnt me."

My finger was still pointing towards him and Vinny fell silent as the man kicked the phone with his foot, turning it as if it was a dead scorpion.

Then he fell to his knees and scooped it up, asking, "What the fuck did you do to it?"

I took two anxious steps back as Vinny yelled, "Donna you had better get over here."

Donna had emerged from the chemist and was now thundering across to us.

The man shot an accusing look at me. "Did you just break my phone?"

I gave a guilty shrug and watched anger flush his face, "You did. You did something to it."

"It was probably a fault in the wiring..." Vinny tried to step between us and got batted out of the way so hard that he sprawled back onto his bottom.

"Shut up, mutant, this has nothing to do with you." He turned back to me and said, "You're going to have to pay for this."

Donna arrived, chin up and chest forwards, prodding the man in his stomach. "Don't push my mate around you moron."

She only came up to his armpits and he sneered back, "It's another freak, and an unfit, fat one!"

"I'm fit enough to take you down," she warned, her West Country drawl strengthening with hostility.

He curled his top lip and shoved her backwards, "Why? What are you going to do, lard-arse?"

"I'm not a lard-arse, I just have a slow metabolism."

"Yeah? That's what they all say!"

"I've warned you."

"Ooooh," he held his hands up and put on a girly voice, "I'm scared, the fat girl's angry," then he set his jaw, "Now get out of my way, porker."

Donna had had enough. She snatched his hand and twisted, wedging her shoulder underneath him and making the huge thug summersault over her head like a small bag of potatoes. He flipped in the air and then landed flat on his back, breath leaving his lungs with a colossal huff.

Then, like a New York cop, she rolled him over, bent his arm up behind him and knelt hard on his spine, spitting gruffly into his ear. "I can take you out faster than you can blink and castrate you in seconds. Just give me an excuse."

"She broke my..."

"She didn't do anything. Your crappy little phone had a fault. Get over it."

"No way, she…"

Donna pushed up on his arm, "I am going to kneel on your bollocks if you argue."

She shifted her weight and he squeaked, "No! Stop! I give up."

She clicked her tongue, disappointed by his rapid submission and let the man stagger upright.

He snatched his phone back and said, "Fuckin' weirdos. You're all friggin' mutants the lot of you!" and then scampered off down the path.

Donna brushed her sweaty black mop of hair back from her face and I stared in wonder, "Donna, that was amazing."

She shrugged, "My mum went out with a martial arts master once and he showed me how to defend myself."

"You were awesome!"

She grinned and tucked her shirt back in, "I love a good tackle in the street."

My short, wide office worker had taken on a new mantle and I gazed at her with admiration as Vinny slapped out a sticky high five, saying, "Nice work ninja. You need to shave your legs though. All that hairy skin flying around was quite terrifying."

She held up a sarcastic finger as Vinny sculpted his hair and shivered, "That man has too much pent up aggression pumping around his body, he should go and spend a week in a koala sanctuary or something."

I asked, "Koalas? Why Koalas?"

"Why not koalas? They're furry, cute and relaxing."

"They live in Australia."

"Do you know, I've always dreamt of going to Australia," Vinny yearned. "I want to get rescued by one of those buff life guards on Bondi Beach."

"Give me a caravan in the New Forest any day," Donna cut in, gruffly. "Oh, talking of which, I need to go and buy the latest Caravan Weekly. I heard there's a new luxury model being released with a convertible roof terrace. Just imagine downing an iced beer up there at sunset."

Donna eagerly disappeared into the newsagents and Vinny sighed, "I dream of hot beaches and she wants a caravan in Hampshire. Life is weird sometimes isn't it?"

We stood outside the shop door, waiting in a long, loaded, silence until I finally braved up and asked, "Why didn't you want your picture taken Vinny?"

"How did you break that phone?" he countered.

I took in a breath, closer to confessing than I had ever been in my life and then sighed, "I can't tell you."

He pulled out his sunglasses and put them on with a nonchalant disregard, "Well, if you aren't going to tell me your secrets, doll, I am certainly not going to tell you mine."

I left them ordering frappuchinos at the coffee shop and wandered back to work, knowing I had just taken a huge risk in front of Vinny.

I was slipping on my promise to Aunty Phyl and had to be careful. If I began using my static to get out of situations, I could get myself noticed and that could spell serious trouble.

Chapter 5

Air-conditioning wrapped its cool arms around me when I got back to Colbert Tower and I stood for a second enjoying the cold chill of air on my face.

Then, rummaging in my handbag, I walked into one of the yawning lift doors and pulled out a biro to jab the button for the 37th floor.

A plastic pen was the perfect gadget for pressing call buttons, I almost always had one on me and it saved my fingers and electrical circuits from severe damage.

However, just as the doors began to close, a sturdy white shoe jammed forwards, and they slid open again to reveal the mouse woman with her carpet bag and half-moon spectacles.

The mouse woman was a well-known figure around Colbert Tower. She was a talkative, black-American cleaning lady with a thick Creole accent and a bust so large, her arms had to form right angles around it. She also spent most of her spare time knitting stuffed mice to sell at the local vets, donating all her profits to The Cat Protection League.

The woman was out of breath as she turned to press the top floor, 45.

"Oh, I'm so pleased to be back," she sighed.

"Have you been far?"

"Lord help me, yes! I normally take a trip to Loop near in Islington during my lunch break but it was a waste of time today, they had run out of royal blue wool. That's the colour I use more than any other to make my mice." She paused to wipe her brow and then continued, "Of course they had acrylic but that feels nasty."

"So what did you do?"

"What did I do? I went all the way across to Stoke Newington to get some." Sighing heavily, she rested her hand against the wall, "Oh my dear, I am so exhausted, all in three quarters of an hour!"

"And it's so hot today."

"My clothes are sticking to parts of me I never knew I had" she chuckled and fanned herself, a sheen of sweat gleaming on her forehead. "Still I've got some now and look what I'm making."

She pulled the half knitted shell of a mouse out with bold blue and white stripes running across it, "Cats can see blues and violets better then reds you know, so they love catching these little cuties."

"Do you have any cats?" I asked as the lift doors opened unexpectedly and the woman began to walk out.

I cried, "Wait, that's not your floor!" and she stopped so suddenly that her needles fell out of her bag, her ball of wool rolling away onto the landing beyond.

She scrabbled to pick up her knitting, saying "Oh, my stitches, my work," and I darted forwards to grab the ball.

However, as I scooped it up the lift doors began to close and alarm thrilled through my blood.

The floor I had leapt out on was Warner and Suma's and if I didn't stop the lift, I would be left stranded there, holding an unravelling ball of wool as the woman travelled upwards.

I panicked and slammed my hand on the call button, an instantaneous and massive electrical impact flinging me back against the far wall. Then the lift doors juddered to a halt and left a twenty centimetre gap for the woman to peer through.

She pressed her face against it and squawked, "What has happened? Open the door."

I scrabbled upright and said, "The lift's fused. Can you edge the door open?"

"I can't, it won't move," she said accusingly, "What did you do to it?"

"I didn't do anything!" I tried to improvise, "It must have been the wool."

"The wool?"

"Yes, it created friction on the door mechanism."

She gave a doubtful frown and I said, "Wait there, I'll get some help."

"I've got no choice, honeychild, I'm stuck in this coffin."

I pulled my pen out to press the button for the reception.

"Warner and Suma, can I help you?"

"Yes, can you phone maintenance please, the lift has stopped."

"I've just had an alarm call to say all the lifts have fused and no-one should use them."

I rolled my eyes and leant my head against the wall with a slight crackle. "Well there's a person stuck in the lift out here and…"

"Wait a second and I'll bleep them for you." There was half a minute of silence before the intercom cracked again, "They just replied saying they would be at least half an hour as another lift has also fused on the ground floor with five people in it."

"Damn." I sparked as I hit my hand against the wall and then went back to find the mouse woman looking out of the lift and mopping her brow.

"This is definitely not good for me; it's getting very hot in here."

"Do you think you can fit through this gap?"

"With a bust like this, it wouldn't be fun. I could end up half out and half in." She fanned her face, "Besides, I'm not feeling too well."

"I'm going to see if I can shift these doors."

"They won't move, I've tried and tried."

"Ok, well stand back anyway."

I rubbed my hands on my skirt and then reached out, but, even as my hand stretched forwards, the metal reacted and another bolt was let loose, this time causing the lift to drop with a huge whump before screeching to a halt.

The woman let out another squark and I groaned, only a narrow oblong of light remained at floor level.

Falling to my knees I bent down to look inside and saw the mouse woman crouched in the far corner with her hands over her head. She shrieked as the lift made another juddering wobble.

It settled and I asked if she was still alright.

"Oh sweet Jesus, I'm going to die,"

"You're not. You're safe," I promised but winced as the cables creaked and the woman tensed again.

"It's going to drop."

Guilt swept over me. I had caused this crisis.

I lay down on my stomach, posting my face against the gap to get closer to her.

"I've asked for some engineers to come and help us."

"It's going to drop and then no one will knit for the cats."

"You aren't going to drop; these lifts have all sorts of safety measures…"

She was gasping in the claustrophobic air and pulled at her shirt collar saying, "I'm suffocating, I'm suffocating."

I tried to calm her down.

"What's your name?"

"Kinky."

Well that was a surprise. "Did you say Kinky?"

"Yes, my mother thought it was cute."

"OK, well, do you have cats, Kinky?"

"No, I live in a housing association flat, so I'm not allowed one, but my cousin, Fancy, has two."

"What are they called?"

"Bernard and Eugene."

"They're unusual names for cats."

"She lets me come over on a Saturday to stroke them and sometimes I cook up some chicken." She sighed, "They'll miss me if I don't visit, they always come purring all the time, rubbing their heads on my legs."

The cable squeaked and we both looked up.

"You obviously love cats."

"Yes, I have a special bond with Bernard, he's really a girl you know."

"That must have been a surprise, when did you find out that he was a girl?"

"Alice?"

Someone called my name and I brought my head back sharply, thumping it on the top of the lift.

It was Adam. Of course.

Of all the people...

"What are you doing on the floor?"

"There's a woman stuck in the lift."

At that point the lift made a whirring sound and Kinky shrieked.

Adam instantly got down beside me and lay on the floor.

I whispered, "Her name is Kinky."

"Kinky?"

"Yes, Kinky."

He blinked twice and then peered through the gap, saying, "Hello Kinky, my name's Adam." His voice was calm and gentle, but she didn't respond. "Kinky do you want to get out of there?"

She nodded and he gave her reassuring smile,

"What I am going to do is put my arms through this gap and push it wider. Then I want you to walk over to me and grab hold of them."

She began to uncurl but then said, "I can't climb up there, it's too high."

"It's alright, I'll pull you out."

"You can't. I'm too heavy."

"I can. I promise."

She whistled and mumbled, "You don't know how heavy I am. My momma used to tell me I had two suitcases packed in my rear end, even when I was little."

"Kinky, if you don't try, you'll have to wait for the mechanics to come and that could be hours," I explained.

"Hours?"

I nodded and she took a deep breath, tapping her hand on her chest before crawling on all fours in our direction. From way above our heads the cables moaned, and Adam and I looked at each other apprehensively.

Then Adam reached his arm out and swept back the immovable lift doors as if they were a set of curtains. I looked at him in astonishment but was distracted by Kinky.

She had reached the side of the box and wobbled upright like a toddler standing for the first time, causing the lift to take on a worrying swing.

Adam extended his arms to a full stretch with his head and shoulders through the opening and grabbed Kinky's podgy hand.

"That's it, give me the other one."

"Wait, you have to take my bag first. It has my needles in it."

He grappled for a second, delivered the bag through the hole and then reached back in.

She put her other arm up and Adam began to wriggle backwards, bending his elbows as Kinky's skin turned white under his tight grasp.

I watched helplessly as Adam dragged her upwards until she was able to hook her elbows on the ledge and be lifted free.

Once he had Kinky lying, traumatised in the hallway, Adam called a beautiful blond-haired woman called Vanessa out of his offices. She produced a chair and a cup of tea for the shocked woman as a squat engineer turned up to check the lift mechanism.

The man in blue overalls stood back and scratched his head, "I dunno, both lifts on this side have shorted out completely. It's a good job you pulled her out it could be hours before we get this problem fixed."

I backed off towards the stairwell as Adam checked that the woman was alright and felt another shock hit my sore fingers as I pushed the fire door open.

Climbing up the stairs, I expected to hear the panel swing shut again, but, instead, footsteps took its place and they rapidly caught up with mine.

"Do you always live your life in crisis Alice?"

"I was just helping her, I wasn't the cause of the crisis," I lied, as Adam fell into step behind me. "And you don't have to walk up with me you know. I don't need a chaperone."

He took three large strides and said, "I'm on my way up anyway. I have an appointment to see your manager." He pulled a business card from his pocket and looked at it, "Ms Drosop."

"Steph? What are you seeing her for?"

"I'm expanding my team downstairs and thought I might use your human resources."

"Oh."

We walked up in silence until he eventually said, "So I still owe you that drink, you know."

"You remembered?" I smiled and then took a reality check, "Actually, I can't, I'm busy."

He rummaged in his pocket and waved two tickets at me.

"What are they?"

"Tickets to see Pedro Distillo in a private audience on Friday if you're interested."

"Pedro Distillo?"

I couldn't keep the longing out of my voice. I loved Pedro Distillo, he was the hottest solo performer on the circuit, and I would probably love this man beside me too, given half the chance. Instead, my shoulders drooped, and a lump of lead formed in my stomach. I was too much of a liability.

"Like I said, I can't. I'm meeting up with friends."

"Is Friday a problem? I can always change the day."

"No, it's not Friday. It's just that... I don't 'do' this whole dating thing."

"You don't 'do' dates?"

I shrugged.

"Is it some kind of celibacy thing?"

"No," I said defensively.

"Are you...do you lean the other way?"

"No." I said and then realised what he meant, "No! Nothing like that."

"Do you have a problem with me then?"

"Oh God, Adam, no. I'd love to go out with you but..." I paused, realising that I had to pick my words carefully.

"But?" he asked, stepping in front of me.

I gazed longingly up the stairs, wishing he would disappear.

"I'm not going to give up unless you tell me," he said adamantly.

I tried to walk around him.

"Adam my life is just too complex. You'd never understand."

He held the other bannister to block my path.

"Try me."

I stopped moving and looked down at my hands. "If...if I get too close to people, I... sometimes I have a problem with..."

I frowned and pressed my lips together as tears of frustration sprang to my eyes. "Oh Jesus, just ignore me. I'm a complete head-case. Why don't you find someone else to go with? That woman who got you the chair seemed nice."

He laughed and stepped aside, saying, "Vanessa?"

I nodded.

"Why would I ever choose her over you? I don't care what you have a problem with."

"Oh, you would do. Believe me!"

I wiped my eyes, sniffed and as a door banged below us, I began to march upwards.

"I have to go."
"But..."
"Don't let Steph bully you too much."
"Alice."
"I'll see you around sometime."

I ran up the remaining steps and slammed out of the stairwell, causing yet another painful burn on my hand. Rapidly I tucked it under my armpit and bolted for the TSI storage room like a hermit-crab retreating into its shell.

I stayed there for over half an hour, hiding like a coward and a fool.

It was only once Steph had reappeared on the work floor and was scouting desks again that I dared to re-emerge, a cloud of self pity louring over me for the rest of my day.

The most handsome man I had ever met just asked me out and I had ended up quaking with fear inside a darkened stationary cupboard.

My life was pathetic.

Chapter 6

I was in Kinley's, a wine bar in Canary Wharf, sitting by a space-age table that made me feel extremely uncomfortable.

It was rimmed with metal and lit by a UV light that shone up through its frosted glass centre. I put my glass down with care, making sure that I didn't touch any part of the electrical death-trap beneath.

Vinny had just sat down to join us and was wearing an orange V-neck tee shirt. A material so bright that it cast his face in shadow and made his teeth loom in the the dark as he grinned around the table.

Donna frowned and said, "What the frig have you been using on your teeth Vin? Vimto or something?"

Vinny raised a hand to cover his glowing mouth. "It's a new tooth-paste I've started using with scorpion extract in it. Is it really bad?"

"Donna's just jealous," Lola said, "Did you enjoy your trip home Donna? How was your mum?"

Donna often went back to visit her family who lived as modern day travellers on a caravan park in The New Forest.

"She was fine."

"Still enjoying her wild Wiccan ways?" Vinny asked with a mysterious wiggle of his fingers.

Donna stared flatly back, "It's her religion."

"Running around dark forests with no clothes on?"

"Have you ever tried it?"

"No."

"Well don't mock then. Besides, she has to take it easy these days. It turns out she's up the duff."

"She's what?" I was so amazed that I leant forward and almost touched the table.

"Preggers. You know, knocked up, bun in the oven."

"But she's old enough to be a grandma."

"I know, funny isn't it. She thought it was all those pickled onions giving her indigestion, but it turns out she's about three months gone."

"It would be nice to have a real baby to look after," Lola cooed with a broody pout, picking up a honey-roasted peanut and staring into space.

"She must have been very young when she had you then." I was still trying to work out the maths.

"Sixteen when she had me, seventeen when she had Lash and eighteen when she had my baby bro, Zac." Donna took another glug of beer. "It's our tradition to get up the duff when your really young."

She burped and peered into her almost empty glass. "Me and my brothers, we broke the mould. I went to work, and they went to…"

"Is the baby's dad around?" Lola cut in.

Donna sniffed, "That's part of the mystery, we don't really know who the dad is. My bet is on our lodger, the bearded woman. It turns out that she wasn't quite a woman after all. I should have guessed when I kept finding the toilet seat up in the caravan."

Donna flashed an accusing look at Vinny, and he shrugged.

"Don't look so scathing hon, I sit when I can, just like the rest of you girls."

"Has she got anyone around to help her out?" Lola quizzed.

"Yeah, Zaza, my mum's fortune telling next door neighbour said she'd look after her. She even said she would help out with the delivery."

Vinny raised sceptical eyebrows and asked, "Did Zaza predict your mum's pregnancy, then?"

"Not everything is visible to clairvoyants, Vinny. Zaza is allowed to miss the odd little thing."

"Pretty bloody big one if you ask me!"

"I love you Vinns," Donna warned, "but I'm about to belt you round the chops. Go and buy me another beer before I smash your pearly whites to pieces."

Vinny nodded obediently and disappeared while Donna turned back and confided, "Zaza did a reading for me while I was back at home. Apparently, I have a problem with my gallbladder, shouldn't wear flip flops and need to avoid small spaces next Tuesday."

Lola looked intrigued, "I'd love to know my future." She turned to me and said, "Do you believe in destiny Alice?"

I shrugged, "Not really but then I don't believe a woman can have six children from two uteruses. So what do I know?"

Donna laughed, "Life's what you make it isn't it, Lola Rose? How's it going with Zac by the way?"

Lola gave a sumptuous smile, "Very well, thank you. Did you know he has created an online avatar which looks and speaks exactly like me?"

"Exactly like you?" Vinny asked as he put down a new glass of stout for Donna. "Does she even have the tattoo on her back?"

He made a slight popping sound as he released his fingers from the side of his glass and then put on a high pitched voice as he slid back into his seat, "Oh, I love you, Zac, fight like a hero in Assassin's Creed and I'll show you the vagina flower on my shoulder!"

"That's my brother you're talking about!" Donna protested.

Vinny shrugged, "He probably likes it. Most men don't have the benefit of having two to choose from."

Lola bustled like an indignant chicken, "Actually, Zac says he doesn't care what a person looks like on the outside. It's what's inside that counts."

I gave such a big snort of laughter at this, that my wine shot out of my nose.

"What? What did I say?" Lola asked.

Vinny shook his head, "Lola you can't say things like that to Alice. You're going to have to buy her another drink now."

"I don't know what I said!"

I made my lovely, unconventional friends when I joined TSI six months ago. We had all begun during a big recruitment drive and were thrown together by the social hub of the coffee machine.

I kept my distance initially and turned down their various invitations, stressed about revealing my problem, but they kept inviting me to their events and eventually I gave in.

Then, one night, after I had far too much to drink, I confessed to having body space issues. To my amazement, they were fine about it, they accepted my failings and still wanted to know me.

Since then they have never pressurised me to join in, never crowded my space and never tried touching me.

Of course, they all probably think I have major psycho/social problems but, as long as no one discovers my real antisocial secret, I'm happy to roll with whatever theory they've formed.

"I think you're lucky, Lola," Donna confided, "My brother will make a great boyfriend, that's if you can keep him out of prison of course."

I didn't respond or hear the reply because I had just looked up and seen Adam standing at the bar, talking with a group of men.

He glanced across, caught my eye, made some excuse to his companions and started walking in my direction.

I returned my focus to the table and said, "Oh God," as my heart went into free fall inside my chest, "What is he doing here?"

"Who?" Lola asked.

"Hello Alice. I didn't expect to see you tonight," Adam said amicably, looking around the group.

I gave a reluctant introduction, "Everyone, this is Adam."

"Ah, the 'bank' Adam?" Lola said. I had, of course, given them the potted version of my bank heist. "Alice never told me how good looking you were. That puts a different slant on everything."

I blushed as she pulled out a stool and said, "Come, sit down and join us."

He sat next to me and I scowled at him suspiciously, asking, "So, do you visit this place often on Fridays?"

"Don't worry, I'm not staying, my clients are off to The Attic in a minute," The Attic was a very exclusive bar in the nearby Pan Peninsula Square.

"I thought you were going to watch Pedro Distillo."

"I didn't bother to go, I was blown out by a hot date."

"The hot date can't have been very interested then."

"She could still join me in The Attic if she wanted."

I shook my head and he grinned.

"I'm still trying to bring her round, give me some credit."

"Didn't I see you in our offices the other day?" Vinny asked, flicking his hair with one hand and knocking all the peanuts off the table with the other, "You wore a Gaston suit didn't you? Only it was rather rumpled."

"Ah, that was because I had been rolling around on the floor with Alice."

I hadn't told them about the 'Kinky' episode and said defensively, "It wasn't exactly rolling!"

"No, you're right, it was more like lying side by side."

Donna did a long slow take in my direction, "You and I need to talk."

"I was saving a woman in a lift alright!"

Lola smiled at Adam and asked, "So, handsome stranger, are you here to invite Alice out on a date?"

"No," I snapped back and he shrugged.

"Evidently not, but I do have a different option."

"Which is?" I asked cautiously.

"A group invite."

Everyone else around the table perked up as he explained, "I have some spare tickets to go to the British Film Awards party on Tuesday."

"The...?"

"British Film Awards," he repeated for me.

I knew exactly what they were but bit my teeth together and said, "I can't."

"The party after the awards? The actual party?" Donna checked, not listening to me.

"Did you say group tickets? Does that mean more than one person?" Lola seconded.

"Yes, my ex-girlfriend gave them to me," Adam said simply.

"What kind of ex-girlfriend gives people tickets like that?" I asked and he shrugged.

"She told me to pass them on to someone."

"How many tickets?" Vinny asked.

"How many do you want?"

"Four," he said.

"No five," Lola corrected, "We would need five."

"It's a date then. I have some...," he rummaged in his top pocket, "here."

The golden tickets were laid in front of us and three hands reached out to snatch them from the table.

"We would love to come."

"Wouldn't miss it."

"We'll see you there," beamed Donna. "Won't we Alice?"

I was in catch-up and looked at Adam, who raised his eyebrows.

I took my ticket from Donna's flapping hand with a reluctant frown as Adam bent towards me and whispered, "Some dates are impossible to turn down, Alice."

I only just had time to grasp the metal leg of my chair and brutally discharge myself before he leant closer and kissed me on the cheek.

"See you there."

The impact of physical contact was like a flashgun firing off through my body and I sat in shocked silence as the tickets were stroked and sniffed by the hyenas sitting at my table, their comments rumbling around my head like distant thunder.

"Just think, I can take Zac and ask him the big question while I'm there."

"I'm more worried about getting a designer suit made up in time, Lola."

"Amanda Demelitov and Gabrielle Hall are both going. I've always fancied them. Do you think my height will put them off?"

What was I going to wear? How was I going to cope? And why had I ever agreed to go?

Tuesday had turned into a life-engulfing plug hole and I was a tiny, helpless plastic duck being sucked towards it.

Chapter 7

I went shopping on Saturday with Vinny and Lola who took great joy in handing out couture advice and screwing their noses up at most of the dresses I tried on.

I settled on a milk chocolate, full-length, fish-tailed, strapless number from Debenhams that had fitted well enough to gain their approval.

It wasn't the most exciting thing I had ever come across, but my budget had limits, even if this was the fashion event of the season.

Lola then surprised me by choosing a low cut, plain, cream 1930s dress in a second-hand shop in Soho.

"No flowers?" I asked as she paid for it.

Her eyes sparkled, "Just wait until I've worked my magic on this little number, you won't recognise it by Tuesday."

After a four-hour stint, I arrived back at my flat in Stratford and scrunched the rest of my clothes to one side of my wardrobe. Then, after hooking my new evening gown up, I flopped, exhausted and shop weary onto my bed.

I began renting my flat because it was under an hour's walk to work and because it was very cheap.

The building dates from 1910 with tall rooms and long sash windows. Although this sounds attractive on paper, a shoddy 1980's conversion left a tiny scrap of a room at the end of each floor.

This claustrophobic box, not much bigger than a double bed, was my bolthole from the world, a snug footprint that I could call home.

When I moved in, I had the entire place transformed into a safety zone, employing one of my aunt's electrician friends to fit a circuit breaker on my electricity panel, a safety measure to stop me fusing the entire building too often. He also tied string pulls to all my lights and attached plastic covers over every plug.

My kettle and all my pans have fibreglass padding around their handles, and I use one of those claw sticks to turn on the gas on the oven.

There was just enough space for a daybed, a bedside table, a narrow wardrobe and a desk in the main room, but I didn't need much more than that.

All other electrical items like TVs and computers weren't worth the effort because they'd simply get fused too often.

I put the kettle on and was pouring milk into my cup when I spotted the singleton stiletto and trainer still standing under my bed.

I walked across, picked them up, clicked my tongue with irritation and threw them into the bin. What was the chance I would ever see their other halves again?

Two seconds later I heard a knock at my door.

It had to be Paul.

Paul was the rather podgy, goatee-bearded, downstairs neighbour who had given me the Jill Valentine model.

He is the perfect example of a geeky tech who does something complex with computer programming during the day and by night morphs into a Dungeons and Dragons, war re-enactment enthusiast, who would happily be a train spotter if he had a raincoat and a clipboard to hand.

I pulled the door open to reveal his beaming smile.

"Come in Paul," I said. "I'm making some tea. Do you want one?"

"No, you've got to come down to my room because I've got something to show you."

"Does it involve role play because I've told you a hundred times that I'm not into..."

"No, it's all to do with my rebellion. I'm breaking the law."

I had forgotten about Paul's uprising.

"What are you doing?"

"Do you want to see?"

I gave him a suspicious look, "Where do I have to go?"

"My room."

"Have you hijacked The Pentagon website or something?"

"No."

"Posed naked on Facebook?"

"No, nothing like that, but you have to promise you'll keep it a secret."

I rolled my eyes "Alright then." I picked up my mug, "Can I bring my tea?"

Paul lived directly below me in an identical flat to mine except that his looked like a teenager's fantasy room.

It had warrior posters stuck up on every wall with Jill Valentine clad in revealing leathers stuck, rather worryingly, on the ceiling over his bed

The fact that I sleep in the exact same space on the floor above, made this seriously disturbing but, it's a free country, and I try not to imagine the thoughts that go through Paul's head every night.

The main centrepiece of his room is the giant computer screen that engulfs Paul's attention day and night but, despite the giant alien face blinking at us on his screensaver, my focus was fixed on

Paul, who had turned to face me with something in his hands.

"Oh my God."

"You can hold it if you want."

"No way."

"What do you reckon?"

"Paul what were you thinking of? You can't have something like that in here."

"But it's only little."

He held up his small hamster and it yawned, almost turning its entire skull inside out.

"It's banned in your rental contract."

His eyes shone, "I know, I am turning into real a rebel these days, Alice. I even jumped over the underground turnstile in the station last night."

"They have CCTV cameras on those things you know."

"I know, I was so worried about it afterwards I had to go and find the guard and show him I did genuinely have a ticket."

I laughed, "Nearly a rebel then."

"I'll be developing superpowers next."

I sat down on his bed and he held the little creature out.

"Do you want to stroke it?"

"No, I have a habit of maiming hamsters."

Paul pulled his chin in and shovelled his hamster back into its cage. Then he sat back beside me while I drank my tea.

"Do you think there are such things as real superpowers, Paul?"

Paul gave the subject careful consideration and spoke as if he was some philosophical prophet,

"Considering recent scientific advances, superhuman powers are only just around the corner, Alice. You could easily have a bionic arm with different weapons or a digitalised eyeball to focus your sights on the enemy. Just imagine warriors that could…"

"No, I mean naturally."

He held his breath and looked at me before blowing out a raspberry laugh.

"What do you mean? Someone that could reverse time or freeze an entire road with their eyes?"

"No, things like…like dislocating all your joints to squeeze through a hole or having powers over bees or…or generating static build-up really badly."

"I like it," he nodded, "Imagine that your army was boosted by a gigantic swarm of hornets that hovered overhead. They could herd the enemy into your traps and sting them until their evil warlord submitted. Then, once you have infiltrated the enemy lines, you slither out of your own suit of armour and…"

"I didn't mean you would have them all at once."

"Oh."

"And not for use in a war game either, just extreme forms of normal, like the fastest growing fingernails or amazingly strong hair. After all someone in this world must have stronger hair or harder teeth than anyone else, only they'd never know it." I shrugged, "Maybe everyone can do something exceptional."

"I see where you're coming from but look at me. What could I ever do like that? I'm just a fat computer gamer who gets breathless running for the bus."

"I don't know, it could be something really small."

I sipped my tea and smiled, "You'll have to go out there and 'find the force', Paul."

"God Alice, you have to come to a Dungeons and Dragons meet with me. They would love to hear you talk about superpowers like that."

"No, for the thousandth time I am not going with you."

He sighed, picked up a dart from the side of his bed and threw it at a vicious looking dragon poster on the far wall. "If you just came once they would see that you actually exist. I talk about you enough!"

Chapter 8

I looked absurd as I left my flat for the party on Tuesday evening and Paul was so enthralled that he tried to take a photo of me with his phone.

Fortunately, I managed to lift my bag in time to block my face and warned him that I would never talk to him again if he tried to take another one.

I think he got the message.

I make a point of avoiding photos whenever possible because I can do without plastering my face up on social media pages.

Of course, Gavin threatens to post something about me every day but he's all talk and no trousers and has never actually gone on to carry out the threat.

I spent the next fifteen minutes wishing I had an invisibility cloak on as I made my way across to Leicester Square.

The train was busy which was unusual so late at night and although I got a seat there were a few people who had to stand.

One of these was a Mediterranean man with bad skin and pointed shoes who hovered close to two women chatting by the exit.

Every jolt swung him close to them, bringing his creepy groin into contact with their tight fitting jeans.

They got off, the train emptied out and the man, licked his lips as he ambled down the carriage towards two young French girls who were waiting by a different door.

In the grimy light of the underground he looked sallow and greasy with hollowed out eye sockets.

Deciding that I couldn't subject the French students to this slime-ball's approaches, I stood deliberately up from my seat and ran my hands down my hips, straightening my dress.

This drew his attention and, as I sashayed past, he veered like a magnet towards me.

The train windows reflected back a sickening tableau, me in vulnerable satin with the thinnest vale of material coating my skin and him, leering, hawk-like behind me, standing close, uncomfortably close, in a nearly empty carriage.

As the train approached Leicester Square, he blew on my neck, huffing garlic-breath at me and making my skin creep. With a surreptitious shuffle of my feet, I made sure that I was charged to full capacity and then waited for him to make his move.

Contact occurred as the train slowed down and his hips thrust forwards to brush against my bottom.

I had the satisfaction of feeling a sharp shock fire off from my rear end and knew it was gigantic. The fire-bolt must have hit the metal zip of his fly and carried enough heat to cause instant injury.

The man let out a muted squeal of agony and I heard his knees hit the floor.

When I stepped off the train, I glanced back to see him gripping his groin as an elderly Italian couple closed in, wondering what had happened.

Explain that one to the casualty nurses, I thought with a smug smile and felt like a brave vigilante as I waddled up the stairs to step out into the fresh night air. At least there were some benefits to static build-up.

It was late and I expected to surface into a wacky world of sleepless tourists and social misfits, but instead a buzz of excited chatter hit my ears.

A galaxy of celebrity spotters had gathered to stake out the scene and I realised that the crowd was even denser by the gleaming, glass-fronted cinema hosting the prestigious evening.

How was I ever going to get into the place?

I began walking, or rather wiggling as I couldn't move my knees very well and noticed that curious looks were being cast in my direction.

Before I made it halfway across the square, a group of Chinese tourists came up and asked to have their photo taken with me.

I held a hand up and shook my head, but the action attracted other people and they began to whisper, "Who is she?" and, "Didn't I see her in that film with Kit Milner?" I blushed fiercely and had to do a quick scuttle sideways to get away from the excitable babble.

Taking shelter in a pizza bar, I hid behind a pillar and peered out at the animated tourists, waiting for them to become distracted by a clutch of real VIPs.

This didn't take long and, once the square had cleared, I cautiously headed back out to try again.

I soon realised that going into the party via the red carpet route was a no-no. After all press cameras meant photos and photos meant unwanted publicity. Therefore I had to find another entrance.

Edging around the back of the crowd, I discovered an inconspicuous grey door to one side of the building with a surprised, burly doorman standing beside it.

"Can I help you love?"

He was about six foot three with a heavy cleft chin.

I cleared my throat, rummaged in my handbag and held up my ticket. "Do you think I can come in through this door?"

The man pulled his face back with concern, "Don't you want to go through the main entrance?"

I shook my head, "No, I'm not a celebrity, so I'm better off sneaking in unnoticed."

He dipped the edges of his mouth and asked, "Are you media then?"

"Definitely."

He nodded, "I thought so, everyone else is clamoring for starry lights and long lenses."

I laughed and shivered, "Who would ever want a close up like that? And all the photos make you look fat anyway."

He gave a mournful sigh and gazed towards the crowd. "I was meant to be on the main door you know. But when it came to allocation, they shoved me round here where all the catering staff come in and out. Not a bloody film star in sight."

"Well, at least I'm not catering, and I am wearing a long dress."

"Well you might just be the highlight of my evening Miss." I handed him my invite, "You are welcome to come in via this crumbling and smelly entrance."

Then he added on a more practical note, "Mind you don't step on any cumquats as you go, one of the delivery men split a box open and they went rolling everywhere." His fat forehead wrinkled in exasperation, "You can't get the staff these days, can you?"

I laughed and he pointed through the open door, "Follow this corridor until it opens up and then you need to head down the stairs to your left."

I nodded, "Corridor, opening, stairs."

"You've got it. I hope you enjoy the evening."

He let me through and then called on an afterthought as I walked away, "Don't do anything I wouldn't do."

The entrance took me through into a shabby corridor that was obviously doubling as a storage facility. Boxes were stacked up to toppling point all along one wall and the smell of damp cardboard mingled with cabbage and fish. I stepped over a small squashed fruit on the floor, ignored the corridor to the left that led to the kitchens and pushed against the large door ahead of me, walking into the bright lights beyond.

A radiant scene hit my eyes like a wall of water, and I was swept up into a noisy whirl pool of gold and glitter. I had emerged on a mezzanine level where women were draped in exquisite dresses and men wore wrinkle free suits that undulated across sculpted torsos. Platinum cuff links, patent shoes and diamond necklaces glinted in the bright lights and my jaw dropped in awe.

Two, very tall women were deep in conversation next to me. Both had pancaked, heavy makeup on and one was dressed in a shimmering green, jewel-studded gown.

The other wore a white dress which was open down to the waistband on her front with two pieces of liquid gold material that ran up, over her shoulders and hung to floor-length behind her.

Her hair was almost white and pulled back into a shining hip-length ponytail that swished down between the drapes of her dress.

I put my hand up to check my fraying bun and felt shabby and uncomfortable. Wanting to hide in a corner, I headed towards a brightly lit metallic bar to my right and spotted Vinny beside it, dressed in a suave, gold lamé suit, chatting with a handsome, blond barman.

"Vinny!" I called out in relief, "It's so good to see a familiar face."

He shook his head, as if I was mad.

"Are you joking, Alice? You are in a room that is spangled with familiar faces."

I chewed my lip as I looked around me, "I'm not very good at recognising famous people, Vin, and they all look different in films."

"Feel the vibe honey. This is just like...like..." He looked for inspiration from the room and took a deep inhalation of breath... "locusts on sticks!"

"What?"

A muscular waiter in a sequinned dinner suit stepped up and wafted the tray of skewered insects between us.

I screwed up my nose, "Ewww."

"Locusts are trending at the moment," the waiter said in a surprisingly high voice, "and are recommended in the entomophagy diet."

"Err, I think I'll pass."

"How are they prepared?" Vinny asked with a playful pout.

The waiter replied flamboyantly, "They are coated in sesame seeds, deep fried and served with a lemon-based dressing of za'atar pesto."

"Oooh, tasty. They sound lush. My name's Vinny Vain, by the way, I'll give you my card later. I have a movie that is crying out for your jaw line." Vinny licked his lips, "Can I take two?"

"You can take as many as you like with a suit like that Mr Vain."

Vinny reached across, picked up two sticks and twiddled them, saying, "It's a Vitriano, of course."

The waiter gave him a wide grin, "Of course.

But I wouldn't expect anything less in a place like this."

He flicked his eyes in my direction without saying anything and I wanted to curl up on the spot and disappear. My department store dress was feeling like a hessian sack.

Vinny took a seductive bite out of one of the appetisers, his eyes steaming with allure towards his new flirt mate and a little part of me rejoiced when a locust leg stuck on the outside of his lip.

I tried to gesture to him, but the waiter stepped between us saying sensually, "You've got something on your labia." Then he put his hand out and gave a erotic swipe across Vinny's lips.

I poked my tongue in my cheek and tried not to laugh as the waiter backed away giving Vinny a twiddle of his fingers and said, "Catch you later alligator."

"In a while...daddy locust legs," Vinny twiddled back.

Shaking my head, I said, "I can't believe you just called him daddy locust legs."

"I know, it wasn't the most provocative phrase, was it? I couldn't think of anything else though, my hormones were raging. Do you think he liked me?"

"Too much for your own good. I'm impressed that you managed to flirt over a plate of insects."

Vinny shivered all the way down his body, "Flirt, maybe, but he's out of my league, he's only interested because he thinks I'm a director."

Vinny brought his attention back to me, having watched the waiter wiggle away.

He popped the second locust into his mouth, saying between crunches, "Alice, you are looking..." crunch "...uneasy," crunch crunch. "I think you need..." lip-lick, "...an ice breaker."

He ran his tongue around his teeth and turned back to the bar. "Have you ever had a Balkan vodka shot?"

"No," I replied cautiously. I tried to avoid getting drunk in densely packed places.

"Well, we can't have a Balkan virgin at this party. A quick fix will give you Dutch courage."

He rapped on the counter, "Especially when the barman, Sam, has a soft spot for me and a completely free supply of drink."

The smiling, deliciously handsome bartender walked back to us and winked at me as he pushed two shot glasses into the middle of the counter, filling them with a luminous green liquid.

"Isn't vodka normally clear?" I asked.

"It's Vodka, lime juice and rum," Sam put the cocktail shaker behind the bar. "You have to down it in one."

He pushed the drinks towards us and walked away to serve someone else.

Vinny looked at me, "Shall we do it in three?"

I nodded.

"Three, two, one... go!"

Vinny stepped up and knocked his back as I reached out to grab mine. However, as my hand neared the glass, I felt a familiar crack jump out and fire into the metal counter.

My vodka ignited and rippled with a blue light. Keeping calm, I tried to grab the glass before it got hot, but a second shock made me jump and I knocked the drink over completely.

A long lick of flame spread sideways as the blazing fluid splayed out across the counter.

"Oh Christ!" I backed off, realising that something beneath the bar was kicking out electric shocks, "Vinny!"

I yanked on his jacket, "Vinny!"

"Oh my God!" he gasped, seeing what had happened and grabbed a bar towel, throwing it onto the liquid.

The towel must have been soaked in alcohol too, because it instantly lit up in flames, making Vinny jerk backwards. The cloth stuck to his fingers and flicked onto the floor.

I heard gasps sound out around me and the crowd backed away as Vinny repeated, "Oh my God. Oh my God," as he stamped on the blazing cloth.

Then, my hands over my mouth, I watched the flames fan upwards, catching his lamé trousers and blazing up his legs.

Just as panic and disaster were about to kick in, Sam, the beautiful barman, jumped over the counter with a small fire extinguisher in one hand and pointed it at the ground.

Seconds later a puff of white powder smothered our corner of the room, the fire was doused and everyone coughed as they fanned the air.

When the haze cleared, I found Vinny examining his scorched trousers.

"Are you OK?" I asked anxiously, peering down at his legs.

"Fine. I'm fine," he said, tensely, brushing at his exposed skin, "It was only the material that caught."

"I'm so sorry."

He looked back at me with surprise, "I don't know why you're apologising; this bar is obviously a fire hazard. We should sue them."

"I'm not sure that the bar was..."

"In the meantime, what am I going to do?" Vinny continued, flapping the ragged front of his trouser legs, "I can't spend the whole evening walking around like this."

He looked crestfallen.

"I could always lend you my dress," I said unhelpfully, and he raised a derisive eyebrow.

"If you were in Dior darling, I might have actually accepted."

"Perhaps I can help." A very tall man had walked up beside us and we both looked up in awe.

"Oh?" Vinny squeaked.

"Would you like to follow me please?"

Vinny nodded and smoothed his fringe into place and then he gaped back at me, mouthing, "I'm in heaven!" as he scuttled after the man.

I watched them head off across the room as the beautiful barman bent to sweep up the debris from the floor and a large hand closed over my arm.

"You need to come with me."

I reached out, grabbed my bag and was tugged along the corridor.

This man was obviously a bouncer, judging by his broad frame and boxy black suit, and he was obviously going to march me straight out of the back door.

I said, in a strangled voice, "I'm not an imposter. I know someone here. Look, I have a ticket."

I yanked back on his arm so I could swing up my handbag and get my ticket out. But, as luck would have it, he stopped and turned at that point, and my black bag travelled in a neat arc right into his crotch.

He bent double in pain and said through gritted teeth, "Ouch."

"Oh, I'm really sorry." I put my cool hands against my head, grabbed some napkins from the counter and tried to pass them to him.

He fluffed them away and stood up, his mouth still tight with pain.

"I was just taking you to the back stairs, all the standard ticket holders are meant to be down there. Only award winners and selected celebrities are allowed up here."

"How can you tell I'm a standard ticket holder?" I asked, still trying to dust the white powder off my dress.

"Do you honestly want the low down?"

"Well you've made your decision about me already haven't you?"

"Fine if that's what you want," he had managed to straighten upright by then but still had to hold onto the counter, "There is the dress, bag and shoes that don't match. Your hair is falling out of its clips and you have no nail varnish on. Oh, and cultured celebrities don't set fire to the bar as a rule."

I stared down at my fire-extinguished, factory-finished gown, knew my hair was feeling loose and tried to hide my burgundy shoes.

"Do you want me to go on?"

"No, that's enough… Do you want me to leave? I've only just got here but if you see me as a security risk then I'd understand. You'll have to let my date know that I've gone."

Well it wasn't quite a date, but I wasn't going into any detail with this man.

"Who are you meeting?"

"Err...he's called Adam..." I stammered to a halt, realising I didn't even know his surname.

"Adam?"

"Yes...Adam...something."

"Oh Christ, you're Alice, aren't you?"

"I...?"

"And you still don't know anything. Ok, I'll have to get you back to socialising then."

I had no idea what this conversation was about but walked obediently beside him as he took my hand and led me down some side stairs.

I said, "I assume that you know what you meant by that last comment?"

"I did."

He paused to lift a woman's diamanté covered hand off the bannister, asking her to step aside. I followed like a prisoner being led to the cells.

'I still didn't know anything?' What was that meant to mean?

The bouncer turned and looked back at me, saying, "You don't know his surname, do you?"

"No, not exactly but...Wait a minute, how did you know my name?"

"It's Warner."

"No, it's not."

"What's not?"

"My name, it isn't Warner."

"Oh, for God's sake, no, it's his name. His name is Warner." The bouncer ran his hand through his hair and said to himself, "Oh Jesus, this is harder than I thought it was going to be."

"Ah, his name is Adam Warner you mean?...So you do know him after all," I began to relax.

"I know of him."

"Does that mean he's famous or something?"

He seemed to debate this. "In some ways I suppose. Not as famous as you though." He stopped as we reached the edge of the room, "Lola's over there."

I bumped into him and was about to ask how he knew Lola, but the words stuck in my throat.

I was looking down at my hand in his.

The bouncer had taken hold of it upstairs and there had been no click, no shock, no electricity. Time stood still as I studied the anomaly.

He looked down at it too and I said quietly, "You're holding my hand."

I was aware of him staring at the link between us for a long moment before he let go.

He stepped back with both hands in the air, "Look, just stay with your friends and you will be fine."

I was gobsmacked. He hadn't received a shock when I had touched him, he had also lifted the diamanté hand up from the bannister and hadn't passed a shock on.

Normally, if I touched a person and didn't let go of them, they would feel all my shocks for me. I turned to him, wanting to find out why he was immune, but his square hands twisted my shoulders and launched me into the room.

I was engulfed by hot air and pale faces, panic tightening my throat as I wove through the dense throng of people that had gathered by the main stairs. Pinning my arms down, I tried to zigzag through to a clearer space, hearing one woman gasp and another man grunt as I brushed against them.

Finally reaching Lola who was standing by the back wall where the crowd tapered out, I began to breathe again.

Lola had her eyes shut in bliss and was surrounded by three men.

One of them was stroking her arm with tender adoration, the second had bent to caress her leg and the third was licking her neck.

She was wearing the same figure-hugging dress I had seen in the shop but now it had tiny red and gold petals glimmering all over it.

"I hope one of them is Zac," I said and watched her eyes flick open. All three men simultaneously dropped their interest and walked away.

"He went to the toilet."

"While the cat's away and all that?"

"Don't tell him, Alice. I'm trying to drop my nightclub habits, but, every now and again…" she sighed and puffed a little waft of rose blossom into the air.

"Well your dress looks amazing; did you sew all of those petals on by hand?"

Lola nodded, "What do you think?"

She did a little spin for me, letting her pashmina fall from her shoulder to reveal her large, ugly tattoo.

Lola blushed and tugged her shawl back up, "I know, I know, just ignore it. I've booked an appointment to see a specialist and he said he might be able to change it into a butterfly or something."

Her eyes began to twinkle as she pointed towards her new boyfriend who was walking back to us from the toilets.

He was a thin, blank-faced man in an ill-fitting grey suit, wearing a large gold necklace.

Lola introduced me to him, "This is Zac. Zac this is Alice, you know, that 'friend' I told you about?"

He said with a slouchy voice, "Hi famous Alice, your neighbour, Paul, is seriously bad at Warhammer you know."

"How did you know Paul was my neighbour?"

"Because he's a tech head," Lola explained.

"What's a tech head?"

"Somebody that plays on the internet for hours, I don't really understand it. This whole internet connection thing is double Dutch to me."

Not understanding it either, I said to Zac, "Can you beat him?"

"Yeah, but he's zero cool!"

I wasn't sure whether 'zero cool' was good or bad and was relieved when Lola cut across me.

"Have you heard my wonderful news?"

"No, what's happened?"

"I asked Zac to marry me and he said yes."

She held her hand out and wiggled a ringed finger at me. I looked between her and the blingy man in disbelief, "When?"

"This evening! It was so romantic. I had the ring in my bag of course, just in case he agreed."

I blinked in shock, they had only known each other for two weeks, if that.

"Isn't that a bit quick?"

"Perhaps, but I knew from the first moment I saw him. Plus, I planned it all already, he just had to be willing." She clapped her hands with delight and asked, "Will you be one of my bridesmaids, Alice?"

"A bridesmaid?" I said in a strangled voice.

I had never even been to a wedding before, let alone been a bridesmaid. The idea of spending a whole day at a crowded party terrified me, but how could I say no to Lola?

I mustered an artificial smile and said, "Of course I will."

Lola's eyes lit up and a puff of rose perfume filled the air as she clapped her hands together, "Oh, I'm so excited. I've already asked Vinny and Donna and they are going to be my other bridesmaids."

"Vinny?"

"If you want my honest opinion, I think he is happier in a dress."

"He would be happy in anything that isn't melted to his skin this evening," I murmured.

"Where is he, by the way?"

"I set fire to him upstairs and haven't seen him since."

"But now I have miraculously been raised from the ashes!" Vinny announced and I turned to see him standing behind us with his arms spread wide.

He had changed into a black and red suit with black tassels hanging down from each arm.

"Vinny, you look amazing," I said.

"I know, don't I just? You'll never guess what happened to me," he brushed his own arm in self-admiration, "That gigantic man I was with, and I mean gigantic! Took me over to a changing room and told me to wait, then, after a couple of minutes, who should walk in? Only Milo Topen!"

Lola squealed with delight and tugged Zac's shirt, "Did you hear that Zac?"

Zac stared vacantly into space.

"Anyway, he came straight up to me and put his arm on mine."

Lola's eyes grew bigger, "No, he touched you?"

"Better than that, he actually spoke. He said...," Vinny paused and cleared his throat, "Hang on, he has a very deep voice, but I'll try and do it. 'That was a very heroic thing you did there with those flames.' Oh God Lola I was so excited I thought I was going to wet myself and then he said, 'I saw your suit was damaged in the fracas, I want to offer you a replacement.'"

"No way, is that one of his suits?"

Vinny nodded, his mouth almost splitting his face he was grinning so much. "The trousers are a bit short though and they weirdly have two zips, one at the front and one at the back," he lifted his jacket to reveal the strange, extra zip.

Vinny patted his suit back down around his bottom, "Can't imagine why he'd need quick access on 'that' side," he quirked his mouth scandalously and began scanning the room, "OMG. Wait till I tell Donna, where is she?"

Lola stroked the arm of the new jacket in awe, "She's been checking out the toilets for the last half hour to see if any of the superstars would chat to her in a vulnerable moment."

"Alice!"

Adam was weaving his way across to us and the coward in me wanted to shelter behind Vinny and Lola, but I knew I had to face the music and talk to the man. He had invited me here after all.

I made myself walk towards him.

"I've been looking for you for ages have you only just arrived?"

I nodded, "I came in through the side entrance because I wasn't up for the red carpet."

"Was security a problem? I'm sorry, I should have thought about it and met you outside."

I had forgotten how attractive he was.

"I see your friends are enjoying themselves."

Donna had joined the group and was demonstrating a rotating karate kick to Vinny. Halfway through she flailed and lost her balance, booting a glamorous black supermodel up the bottom.

Lola, meanwhile, had grabbed a glass of Champagne from a passing wine waiter and spilt some down her front.

Instead of dabbing it with a tissue like a normal person, she pointed at the stain and said something to the waiter who instantly fell to his knees and began to lick it off while Zac stood in oblivion, staring up at the ceiling with his mouth open.

I tried not to look embarrassed.

"They like their night life," I explained, and Adam lifted his eyebrows.

"They certainly make a party go with a swing!"

I nodded awkwardly and then he looked at me, laughed and shook his head.

"What?" I asked.

"I can't believe I had to invite all your friends out just to get a date with you."

"I'm only here because of them," I warned.

"I'll take what I can," he smiled, "At least I'll get to know you a little. We missed out on an excellent concert apparently."

"You could have gone to see Pedro alone."

He shrugged, "It doesn't matter. His agent also gave me a couple of backstage passes for Wembley if you're interested."

"Generous, but, with my disaster record, I think I'll give Wembley a miss." I shivered, "Just imagine all those backstage wires."

The last part of my sentence had popped out by mistake and I snapped my mouth shut. However Adam didn't seem to notice and was still looking at me amicably, I changed the subject.

I asked, "Did you find out what happened to Kinky?"

"Kinky?"

"Yes, the woman who was stuck in the lift. I tried to check up on her, but the cleaning manager told me she had left."

"Oh, that Kinky," he pulled at his shirt cuffs, "I found her a new job."

"You did?"

"Yes, Vanessa told me she loved cats and I have a friend who works for the RSPCA. She is now pampering lost kittens every day."

"That's incredible. I can't believe you did that."

This act of generosity painted Adam in an even brighter light.

"She deserved a break; I try to help people when I can. It's one of the few perks of being rich."

He didn't look particularly happy about being rich.

"I think there must be a 'million' perks to being rich?" I said and his brows drew together.

"They are overestimated. Money can't make you happy, Alice."

"It made Kinky happy."

Adam grinned finally and said, "Do you know what? You are right and you being here makes me happy. Will you come and meet some friends of mine?"

He tried to catch my elbow, but I sidestepped as a bright flashgun fired off. I was jolted backwards and blinked, half blind, as Adam pushed a black camera out of my face.

"Get lost Marcus and leave us alone."

The photographer shrugged and Adam swore, "Bloody Denton, I told him no photos."

As my eyes refocused, I found myself staring at the tiny black buttons glittering on the front of Adam's shirt.

"Are you alright?"

I was close enough to reach out and touch them, to trace the starched shirt up until I felt the fine point of his collar to smell the aftershave on his neck...

"Alice?"

"Hmm? What? No, I'm fine."

"Are you sure?"

"Yes of course."

"Follow me then."

Being anywhere near Adam was very high-risk for me. I walked as tight as a pencil to avoid touching anyone and was relieved when he led me to a bar with a thick metal pole running along the front of it.

I reached out and slid my hand along the ice-cold metal feeling a sharp click of static release as I discharged myself. I was safe and grounded for now.

Adam approached a rosy cheeked man with a yellow waistcoat who was downing a whisky.

"This inebriated lout is George Canther, one of my very best friends."

"One of your most unlucky friends," George corrected with a slight slur.

"Why unlucky?" I asked and George sighed.

"I spend my life burdened by bad karma. In fact, I only got here tonight because Adam saved my life. Again."

"That's only because you were texting your editor and not looking at the bus about to hit you."

Adam turned back to me and explained, "When George isn't attempting harakiri he is a very fine politician and an author. George, this is Alice."

"The famous Alice?" George leant towards me with a smile, "Adam's been telling me all about you."

Adam cleared his throat and I wondered what he had been saying as George added, "I'm on a quest too you know."

"Oh?"

"I'm here to fall into the arms of a goddess," he explained in an exaggerated whisper, "Adam is going to find one for me." Then he pointed at the floor with a slight stagger, "Tonight!"

"You will have to stop drinking George or it's game over."

George laughed, "You live life too seriously Adam."

Another man appeared beside me and Adam said, "Alice this is Cornelius Stryx."

"Ah, Alice, how interesting."

Cornelius Stryx held his hand out and because I was attached to the metal bar, I was actually able to shake it.

"Strix is a scientist."

"I have a doctorate in electromagnetism, if you want to be exact, Adam," Stryx explained.

He had grey, wiry hair, round, metal rimmed glasses and an accent like a German psychologist. "I have been writing a paper on action potentials and electrochemical gradients recently and...."

"And more importantly, he has started doing some field research for me," Adam cut him off.

Strix smiled, "Ah, yes. Research into a very unique field," he looked at me and repeated to himself, "Very unique."

George slapped the bar, "Enough of the boring introductions, let's get some more alcohol in. Who's calling the shots?"

"I'll go," Adam laughed, "Can I get you something Alice?"

"Yes, but not a shot," I said alarmed, "I'll just have a white wine please."

George held up his empty glass, "You're a God, Adam. Pick me up a large absinthe while you are there."

Adam headed off to find the barman, and Strix pushed his glasses up his nose, saying, "Do you know why dripping sugary, iced water into absinthe makes the liquid become opaque?"

"No."

"It's because the terpenes in the spirit precipitate out of the solution."

"Oh? How interesting," I smiled blankly back and heard George chuckle.

He said, "I'll tell you what, Cornelius. Why don't you toddle off to look at the white packet that just fell out of Demelitov's bag over there. I bet that would have an interesting effect on my absinthe."

"White powder? What's in it?"

"I have no idea," George declared innocently and Strix's face lit up.

"I'll go and find out."

He headed off towards the woman who had been booted up the bottom by Donna and George rolled his eyes, "I don't know how Adam puts up with him, he's so dull."

"Did you understand that whole opaque absinthe thing?"

"I did, actually," George replied, and I looked at him surprised.

"I used to teach science at a jolly posh prep school."

I laughed, "You don't look like a science teacher."

"No? Lots of people say that." George wrinkled his nose, "I wasn't very good at it."

"Do you still teach?"

"Not now, after a bit of a life crisis, I decided to give politics a try and rather enjoyed it. Still I'm putting that all behind me tonight."

"Because you're here to meet a woman?" I deduced.

"Not just a woman, Alice. I'm here to meet a goddess," George corrected, "She has to be incredibly beautiful."

"Well you have plenty of women to choose from."

I gestured towards the room and George asked, "How did Adam end up meeting you?"

I winced, "I met him during a bank robbery."

"Ha! Now that's one for your grandchildren to hear."

"That's jumping the gun a bit George!"

A small Indian man with an elaborately embroidered coat suddenly appeared beside us and began shaking George by the hand.

George introduced me, "Alice this is Raffi Suma, Adam's business partner and a famous Bollywood celebrity."

Raffi huffed modestly, "It's my wife, Sati, who is the celebrity. I am simply an ordinary businessman working with Adam."

"Is Sati here?" George asked looking beyond Raffi.

The small man pressed his hands together. "Unfortunately, my wife couldn't come this evening, she is busy filming in India."

"What a shame, I was hoping that she would introduce me to some of her friends." George looked crestfallen and Raffi patted him on the back.

"Don't worry too much George, Adam has plenty of other famous women fanning around him."

"Really?" I asked, feeling inferior in my off the peg dress.

George hopped with excitement, "Yes, just wait Alice. Adam knows everybody! And I mean everybody. His ex-girlfriend is one of the most beautiful women I have ever met."

Raffi had begun zipping his mouth frantically, trying to stop George talking, but George bumbled on.

"I mean seriously she was so hot that most men would...."

"A cold glass of water, George?"

Adam had arrived back and cut him off by thrusting a clear tumbler into George's hand.

George crowed a loud complaint but restrained himself as the room hushed and people began to turned towards the balustrade.

In the calm that settled I sipped my wine and thought about the conversation I had just had. George had said Adam and Raffi were partners.

The slow cogs of my brain also worked out that their surnames made up Warner and Suma, the lead names in the company five floors below mine. Did that mean that these men actually ran the company?

When Adam said he was rich he meant seriously rich! And, if that was the case, what on earth was I doing here? I had spent most of my life struggling to find the bus fare home and now stood in the company of business giants and film star millionaires.

This was all so out of my depth. I should be tucked up drinking a cup of cocoa now, watching this event occur on Paul's computer, not actually being in it.

A young DJ with red headphones on dipped the music in the room, holding one hand up in the air as the crowd fell into an expectant silence.

Adam stood behind me and fed details of the unfolding spectacle into my ear, "All the award winners are about to come down to join us."

I gasped, realising I would have ended up walking down the wide main stairway in the midst of them like a complete dork if that bouncer hadn't transplanted me.

"Look there's Carla Clandi and Jasper Laplage. Tinsel town's most adored couple."

They had chewing-gum white smiles, all-over tans and glided with effortless grace down the stairway.

"And that man coming down now...," this was a very thin older man with artificially big teeth, "is

Milo Topen, a famous film director who lives by his casting couch."

I recognised the name and twisted back to catch sight of Vinny jumping up and down with glee as the personality gave a twinkling wave in his direction.

"There's Anthony Lecturn from Space Voyages, the film that scooped all of the awards."

"The man with false looking hair?" I whispered back, "Do you think he is wearing a wig?"

Adam said quietly, "Probably, but aren't we all hiding something in this place, Alice?"

I turned to look at him, but he caught my shoulders and held me in position, murmuring, "No don't move, I didn't mean to say that."

"What did you mean to say?"

"I meant to say you look stunning tonight."

I shook my head, feeling awkward, "How can you mean that with all of these beautiful people around me?"

Adam moved his mouth closer and whispered, "Don't wish yourself away Alice, you're worth a thousand of them."

I swallowed, concentrating on slowing my breathing, aware of his jacket brushing against my dress and the warmth of his body behind my back.

He ran his fingers down one arm and I pressed my lips together, trying to maintain control as I clung rigidly to my metal bar.

Nobody except my aunt had touched me before and letting a man into my deadly static zone made me feel sick and ridiculously excited at the same time.

Then Adam looked up again and said, "The woman in white coming down now is Zara Capaldi and that's Gabrielle Hall."

Zara was the woman in white drapes I had seen earlier and the other was a stunning, dark-haired woman in the tightest, deep-red dress, stitched from top to bottom with shimmering sequins. She swam down the steps with effortless grace.

"Gabrielle Hall the supermodel?"

I almost withered on the spot when he nodded, and his lips brushed against my ear.

This was an insane form of torture. I was not allowed to do this, couldn't let someone get close to me, but god did it feel good.

"She's the ex-girlfriend that gave me the tickets."

"Oh." My wax wings of love shrivelled and burned. She was stunning. "Well I knew you had one of course, she's incredibly beautiful."

"Gabriella and I weren't really...," but his explanation was broken off as George tugged on his arm.

"Adam," he demanded in an urgent voice, "You need to introduce me to Zara."

I edged my shoulder out from under him and stepped away to put my glass down.

"She's a supermodel who only goes out with multimillionaires, George."

"But with a good word from you, she might look my way."

Adam hesitated and George's pleading voice took on a covert edge.

"You promised to help me in Cyprus, remember."

Adam let out a breath and shook his head, "How many times can I keep trying, George?"

"This is the last, come on. Pull a few strings for me and do the honours." He waited with a hopeful smile fixed across his face and then added, "After that I vow, I'll give up and leave you in peace."

Adam turned to face me, holding his hand out as he asked, "Do you want to come and meet some film stars?"

I shook my head, reality weighing like swamp water in my lungs. I would almost certainly end up shocking him and exposing the secret that had been my loadstone for so long.

"I...I need to go to the ladies first. Do you know where it is?"

"I think it's by the doors back there," Raffi replied.

Adam looked worried, so I gave a casual wave and said, "You go on, I'll catch up."

"But..."

George tugged on his arm.

"I'm fine," I said, turning away, "I'll come back and find you in a minute."

Chapter 9

I weaved across to the toilets and side-armed the door open to find the cool room blissfully empty.

Walking over to grab the porcelain sink, I saw my ordinary face with its amateur make up and collapsing hair staring back at me and wanted to punch it.

Shrinking backwards, I crouched in a corner and put my hands up against my cheeks to stop myself from melting into tears.

What the hell was I doing here? And why was Adam even talking to me? I was a poverty stricken, socially inept, badly dressed virgin with serious electricity issues.

If I went back out there, what was going to happen? A quick snog by my metal bar and then contact burns as soon as I let go?

If he was after a one-night stand, he wasn't going to get far. Not with my defective torture hands.

I hit the pipe that ran behind my bottom and felt a spark whip into my fingers. Then I stared at my painful hand and scrunched my knuckles tight, flicking them from me as if to throw the curse away.

I hated myself, hated my hands, and hated my life. Why couldn't I enjoy one night of freedom, just one simple date with no shocks? I didn't care if I was a bored man's diversion or even a quickie behind the back wall, one night of contact was better than growing old as a virgin spinster.

A tear brimmed, rolling down my cheek and I shut my eyes.

If I snuck away now Adam probably wouldn't notice or, if he did, he'd just be pissed off for a few days, never talk to me again and live the rest of his life wrapped in the long arms and legs of his million-pound lovers.

"Uh-oh, this looks like crisis management."

A woman just came into the room. No, not just any woman but, oh my God, it was the million-dollar Gabrielle Hall.

Bloody great, I thought to myself, the ex-girlfriend of my ex-boyfriend.

She walked into a toilet and grabbed a handful of tissues, holding them out to me, "Was it the awards?"

She was Australian and her accent captured exotic sunshine. She turned back to examine her eyebrows in the mirror.

I sniffed and said, "No, it's something far more basic than that."

She hitched up her lavishly embellished dress and sank down beside me, I fixed one of my hands on the metal piping behind my bum and clung tight, just in case I was carrying a charge.

Her slender shoulder slotted comfortably next to mine, "It must be a man then."

I nodded and she screwed up her nose, "It's always men. Do you smoke?"

"No."

"I wish you did; I'm dying for a fag."

To my surprise, I said, "Can I ask you a question?"

She shrugged, "Ask away."

I swallowed and then asked, "Do you know Adam Warner?"

She ran her tongue around her teeth and then picked a piece of fluff off her lips with long scarlet talons as the door slammed open and Donna strode in, shooting an imaginary gun in my direction.

"Ooooh, Gabrielle frigging Hall no less. You nailed it, Alice my girlie. Talk about picking a juicy one. Can I sit down too?"

She wiggled into the tiny space beside me, able to condense herself into the surprisingly narrow slot somehow. Then she shuffled into a comfy position and grinned, looking at each of our faces.

"Don't stop. Keep talking, I'll just sit here."

"Do you have a fag?" Gabrielle asked and despite my frantic actions to say no don't do it, Donna had shoved a hand down the front of her dress, rummaged around inside her ample bra and produced a giant splif to wiggle in front of us.

Gabrielle's eyes lit up and I half choked, stammering, "I don't think that's a good idea."

But even as I spoke the paper tube was being lit.

"Er...no. Are you allowed to do this?"

Gabrielle ignored me, took the splif, sucked hard and rested her head back against the wall in a bliss of relaxation.

"Sod the rules, this is good ganja. What's your name?"

"Donna." Donna also rested her head back and shut her eyes, "And this is Alice, she's here with Adam."

"Jesus Christ. My Adam? Is that why you were asking about him? Are you his new bitch of a girlfriend?" Gabrielle asked abruptly and my mouth dried in alarm.

"Er...well...I..."

I hadn't counted on her being jealous and panicked, taking the joint and giving it a desperate suck.

I had never let myself smoke anything before because I was too high-risk to be out of control, but my evening with Adam, Vinny and the bouncer had taken its toll and a fight in the toilet could be my final straw.

I coughed and said in a husky voice, "I'm not exactly going out with him."

"But he's invited you here tonight?"

My head swam almost instantly, "Kind of."

She lifted a hand to give me an unexpected punch on the shoulder and said, "Good for old Benny Boy. But I warn you, if you're planning to melt the ice king's heart, you're going to have to perform a bloody miracle."

"Ice king?"

She laughed.

"Oh, don't get me wrong. Physically, he blew me away. I mean, he was sensational in bed, but he was always in control and made it quite clear that he could never love anybody, ever." She sniffed and did some yoga rotations with her neck, "It was probably just an excuse to get rid of me. You know what men are like."

"Did he say why?"

Gabrielle shrugged, "No, we never talked about it. We were only shag buddies, it did us both good."

She waved her slim, suntanned fingers, "It gave the illusion to the press that we were in a long-term relationship to stop them hassling us."

Shag buddies? Well, that summed up the kind of world he lived in. Perhaps I did myself a favour by walking away.

I stretched my feet out and realised they only reached to two thirds the length of Gabrielle's and saw dear Donna's were even shorter.

"Alice," Gabrielle said my name as if trying on a new coat.

"Yes?"

"That's a pretty name, your mum and dad must have liked you when you were born. I wasn't born Gabrielle you know?"

She took a lung-filling suck and held it for a long time before relaxing and passing it back to me. I took it, having crossed the pot-taking boundary already, what difference would a couple of extra puffs make?

"Nope. My Mum and Dad thought it would be really cute to call me Brownie. Brownie Hall, what kind of shit name is that? It stuck until I was 14, when my agent said that it sounded like a public toilet, so I forced them to change it."

I held the joint out to Donna who shook her head, enjoying her moments of superstar toilet revelation.

Gabrielle took it back again with practiced fingers and shook the joint, "I know I shouldn't smoke this but, when you've had to sit next door to gropey Milo Topen all evening, you need a point of release."

"Milo Topen? He is really famous though."

"Yeh, what is it with all these scumball men? He had his hands halfway up my skirt the whole time, as if he would ever stand a chance."

"I could easily put him out of action if you wanted," Donna offered.

"Do you know, I might take you up on that when he does it next time."

"I've seen her in action, she's scary," I told Gabrielle and Donna grinned.

"I have my techniques."

Gabrielle twisted upwards to flick the ash into the sink.

"So, do you have any vices, Alice?"

I made a guttural sound in my throat, "God yes."

"It isn't prescription meds is it? I have a ton of friends addicted to those. They completely screw up your acting of course. But that doesn't affect me I'm just a clothes horse."

"But a very beautiful one."

She snorted, "A lot of good it's done. I've had more men than hot dinners and never loved any of them."

"Oh."

I coughed, feeling my brain elevate up to the ceiling and stare back down at the three of us sitting like dollies on the floor.

"Well you're luckier than me. I've never even been kissed properly by anyone, let alone had sex with them. I'm going to end up like a closeted, electric bloody Nun. How sad is that?"

"Do you know what?"

"What?"

"You're probably gay and you don't know it yet."

"Gay?"

She took a deep inhalation, held it and nodded, "I can snog you now if you want. So you can check out how it feels. It wouldn't bother me, I'm fine with either. Kiss you just as happily as the next man."

"Or woman," Donna piped up, perking up beside me and looking across with interest, "I'm in!"

I blinked and tried to pull myself together. I had just been labelled a lesbian by a spliff-smoking goddess in the back toilet of the BFAs and was about to be squashed in the middle of a hemp-packed love sandwich. How much more bizarre could my life become?

"I think that I should get going before I do something I might regret," I said, pushing myself upright. Then I tried to stand on spaghetti legs as the other two made ungainly attempts at moving too.

"No don't stand up. It's far better down on the ground believe me."

I stared back in the direction of the reception room and asked, "Do you know how to get out of here?"

"Well, if the door looks too extreme, you could always try the window." Gabrielle pointed up towards a tiny, ruler-sized window in the wall above their heads.

Donna agreed, "Windows are always a good on a dodgy date."

She finally accepted the joint and took a long pull, realizing it had almost burnt through. "Have you done many windows, Gabrielle?"

I tried to refocus their conversation, "No, no, hang on, not the toilet," my hands formed a circle, "This whole building."

"Well we could always roll you up in the red carpet and you could go home like Cleopatra," Gabrielle sniggered.

"I roll very well, you know," Donna chipped in.

"I bet you do, you little minx."

I said, "Can you tell Adam I wasn't feeling well or something?"

"Sure will." Gabrielle shuffled towards Donna, "That was bloody strong stuff you know."

Donna's eyes twinkled and she started rummaging inside her bra again.

"I've got another one in my other boob."

I gave up, grabbed my bag and left them to it.

Chapter 10

A back exit avoiding the mezzanine stairway was harder to find than I had expected, partially because the corridors kept looming in on me, but also because my balance was shot to pieces and I kept bumping into the walls.

After three attempts at back routes, I finally spotted an emergency exit in the corner of the main hall, a space that was still teeming with people.

It would only take about ten steps to reach but Adam was standing by the bar, scanning the room. I debated my chances of making it across without him seeing me and hovered on unsteady feet, peeping through a glass door.

Then Pedro Distillo stepped up to the microphone, ready to begin singing and I gave a sad little moan, longing to stay and listen.

"Ground yourself, Alice," I muttered and slapped my cheeks, forcing my fuzzy thoughts back to escaping, after all, my absence would be noticed at any minute.

In fact it had been noticed already and Adam, seeing that I hadn't reappeared, drew his eyebrows together, pushing through the far door that led to the toilets.

I grinned and high-fived myself, his timing couldn't have been better. My escape route was clear.

Dashing for the emergency exit, I pressed the heavy metal bar down and felt it splatter with electricity. Its stiff hinges resisted until a second, harder shove broke it open and I fell through the gap, stumbling free from my danger zone.

The door clanged shut behind me, and I staggered upright, breathing in the silent, fresh, dark air. I closed my eyes and spread my arms wide, feeling like a hot air balloon that had been released into the limitless sky.

Feeling the world lurch, I cursed the dizziness that kept sweeping over me and turned in surprise as the door opened again, almost immediately.

The mystery bouncer from earlier slipped through it, reached out to grab my elbow and pushed me back into an alcove with his hand over my mouth.

I tried to protest but within another five seconds the door opened a third time and Adam stepped out. He took a silent look up and down the street before swearing and turning to go back in, slamming the door closed behind him.

"Yikes that was close," I whispered as the bouncer moved his hand.

"I was guessing that you wanted to avoid him."

"Hell yes. Adam isn't luring me in tonight, even if he is a God in the bedroom." I began to react now and pushed him away, "I don't even know who you are. Why are you out here with me?"

"I saw he was following you and I didn't have time to explain, so..."

Oh my God this bouncer had done it again. I looked at his shock-free hands, "How did you do that?"

"What?"

"Touch me?"

He drew his eyebrows together and asked, "Is this a trick question?"

"It's a bloody shocking question!"

Then he bent his head to one side to look at me, "Are you alright?"

I bent mine to one side too but looking at someone with a horizontal face wasn't ever going to do my balance any good and I stumbled as he said, "Oh Christ, you're high aren't you?"

I shook my head, "No, Gabrielle Hall is definitely higher than me. She did weed in the toilet."

Then I giggled, realising what I had just said, "Weed in the toilet! That's quite funny, actually."

The bouncer, who had his arm locked around my waist, didn't seem to have a sense of humour at all.

"How are you getting home tonight, Alice?"

My knees gave way and I slid down his front. "I don't know. How did you know Lola's name earlier?"

"Concentrate. You need to get a taxi."

"Donna's bra was the problem; it was fully loaded!"

"You're not making any sense."

"I am, it's just that you don't understand me."

He tried to walk me forwards, but my struggling legs became knotted underneath me and gravity dragged my face down towards the ground.

I watched my bag spill coins everywhere as it hit the pavement, heard him swear, sigh and say my name, heard a taxi being called, and then felt solid hands gather me up from the cold concrete before the doors of consciousness finally closed.

I had strange, elongated arms in my dream. Arms that dragged behind me as I sauntered up a deserted catwalk.

Lola appeared, picked one up off the floor and looked at my stretched-out fingers. She clicked her tongue disapprovingly and said, "You will never get a wedding ring on these hands, Alice."

I pulled away from her and a metallic lift door opened revealing Stephanie, my line manager inside.

She had covered its corners with thick black thread and was calling me over to look inside a disturbing, funnel shaped web.

Backing off in alarm, I tripped over, Donna, who had twisted herself up in my bedroom carpet and looked like a giant rolled up cigarette.

Reaching a spaghetti arm out to help her, I missed and dangled it through my window and picked up Milo Topen's burnt trousers lying on the pavement below.

Trying to give them back, I found that the famous man had changed into a bearded lady with insects in his mouth.

He smiled and revealed hundreds of segmented legs wriggling between his teeth, asking if I had any dental floss going spare.

I snapped awake and blinked in the pale wash of early dawn. Swallowing against a throat like sandpaper, I cradled my exploding head and rolled onto my side, after all strange dreams were better than throbbing headaches.

Then I froze.

The pillow under my face wasn't my pillow. This was spongy and hard. I stretched out an arm and felt a rough woollen blanket scratch back.

Alarm bells fired and kick me into full, painful consciousness.

Where the hell was I? I sat upright, struggling to bring an unfamiliar room into focus as panic swept over me.

Had I been abducted and date raped by some weirdo?

I pushed back the blanket to check and found that I was still dressed in my evening gown with my tights and knickers on.

My evening gown. Of course!

I had been to the British Film Awards to meet Adam.

Perhaps this was Adam's house. I looked around me and scowled, did Adam really sleep in a bedroom like this?

The room was barely larger than the double bed I was lying in and had strange forest wallpaper claustrophobically plastered onto every wall.

Feeling dizzy as I pushed myself to the edge of the bed, I levelled my unstable feet on the floor and squinted at a small alarm clock on the bedside table.

It was still only 4:35 in the morning, perhaps I could sneak out unnoticed.

I staggered upright, caught a sharp thwack from a cold radiator, and shook my fingers, swearing under my breath as I crept across to the bedroom door, inching it open a crack.

Pressing one eyeball up to the narrow gap, I observed a small sitting room with white walls, polished floorboards and pine furniture.

This opened onto a wood-clad galley kitchen at its far end with a breakfast bar and two pine stools pushed up against it.

All the wood everywhere gave the place an alpine lodge look and there should have been a set of skis defrosting by the door.

Instead, in the middle of everything, unmissable, large and snoring on a futon settee, was the bouncer from the night before.

Oh God. I closed my eyes and leant against the wall for reassurance as the memories from the previous evening crowded in.

Adam, the toilets, the supermodel, the ganja cigarettes.

But what happened next? This man had obviously brought me home with him, but why? How?

I couldn't remember any details after being in the toilet and screwed my face up. Forcing my mind back, I conjured a fleeting image of him talking to me at the back of the cinema, but I had no idea what had happened.

Had I snogged him? Collapsed on him? Did he find out that I shocked people? My skin crawled with every predicament.

My only option was to escape before he woke.

Easing the door open, I tiptoed into the living room and found my bag and shoes stacked in the far corner.

I scooped them up and then turned, standing in silence as I studied the person who had brought me home with him.

He was a heftily built man with chestnut hair, blunt features and a heavy chin, now dark with stubble. His breath was deep and rhythmic and there was a feeling of solid stability about him that made me hesitate.

I half wanted to wake him and find out what had happened, ask him who he was, but then sensibility returned. I was in a strange man's flat, all alone, god knows where in London and I had to get away.

I walked across to a large dresser taking up most of one wall, found a post-it note and scribbled a rapid sentence.

"Sorry for causing you all these problems, hope I wasn't too much trouble, love Alice."

I shoved a couple of happy crosses underneath it and then left it on the bottom shelf next to a thick book entitled, "The Beginning of Life's Secret."

Inching the chain-jangling front door slowly open, I winced as it let out a loud creak, freezing in place as the snoring hitched.

I counted to ten, waited until the low rumbling sounds had begun again and then smushed my body through the slim opening.

As the snoring stopped altogether, I scooted down three flights of steps to the ground floor and threw myself out of the communal entrance.

The gardens of the squat 1970s apartment block sat quiet and undisturbed as I sprinted through them expecting a hefty bouncer to barrel after me.

After five minutes at high speed, my pace dropped off and I began looking for a distinctive landmark to place myself.

This proved harder than I thought, because the tightly packed houses in this part of London shouldered together, blocking my sightline.

The identical streets around me seemed empty and old fashioned. Dawn nudged colour onto their broad bricked chimneys and I imagined Mary Poppins hopping along each one with her cheerful chimney sweep, his circular brush sticking out like a parasol over one shoulder.

Eventually I emerged by Camden Lock Market and wandered along its riverbank, accompanied for a long time by a hungry duck. At least <u>he</u> didn't care if I walked home at 5am wearing zombie makeup and a very grubby evening dress.

Chapter 11

"What happened to you last night?"

I had my head buried in my hands, my brain in danger of imploding. Three hours of drugged sleep in a stranger's bed and an hour and a half's walk home had done me no favours.

I twisted to lie my cheek against the cool wood as Adam rested his hands on my desk.

"I looked everywhere for you."

It was eight fifteen and big-eared Megan (and I mean big-eared) had little else to do with her morning other than listen and gossip. She had even moved her chair closer to me in order to get a clearer take on the conversation.

"I didn't feel very well."

"You didn't feel well? You could have told me you were leaving."

"It wasn't exactly a one-on-one date was it," I countered dryly.

"It was as much of a date as you would give me, Alice."

"Alright, I'm sorry, perhaps I should have let you know."

He began to calm down and asked, "Where did you go?"

Stephanie walked up behind me with a black coffee, hopefully loaded with sugar.

"I don't allow visitors on the work floor, Alice."

Her shrapnel voice bore no nonsense as the cup clunked down beside my head.

"He's about to leave Steph, can you give me two minutes?"

She grunted and then bent to study Megan's monitor, both of them earwigging on my crisis.

"I..." I lowered my voice, "I came across dizzy and had to get some fresh air."

"So you just left?"

"I didn't just leave. I told Gabrielle I was leaving."

"You told...?"

"Gabrielle, your ex-girlfriend."

He shook his head and bent to whisper, "You trusted the biggest pot-head alive to pass on a message to me?"

I nodded.

"Did you know that, by the end of the party, she got herself stuck in the toilet window and has now hit the front page of every newspaper?"

"No!" I bit my bottom lip. "Was she alright?"

"Yes fine, eventually."

"God, I feel so guilty, I started the conversation about the window."

He crouched down and cleared his throat with an irritated click. "I have been worried sick, where did you go when you left?"

"Where did I go?"

"No-one knew where you were."

"I...I went to a friend's." I realised he was still in his dinner suit, "Haven't you been home yet?"

"All your friends were still at the party."

I couldn't exactly tell him that I'd ended up sleeping the effects off in an unknown bouncer's bed, could I?

"Adam, please don't ask me all these questions."

"Alice," Stephanie's sharp voice prodded me back to work.

"Come out for supper with me."

"You're joking."

"Why not?"

"Why not? I have just been to one of the most disastrous parties of my life, set fire to someone, caused your ex-girlfriend to get stuck in a window, smoked pot and then got yelled at for skipping out on a date. It wasn't exactly a success."

"I didn't yell."

"You didn't need to. Everything counts as a yell inside my head this morning!"

He looked at me for a long five seconds and then said despairingly, "Alice, I just tried to spend an evening with you."

"I know but I don't do dates well. Give up on it, Adam."

"Alice…"

"No," I pulled my keypad towards me and pretended to type, "I have to work."

He dragged his hands off my desk then backed off. I watched him walk away and felt acid fill my stomach as Steph ordered, "Drink some caffeine Alice, you can't work in that state."

I picked up the hot mug and burned my lips on the scalding black coffee.

I'd screwed everything up. Adam could be the one and only handsome man that ever wanted to know me and I had effectively kicked him in the bollocks. Clever self-destructive mutant Alice does it again. I might as well go and live the rest of my life out in a frigging nunnery.

Donna crept into the office looking very pale and wearing dark glasses at nine thirty and, after receiving a rollicking from Steph, slid, slug-like into her seat.

Seeing that she was in a worse state than me made me feel a little better and I caught Lola speaking to her by the drink dispensers at coffee break.

"It's not just that. You left your post Donna. We had to cover for you."

Donna went even whiter if that was possible. "I...I got carried away."

"It could have all gone wrong. Thank God Max had the sense to…"

"What could have gone wrong?" I asked poking my head into their conversation and Lola jumped before holding up a picture on the front page of her Daily Speculator.

A red sequinned bottom and long legs were sticking out of a very small window. I grabbed the paper and scanned its headline.

"Supermodel spends glitterati evening stuck in the crapper!"

Lola flung an accusing glare at Donna as I continued reading.

"Supermodel Gabrielle Hall was so stoned last night she tried to make a back exit out of the ladies toilet window. Despite help from other guests, the fire service was eventually called and had to soap her up in order to slide her out through the tight opening. Unruffled by the undignified experience Gabrielle waved as she left the building shouting, it was just like being born again boys, you should try it some time."

I gasped, "Donna what did you do?"

"I just bet Gabrielle she couldn't climb through it," Donna downed a cup of water, "So she said, I'll do it if you do it first."

"Are you telling us you fitted through that tiny hole before her?" I was astonished, small windows and wide stomachs do not normally mix, "How?"

She shrugged and pushed the hair out of her eyes.

"I have small bones."

I shook my head in disbelief as Lola cut in, folding up the newspaper and deliberately changing the subject, "Let's not talk about it anymore. I'm having my bridesmaids' fitting next Wednesday. You need to book the afternoon off, Alice."

Vinny appeared from nowhere and stood beside us, pressing his palms together.

"Did I hear talk of bridesmaids? When are we doing the deed?"

"Next Wednesday."

He covered his mouth in mock outrage, "Wednesday?...Jesus that's quick! Have you really thought this through, my honey?"

"Vinny, I have met my fantasy man."

He sulked, sticking his bottom lip out, "Some girls get all the luck. Milo hasn't called me back yet."

I remembered Lola's pale skinny man in the night club and wondered what his secret was. Then I thought of the fantasy man I had just ejected from my life and slumped morosely.

"Now bear in mind that you are all going to be flowers."

"Flowers?" Donna asked, frowning, "What do you mean flowers?"

"It's part of my floral theme. The outfits may seem a little strange by themselves, but I promise that they'll look magnificent when we all walk down the aisle together."

I drooped even more, what were we going to end up looking like?

"Oh, and I have the perfect outfit for you Vinny," she laughed and cupped his cheeks with delight.

"Is it?"

She nodded, "Lilac and cream. Can you handle a man skirt?"

"Oh God yes. Lola Rose you are hitting my fantasy outfit now. Why didn't you get married earlier?"

"Believe me, I've tried."

She tapped her fingertips together with glee and turned to walk off with shining eyes, smelling more strongly of rose perfume than I had ever noticed.

I looked back at Donna and raised my eyebrows, "Have you ever been a flower before?"

She sighed, "God, I bet I'm an onion or a thistle, I always get typecast."

"How did you manage to get through a hole too small for Gabrielle Hall to fit through?"

Donna shrugged, "I'll explain it all to you one day, Alice, just not now perhaps."

She mimed her head exploding and walked back to her department. There was something about Donna that simply didn't add up.

Chapter 12

The following day I had fallen behind with one of my spreadsheets and had to stay late at lunch time to finish it.

Having arranged to meet up with Lola and her tec-head fiancé in the park, I sped through my list and then stopped, puzzling over the last entry.

It had the same name and credit card number but two different billing addresses. This was easy to rectify but took time, so I'd have to finish it later.

I knocked on Stephanie's door, waited a couple of seconds and then pushed it opened to find her hunched over, her attention fixed on a Mills and Boon romance.

This, in itself wasn't unusual, Steph hoarded these kind of books on her shelving units, what <u>was</u> unusual was the wide curtain of spit that was dribbling out of her mouth.

This bubbly slime overflowed her lips and puddled down onto a plate, drowning a mucousy lump of ham in a frothy soup of saliva.

I stopped in shock, hanging like a puppet in the door frame as she opened her eyes wide, grabbed several tissues to break the spit trail and then twisted away from me.

I backed off, mumbling something about coming back later as I dragged the door shut, struggling to cope with the bizarre and revolting scene inside.

Unsure what else to do, I walked across to my desk, picked up my sandwiches and headed for the exit as her door swung open.

"Wait, Alice. It's a hormone problem. I have to do that to digest my food!" Steph shouted across the empty room.

"Don't worry about it, Steph, I didn't see anything," I waved back, cracking my shoulder against the swing doors.

"Nothing?"

"I promise. Nothing. Your lunch hour is your own business."

She threw me a grateful smile and called out, "You can take as long as you want for lunch!"

Lunch? The last thing I could think of was lunch. I staggered out of the building and was hit by nauseous, dense heat. London was wallowing in a pocket of soupy, still air that was nearing body temperature.

Milwall Park was a clammy ten minutes' walk from the office and turned out to be incredibly busy. Every sun loving office worker in the area had descended on the green patch and were crowding me out with their sprawling bodies and sweaty armpits.

My lunch-break had turned into a game of 'Where's Wally' and I had to try and find the canoodling woman with the rose in her hair.

I walked around for about fifteen minutes and felt my energy levels drop as I reached the far end of the park. This is where I needed a mobile phone. I sat on a vacant bench and stared down at my unappetising sandwiches. Our lunchtime rendezvous was evidently not going to happen.

That's when I saw it. An ominous and sinister droplet of water hitting the ground in front of my foot with a heavy thud.

London's humidity had pushed the atmosphere to breaking point and I hadn't noticed. I was about to be caught in the middle of a park, in the middle of a thunderstorm.

I jumped up as the overgrown drops began to multiply and watched the people around me grab their picnic things and scamper to take shelter under the bandstand.

But I couldn't do that.

I was a conductor of electricity and anywhere outside during a summer storm was extremely dangerous.

I began walking as more and more droplets made little puffs of sand dance under my feet, while a low grumble of thunder shook the air.

If there is one thing that terrifies me more than anything, it's thunder and lightning. This makes sense considering my problem, but the really strange thing is that this terror existed before I had a problem with static.

One of my first memories from childhood was screaming in horror and shaking under the kitchen table as my aunt's long arms reached across to pull me out. Another time, I remembered sitting on her lap in a darkened hallway clinging to her like a limpet and thinking that I was going to die.

Panic built inside me as I reached the gates of the park, these were the far gates and I still had a long walk back to safety.
The hairs on my arms rose up as heavy raindrops crackled against my skin, my shirt clung to my chest with static and I knew that I wasn't going to make it back to the office.
There was a coffee shop three streets away. If I could just get there I would be alright, but, with each step my muscles ached and a tiny spasm triggered as a distant flash of lightning lit the sky.

The cloudburst was intensifying, dropping the temperature sharply. Rain plastered my hair to my head and water ran down my legs, pooling in my shoes.

Dread crushed my chest and I forced myself onwards, just two more roads and I'd be safe, but even as the café's bright lights shone ahead, my feet began to tingle. Charge was building in the air and it loaded up on me like the spring on a mousetrap.

I grabbed one of the railings, hoping to discharge myself but it made no difference, the dense drops were sparking me up.

I heard myself sob in desperation.

I didn't want to be here, I wanted to be back in the hall with Aunty Phyl, cocooned in my office, sheltering with Lola, hiding with anybody, just away from this lethal park.

Wiping the water off the end of my nose, my head spun and pressure started to build behind my eyes, my knees buckled, and as I was just about to collapse, a car revved up beside me, its door swinging open.

"Get in."

"What?"

"Get in or you're going to get hit by lightning."

I wrenched my hand away from the metal railing, stumbling as I closed the distance to the car. A huge shock sparked as I touched its sleek grey door but I barely flinched, throwing myself in and yanking the door shut with a whump.

I was safe.

Pressing my hands to my numb face, I tried to block out the almost instantaneous flash and bang outside.

I shut my eyes for a full ten seconds before I could breathe again as Adam watched in silence, waiting for me to recover.

"Are you alright?" he asked eventually, and I looked across at him, my fingers trembling as I brushed the damp hair away from my face.

"I think so."

"You got drenched."

I mustered a shaky laugh, "I don't know where it came from, the weather was alright when I left the office."

"Here, do you want a towel?"

He rummaged in the back seat and produced a towel from a sports bag, just as I took it though, another overhead clap of thunder rocked the street and I jumped away from the window.

"You're safe you know. You are insulated inside a car."

"I may be in theory, but I don't trust physics. Especially when a storm is this close."

"Have you had lunch yet?"

"No, I was meant to meet Lola for a packed lunch in the park."

"Where's your food?"

"I abandoned it." I had left my sandwiches on the bench when I fled and the pigeons or some shoe steeling tramp would probably be eating the sodden slices by now.

"If you fancy Italian, I haven't eaten either."

He saw the apprehensive expression on my face and shook his head, "It's just lunch Alice, you need to get somewhere safe and dry."

Another growl of thunder broke the air and I nodded.

"Good. Well there is a place called Lupo near here that sells pasta and has an underground car park beside it."

"Wait. I have to let Lola know I'm alright. She'll wonder where I've gone."

"You can use my phone if you want."

He pulled a mobile out of his top pocket and put in a passcode, making it give out a strange little chirrup.

I looked at the device and gave a derisive snort. "I can't use mobile phones."

"Why not? You're in a car out of the thunder and I should have good reception."

And then I realised he was actually right; a car is something called a Faraday cage (and someone like me pays attention when Faraday cages are talked about in class). All electricity created in them cannot contact the ground due to their metal exterior and rubber wheels.

This was why I was safe from lightning in the car, and it also meant that I would be able to use his touch screen while I was sitting insulated by it.

I tentatively took the device, relieved to find it didn't crackle but being a technophobe, I had no idea what to do with it.

"I don't know how to...,"

I jerked as Adam pressed his hand firmly behind mine and tapped a few buttons with the other.

"You just have to put the number in and press the green 'call' icon."

Then he turned back, put his car in gear and began driving while I sat, awestruck by the painless touch of his hand. His strong, elegant fingers had been warm behind mine.

In this car his fingers could touch me everywhere without a shock. I imagined falling into his lap as he stoked my face, caressed my neck, slipped down to undo the top button of my shirt and then...and then I caught sight of my reflection in the window and realised why he had turned away.

Not only had I been obnoxious to him the last time that we met but I also looked like a drowned ghost.

My hair was dank strands of seaweed plastered flat against my forehead and my see-through shirt stuck to my thin shoulders. A shirt that was now revealing my luminous pink Primark bra which glowed starkly through the material.

I focused, took a reality check and began to dial Lola's number to tell her I was off to Lupo.

"So, it looks like I have to thank you for helping me, again," I said as I gave a slight shiver in the cool air of the restaurant.

He huffed, "It seems that you really do live your life in crisis, Alice."

"More often than you would know."

"I thought you were going to pass out."

I made the mistake of glancing up then and when his eyes locked into mine, a twist unraveled inside me, starting in my chest and travelling all the way down to my toes.

"I was fine."

"You were not."

"I panicked. It was stupid. I feel really stupid now that I'm warm and dry in here."

He took a sip of his wine and I fidgeted in the silence that followed, trying to unstick my shirt from my collar bone. Finally, I addressed the elephant in the room.

"Look, Adam, I'm sorry I was so rude to you yesterday. You just caught me at a bad..."

"You don't need to apologise. You were right."

"I was?"

"I manipulated you into going to the party, forced you to talk to me and then was cross when you left. It served me right."

I sighed and stared down at my napkin.

"You didn't force me to talk to you and I was still horrible."

After a few moments of silence, he laughed to himself and I looked up to see him shaking his head.

"So do you often run out on dates?"

"No," I laughed in return. "Do you often manipulate people?"

His eyes creased with humour, "All the time. It's my character flaw."

"God, I wish that was my worst character flaw."

"I don't believe you have any, Alice."

Well I had walked into that one!

"Where do I even begin?"

"Fine, let's start on a different footing, how about telling me..." he thought about it, "Your first memory as a child?"

A slim-boned waitress delivered a plate containing boiled gnocchi with truffle and walnut paste dolloped throughout a sea of zesty tomato salsa.

I began to feel better as I ate.

"And you've only ever had your aunt bringing you up?" Adam sipped from a permanently topped-up wine glass.

"My aunt? Yes, but she was great, she worked from home mostly."

"Doing what?"

"Oh, you know, beauty therapies and stuff."

"But surely you must have some kind of connection to your parents?"

"No, I only have a picture of my mum holding me when I was a tiny baby."

"What about your dad?"

"I've never known anything about him."

"Nothing?"

I pulled an indifferent face, "No, nothing. In fact,.I don't even know his name."

The waitress picked up our plates and put down a drink that was nothing like normal coffee.

"What is this? It tastes like syrup."

Adam laughed, "You ordered it."

He had ordered one too. It had a thin layer of hot coffee at the bottom while a sweet yolky mixture clagged up the rest of the tall glass. I sipped, I mixed, I sipped again and watched Adam down his with apparent enjoyment.

We fell into silence just as the party next to us left and the cool air of the restaurant drifted to a lull. I sighed and twisted my cup, looking at the thick coffee mixture.

"Do you mind if I go to the ladies?"

He looked up at me and then asked quietly, "Will you come back again?"

My cheeks burned, his uncertainty crushing my wobbly confidence, "Do you think I am that unreliable?"

He lifted a finger from his cup and shrugged.

The underground toilets were claustrophobic and hot. I splashed water up onto my cheeks and looked at my eyes in the mirror. They were a coward's eyes.

Adam was just trying to get to know me and I had kicked him away, unable to trust a genuinely interested person. Why was I living my whole life in fear of something that I didn't understand?

I took a slow walk up the steps into the restaurant and ambled through the rear seating area, lost in my own thoughts, but then I heard a voice that I recognised.

"I'll keep my eyes open; she'll be back soon."

I turned to focus on the table beside me.

"Vinny?"

He looked as shocked as I did and knocked over his wine glass.

"Oh my God, Alice, what are *you* doing here?"

He stood up to air kiss me as I said, "I could ask you the same thing."

"Oh, well. I often try out new places."

"And you came to Lupo? On the same lunch break as me?"

"Yes, what a coincidence," he pulled his earlobe and turned to the person he was sitting with. This was the DJ I had seen at the awards ceremony, the one with red headphones on. In fact, he was still bizarrely wearing the same headphones while having his meal.

If Vinny had got together with this guy, he had stayed very quiet about it and that was not like Vinny at all.

I tipped my head and asked, "And this is?"

Vinny blushed, "Jack, this is Jack. He is a friend of mine from work."

"From work?" I was sure that he was the DJ, plus I knew everyone Vinny worked with.

The blushed deepened and ran down Vinny's neck.

"Oh, did I say that?...I meant to say...this is...Alice. Alice is a friend of mine from work."

He fanned his face, saying, "I'm getting all hot and flustered, aren't I?" Picking up his wine glass, Vinny looked into it and added, "Alice, this is Jack."

The young, fresh-faced Jack half stood, smiling in greeting and I noticed that the end of the head phones weren't attached to anything, perhaps this was the latest fashion whim in the music industry.

I just smiled in return.

Vinny pulled at his collar and then continued, strangely tongue-tied.

"And Jack...Jack is a special friend of mine I have known for a long time...from...school."

Well, to my skeptical eye, he looked about ten years younger than Vinny, but it was prudent to avoid a debate with Adam waiting on a timer. Instead, I asked, "Are you enjoying the food?"

"Yes. Have you tried the Casu Marzu?" Vinny rolled his eyes in ecstasy, "It is out of this world. Jack didn't like it, of course but he isn't a great one for new flavours."

"I don't think I've ever heard of it."

"Ah, you've been missing out in life, Alice. This is cheese with the most exquisite flavour. Look closely and you'll see hundreds of..." Vinny broke off as his sticky hand caught the edge of the small table and it's spindly legs crumpled, tipping the entire setting onto the floor.

I winced as all the food, cutlery, plates and remaining wine cascaded downwards with an almighty crash and then edged backwards as several waiters closed in.

Deciding to make a tactical retreat, I left Vinny to sort out his own commotion and returned to Adam.

Fiddling with my napkin five minutes later, I said, "So tell me something about *your* childhood?"

"Me?" Adam sounded surprised.

"Yes, you know all about me, but you haven't said anything about yourself at all."

"I was born into a wealthy family and grew up just outside London."

"Go on," I prompted.

"Not much more to say beyond that. I was pampered from birth, went to an expensive private school and was given every luxury a child could ever need. Fairly mundane, if I'm honest."

This didn't fit with Gabrielle's description. Where had the Ice King come from?

"Were you happy?"

He gave a tight smile, "What is happy?"

Then he lifted his arm to call the waitress over for the bill and she almost touched me as she cleared the cups from the table. I slid my hand away from hers.

"Did you grow up with any brothers or sisters?"

"It depends which way you look at it. Don't you ever want to trace your parents, Alice?"

I shook my head, wondering why he had changed the subject.

"What has that got to do with…," but I broke off because he reached across the table to put his hand over my fingers.

Snatching my arm back, I clenched my fists under the table.

"Why won't you let people touch you Alice?"

I felt as if he had slapped me.

"What do you mean?"

"I mean you flinch every time I come anywhere near you."

The colour must have drained from my face and I heard ringing in my ears.

"Alice."

This is what I had dreaded. My hands were clammy under the table and I lifted one to pull on the button of my shirt, trying to get more air into my lungs.

"Alice, it doesn't matter."

I was going to have to get out of there, away from this intrusion. Adam had noticed and I had to get away from him.

"Alice, focus on me!"

The command in his voice brought my eyes back to his.

"Listen to me. I don't care."

"I...I need to go."

I began to stand and he went to put a hand over mine to catch me and then stopped himself.

"You don't. I promise I was just trying to divert the conversation. Please stay."

"I've got to get back to work."

"I know but not like this. Just talk to me about something neutral, your favourite holidays, your hobbies, your flat, anything. Just show me you are alright."

I faltered, knowing my legs were like jelly and folded back down again.

He said, "Do you want to know something...something really stupid that nobody else knows?"

I didn't respond.

"I saved George's life with a dinghy once in Cyprus and he has reminded me about it every day since."

Adam raised his eyebrows, trying to pull me back into the conversation and said, "Please, just talk to me Alice."

I eased out of my lockdown and gave a small shrug.

"Will you show me you're alright?"

"How?"

"Tell me something trivial."

"Like what?"

"I don't care, anything."

"Fine, I used to have a hamster called Mootie."

He cautiously repeated, "Mootie?"

"I think it's another word for marijuana."

"Why was your hamster called that?"

"My aunt used to make hashish cakes for some of her clients. Mootie was her code. When they asked about my hamster, they automatically received a happy cake."

I gave him a hint of a smile and Adam's shoulders relaxed. Shaking his head, he sighed, "Alice. How am I ever going to hold on to you?"

I shrugged, "I don't think anyone can."

His fingers slid forwards until they were millimetres away from my edge of the table and then stopped.

"You set the parameters, Alice and I will stay in them. I promise."

Chapter 13

So, I had a slight problem with the printer at work.

I had set it to print a document out eight times and the damned thing started printing eight hundred instead. I called Donna and Vinny in to help.

Vinny pressed the same buttons as me and then tried to take out the feed tray. This jammed in place, stuck to his hands and created a great flurry of paper, carpeting the floor of the small room.

As the machine was beginning to smell hot, Donna decided she could reach the plug at the back of the unit. Unfortunately, after some effort, she managed to fall down the narrow side of it in a space barely more than 15 centimetres wide and wedged in place, her ballooning rear sticking out.

Michael from engineering arrived on the back of an emergency call just as the smell of hot plastic was beginning to get really worrying.

Then flash-pants Gavin came in, helped Michael heave the machine away from Donna and finally revealed the plug socket.

I reached down to yank it out, leant on the printer and managed to give Michael and Gavin a massive punch of static.

Gavin whooped with joy at the thrill while Michael thought he had been hit by the mains current and slumped, sweating with panic on the floor.

Stephanie came in, decided he was going into full cardiac arrest, called an ambulance and had him carted off to hospital where he had to stay overnight for observations.

At lunch time, once everything had calmed down and Stephanie had finished shouting at everybody, I managed to catch up with Lola, who had decided to stay in and read her bridal magazines.

She pointed at an oversized flower arrangement.

"Do you like that one?"

"What, as a bouquet?"

"Mmm maybe it is a bit big. I could take out the gardenias."

I stayed quiet, not knowing what a gardenia was and took a bite of my sandwich. Then I looked up to see the lift door slide back revealing the hefty figure of our chairman emerging with two of his cohorts behind him.

"It's Mr Amery." I dropped my sandwich and turned to Lola, "Oh Christ. We have to warn Stephanie."

"Why? What's wrong?"

"We have to stop them, she's on her lunch break."

"We can't," Lola countered, "They are already walking towards her office."

"You don't understand! The last time I walked in on Steph..." I debated whether to tell her and then realised that I had no choice, "she was dribbling on her food. She has some kind of strange hormone problem Lola; she'll be so embarrassed if they find out!" I leapt to my feet and shouted, "Mr Amery, wait!"

He paused with his hand stretched towards Steph's door.

"We've been having some problems with that door."

"This door?" he asked with an indignant shove.

The door arched open to reveal a salivating Stephanie inside but, simultaneously, the most delicious smell of roses filled the room and all the men's heads snapped across in our direction, or rather Lola's direction, their faces transfixed with worship.

"Mmmm, foxy ladies," Mr Amery purred, "What divine air freshener do you use?"

"Errm...Glade I think," I mumbled and looked askance at Lola, "It's very strong isn't it."

"Yeees," he replied and began to sidle towards us, shimmying his hips, his minions falling in line behind him like an unfit dance troop.

Steph shoved her fluid filled Tupperware box in her draw, as the sixty-year-old man ran a seductive hand down his body, "I could do with some of that delicious aroma."

She hunched over, used the hem of her skirt to wipe all the remaining mucousy spit away from her mouth and then sat back up again.

"You could smear it all over me if you like."

Steph used a picture frame as a mirror to push her hair into place and rested both arms on her desk. Then she nodded at Lola, gave her a tight smile and the smell instantaneously disappeared.

Lola said abruptly, "Well you can't have it. It's out of stock," and flicked another page of her magazine over.

The men bumped into each other with confusion as if coming out of a trance and Steph formally stood up to welcome her visitors.

"Mr Amery, what a pleasure, please come and sit down, can I help you with anything?"

He bumbled about for a bit, searching his pockets and puckering up his lips as if he was tasting something.

"I...Yes, what was I just looking for?"

"A coffee perhaps?"

"Do you have any honey and lemon? I think I have a cold coming on."

Steph put a hand on his back and gave a consoling nod as she guided him into her office,

"No but I have a very nice bottle of Jack Daniel's in one of my draws."

The door closed on them and I asked, "What did you do?"

"Mmmm? Oh that thing. It was nothing really, it was one of those scratch and sniff patches in this magazine. Do you think I should have some baby's breath or would that be too fussy?"

"But you...?"

"And you will never guess what I've got planned for the reception tables afterwards."

"I..."

"White peonies in jam jars, roses on my table of course but I have to think about the other people coming too."

And with that she changed the subject and refused to speak about Mr Amery's behavior anymore.

An hour later, Stephanie walked via my desk and leant towards me with a little smile in the side of her mouth.

"He was congratulating me for outsourcing my personnel to Warner and Suma." She strolled away from me and threw back over her shoulder, "By the way, that boyfriend of yours can visit any time he likes."

Megan looked up and said, "What boyfriend?" but was cut off as Stephanie flicked her shoulder.

"I wasn't talking to you, elephant-ears get on with your work."

"Lola, you can clock off early if you need to this evening."

Lola didn't look up but raised a hand and Steph slapped it as she went past.

I calmed Megan down, cooing that her ears weren't that much larger than normal and anyway nobody would notice them with her hair in a low ponytail.

Then I turned my attention back to work and received an e-mail from Adam reminding me I had to wear a hat for Saturday, the thought made me groan.

"What's the sigh about?" Vinny asked, stopping to peer over my shoulder.

"I've agreed to go out with Adam this weekend and he's taking me to watch horse racing."

"Oh, that's brilliant, you'll love it. Have you ever been?"

"No."

"Why the glum face? Don't you want to go?"

"I'm nervous about going on any date, Vinny. I've never put myself out there before. Plus I need to find a dress and hat to wear."

"I can get you a fabulous dress, I know just the place."

"I have about ten quid left in my pocket this week," I warned him, but he waved me away.

"Don't worry. You don't have to pay anything, these clothes will be 'on loan'."

"'On loan' from where?" I drew my eyebrows together.

"Well…" Vinny perched his rump on my desk and took me into his confidence. "I happen to know that Milo Topen's third wife left behind an entire walk-in wardrobe full of clothes when she deserted him two years ago."

"And how would you know that?"

His eyes glittered, "I might have been in it."

"You went to Milo Topen's house?"

He pursed his lips and nodded.

"But I thought you were going out with that guy in the red headphones."

"Jesus, no, he is way too young for me."

"But I thought he was…"

"Oh God yes, he was an old school friend, wasn't he? Yes, um, he was just several years down from me, besides I like an older man."

"Thanks for offering to help, Vinny. Milo Topen may be a good catch, but I couldn't wear his ex-wife's clothes."

"Why not, they aren't doing anything in that wardrobe."

"It…it wouldn't feel right, it's a bit like wearing dead people's clothes."

"Whatever you want honey-bun, but beggars can't be choosers."

He huffed and flounced off as I called, "I'm not quite a beggar yet, you know."

"You can't buy a dress and hat with ten pounds, sugar," he called back and I scowled.

"I've got lots of hats," big-eared Megan offered, "You can borrow one if you want."

"I would love you forever!" I said and wrote a message to Lola to see if she could help.

Chapter 14

I had only ever seen the posh enclosure at Ascot on the news and had no idea about racing protocol. However, my friends told me I would be fine and had spent the last few days dressing, refining and coaching me.

Lola had given me the low down on how to place a bet; Donna briefed me on odds, bookies and accumulators; Vinny had produced a crimson dress out of nowhere, promised me it wasn't from the morgue or Milo's ex-wife's mausoleum and Megan had given me a pork-pie sized hat that almost matched.

To top it all, I managed to cram my feet into some diva red stilettos that had sat at the back of my cupboard for the last two years waiting for their first outing.

I regretted wearing them when I saw the grassed over enclosure. Heavy overnight rain had left the ground beneath waterlogged and gloopy and I had to keep my weight on my tip toes to stop my shoes sinking.

Making my way towards a small presentation stand at the center of the rink, I found a metal railing that ran down some steps and gave myself a vital discharge.

Around the edge of the crowded lawn ran the parade route for the horses where muddy stable hands were trying to keep hold of colourful bobbing reins. One pint-sized jockey in black and white silks mounted a large grey horse as if he weighed nothing and perched on top like a little chipmunk.

"Alice."

Adam was standing very close and put a handout to tip my chin up but stopped himself at the last second. He was smiling as his eyes explored my face.

"You look beautiful."

I blushed and swished my handkerchief dress.

"I might even look glamorous if I wasn't standing in shoe-sucking mud."

I picked my foot up to demonstrate and left a sulking stiletto in the ground.

"I didn't know whether you would come."

"I said I would."

Adam went to brush a finger against my cheek, but I automatically shrunk back from the contact.

"I'm sorry, I keep forgetting." He looked distractedly towards the racetrack and then said in a lighter tone, "Well, you are going to have fun today."

"I am?"

"Yes. Have you ever been racing before?"

"No, but I've been doing my research and know exactly how to put a bet on."

He grinned, "We have to inspect the field first. It gives us a good chance to suss out the competition."

"Apparently I should be looking for a mudder."

"You dab punter, you've learnt the lingo."

I laughed, "Donna told me to say that. She has an Irish uncle who used to take her betting when she was seven."

"I hope she fed you some good tips then."

"Hmmm, she bets on her fortune teller's predictions and they aren't that reliable."

Adam grinned, "Nothing ever is with horses. Come and say hello to George."

To my surprise, I found George standing, with his arm around Zara, the white-haired goddess from the awards.

"These two got together that night at the BFAs," Adam explained.

"Yes, that turned out to be quite an evening after you left, Alice," George laughed. "Adam told us that Gabriella was stuck in the toilet window, so we decided to go in and give her a hand. I grabbed one leg, Zara grabbed the other and we both give a good pull but that's where it all went wrong."

"For me, yes," Zara took up the story, her accent holding a flamboyant French curl, "What happens next is so disgusting. I gave such a big tug on Gabrielle's shoe that it came off in my hand

and I tripped, falling backwards into one of the toilet cubicles and dipped my hair into the actual toilet water."

George stroked her white mane, "You can only imagine the madness that followed, I had two supermodels in crisis at the same time."

Zara screwed up her nose with distaste, "It seems funny to him now, but I was so upset you wouldn't believe it, my hair had all kinds of actress shit in it and it flicked all over my dress."

I bit my bottom lip, trying to keep my face serious, "Oh, your poor dress. So, what did you do?"

"Well, I got to be the hero for a change, isn't that a turn up?" George grinned.

"He abandoned Gabrielle because her arse was completely stuck and came to help me. He was my knight in shining armour."

She gave George a coy smile and he blushed, "I'm not so sure I'd go that far but I did put her hair in the sink and washed it with some soap."

"Then the firemen arrived and tried to get Gabrielle out. Oh, they pushed and pushed like they were pushing a big fat bus out of a rabbit hole but she didn't move an inch until my George made them use soap which popped her out like a, how do you say... Cochon graissé?"

"Greased pig," Adam translated.

"I took Zara back to sit at the bar, gave her several strong drinks, cut the contaminated end of her hair off with a pair of bar scissors and cracked a lot of bad jokes. Then she invited me back to her place where we ended up having..."

"Too much detail George," Adam cut in and Zara chided,

"Yes George, the don't need to hear all that meat and potatoes information."

"I was only going to say night cap." George was so indignant that his eyebrows almost shot off the top of his head and Zara gave a light laugh, bending to kiss him on the nose. Then she leant on his shoulder and reached down to one of her tiny feet to free up a spiked heel. At least I wasn't the only one struggling with the mud and the lingo.

More horses had begun parading around the small track and Adam lifted his hand to point out a frisky colt.

"That's one of my mares."

"Your horse...do you mean a horse that actually belongs to you?"

"Yes. I have several. Do you want to come and see her?"

He walked across the enclosure and I teetered beside him, asking, "What kind of person has their own horse?"

"Horses. I Inherited most of them."

"Oh, that makes it better does it?"

"What do you mean?"

"I mean that this kind of life is not normal." I gestured to the enclosure, "Only elite people live like this. How ridiculously rich are you Adam?"

He grinned, "Rich enough to pay a mountain of tax."

We had walked up to the dividing rope and the horses, who had seemed quite delicate and small from a distance, became enormous. These snorting, stamping creatures caused the wet earth to shudder and squelch as they crossed in front of us. Several of the jockeys had mounted and looked like colourful sweets on top of the glossy-coated thoroughbreds.

"She's called Titanium's Joy. Come and say hello."

Adam's horse was beautiful but very skittish. The salivating beast had begun to prance and fuss even before it had circled around once and the mounted jockey was working hard to subdue her.

"I don't ride them much these days. I have an uncle with a stud farm in Berkshire and he does all the training for me."

Adam clicked his tongue as the horse drew near, putting his hand up to pat its neck. "You can stroke her if you like."

I shook my head and swallowed nervously, "I'm fine."

"She won't hurt you."

"No honestly…" But at that point all my fake reserve and dignity got shoved down the pan because the horse started to turn, prance and lift its front feet.

The jockey pulled back hard to control it and reversed the huge chestnut's buttocks backwards in my direction.

In an ideal world, I would have simply stepped out of the way, but my bitch stilettos wedged themselves firmly in the wet soil and fixed me in position. I panicked and leant backwards to avoid being touched but the horse kept reversing until I had no choice but to lift my arms and block being crushed.

I felt the kick of electricity jump from my hands into the shining, tender rump and then wheeled around as I toppled backwards.

The only good thing about the situation was that I had discharged my static before I flopped down onto Adam. The multiple bad things that unfolded were catastrophic and drew in a horrified audience.

The horse, spooked by the sharp crack on its bum, reared up with its hooves raking the air, catching the dividing rope as it descended. The rope caught in its legs as it began to gallop off at right angles to the enclosure, and formed a constricting tourniquet around all the feathery-dressed, smart-suited gentry within.

As I watched, hats went flying, shoes were left stuck in the ground and knees thudded into damp puddles as the crowd around me fell like dominos.

Adam and I lay staring at the chaos around us. The horse finally threw its rider and kicked off the rope before disappearing in a fast gallop around to the far side of the grandstand.

Groans of recovery began to be sounded out as I looked at Adam and realised I was lying on top of him.

He pushed up, leaning back on one arm and laughed, "Are you alright?"

I nodded.

"I'm sorry Alice, I'm such an idiot sometimes, she could have really hurt you."

He pushed my hair back and I froze, his body so inter-tangled with my own that I would shock him if I moved, shock him if he kissed me. I wavered as his fingers tightened in my hair to pull me closer but just then, a pair of hands grabbed my shoulders.

"Let me help you up," I turned reluctantly, to see Zara looking down at me.

"You two nearly got hammered by that horse. Have you broken anything?"

"I...err...no."

I came back to my senses as she pulled me away with surprising strength, all the sharp shocks that would have hit Adam, jumping into her hands as I was hitched upright.

Zara blinked several times but surprisingly, didn't say anything about the painful sputters. Instead she wiped her hands with a tissue and asked me if she had any mud stains on her skirt. Zara was the only person apparently unscathed by the galloping tourniquet.

George closed in and hauled Adam to his feet, thwacking him on his arm, "Jeepers that was a close call matey" and then added with a disparaging grin, "A bit of a ringer that mount of yours. I told you she was dangerous."

Adam brushed some of the mud off his trousers, saying testily, "Get out of my face George," before turning to walk towards the grandstand. He went to grab my arm, but I yanked it swiftly away. He grasped air but didn't stop walking.

"He's right, perhaps you'll be safer upstairs, Alice."

"That was quite a scene you generated earlier."

I was standing up on a viewing balcony, having decided to stay a safe distance from all the parade-activity below and turned towards the familiar voice, shocked to see it was the bouncer from the BFA evening.

"What are you doing here?"

"I'm working."

"As a bouncer?"

"As security."

"As security? At a racecourse?"

"Yes, what's wrong with that?"

"Well nothing, apart from the fact that…"

"That you hoped you would never see me again?"

I pressed my lips together and turned away from him.

He lifted a pair of binoculars to look down at the crowd below.

"I see they've reconstructed the parade enclosure."

"Yes."

"Did you get hurt at all?"

"No."

"I thought the horse might have clipped you."

"Why? Were you watching?"

"Of course."

"From up here?"

"Yes." He held up his binoculars.

I felt sick at the idea of being found out but knew he would have just seen the horse rearing up and bolting away from this distance, he couldn't have guessed that I had electrocuted it.

He asked, "Do you know if anyone else was hurt?"

I sighed and nodded, "Slightly, one lady had to go to the first aid tent with a twisted ankle and there is a man with a fat lip where a post came out of the ground and hit him, but apart from that..."

I gestured inside to several women who were still sitting recovering with laddered stockings, crumpled hats and torn pockets and guilt cramped my stomach.

He scanned them thoughtfully and then said, "My name's Max Greenstick by the way, just in case you were wondering, after collapsing on me outside the cinema."

I wasn't wondering anything, I just wanted him to go away. I turned and said, "Look, I'm sorry, you caught me on a bad night."

He raised his eyebrows and nodded as if to say, "and how."

"Don't look like that. I appreciate the fact that you scooped me up and let me sleep it off in your bed but..."

"You could have woken me up to tell me you were leaving."

"Oh, come on, think about it. I was at some strange address with a strange bloke I didn't know. God knows what you might have done if I had woken you up."

"Well I didn't do anything to you earlier did I? That should have been a fair pointer."

I huffed and looked away.

After a short silence, he asked civilly, "Did you get home alright?"

I nodded and gave into his persistence with half a smile.

"I walked back. With a duck."

He laughed and said, "It's good to know you had company, at least."

With the ice temporarily broken between us, I said, "I'm Alice Carter."

"I know."

"Yes, talking of that, how did you know so much about me that night at the BFAs?"

"I only knew your name."

"And Adam's and Lola's."

He looked down at his hands on the railing. "Perhaps I'm just good at my job."

A woman in a white jacket had walked out to stand beside us and asked with a posh, nasal twang, "Have they started yet?"

"No, but I think they are about to."

The last of the tiny, toy figures were being loaded into the starting gate on the far side of the field. She glanced over and then retreated inside, leaving an awkward silence between us until Max cleared his throat and said tentatively, "Can I give you a warning?"

The starter's pistol went off.

I raised my voice, "As long as it's free."

"It's about Adam."

"Why? Do you have a problem with Adam?"

"No, but he has a reputation."

"As what? A cold-hearted womaniser? I think I can protect myself you know."

"No, it's more than that. He isn't…"

"Is Zara out here?" George's head popped out through the open sliding door.

"No!" Max and I both snapped together and then watched as he grimaced and disappeared again.

"He isn't what?"

Max switched his attention back to the giant screen that was tracking the line of sprinting horses.

"Nothing." The two front jockeys were drilling down to find more power for the home straight. "Are you going to see him again?"

"Like it's any of your business…"

"You'll regret it if you do."

I sighed as the cheering escalated around me and half shouted, "Perhaps, but he will probably regret it more than me."

"Well, he'll be happy, at least," Max nodded towards the racecourse, "His horse just won."

I glanced down and saw Adam looking back at me. I waved and gave him a thumbs up to celebrate his success. My five-pound bet had upped itself to twenty quid.

I turned to tell Max, but found him gone and huffed, cross that I hadn't asked for his number. This strange security guard was intertwined with everyone I knew and I had no idea why.

That evening in the car home, I asked Adam if he knew who Max was.

"Max who?"

"I don't know. He was a bouncer at the awards."

"Was he the man that you were talking to on the balcony?"

"Yes."

I blushed, realising that Adam had seen us chatting, "I think he works for a security company or something."

Adam bit the side of his lip.

"What did he talk to you about?"

"Oh, lots of things, horses, racing, you."

"Me?" Adam laughed but his voice had an edge to it. "What did he say?"

"He warned me not to go out with you anymore."

"Why? He doesn't even know me."

"He said he knew *of* you."

"Meaning?"

"Just your reputation, probably."

Adam drove on in silence as he absorbed my words and then he sighed with some internal resolution.

"Perhaps he's right. Perhaps I'm not good for you."

"I think I'm old enough to make my own decisions. I don't need some pompous security bloke to tell me what to do."

"You said you met him before at the awards?"

I nodded as he asked quietly, "Do you know his surname?"

Now I didn't want to get the man in trouble. He had scraped me up off the floor after all and put me up in his bed for a night.

I shook my head innocently, "No, like I said, I've only met him twice."

He drummed his fingers on the steering wheel and then said in a lighter voice, "Talking of surnames, have you ever wanted to find out about your own history, Alice?"

I shrugged, "I suppose. I did try to find my birth certificate a couple of years ago but couldn't trace anything, probably because I was born in Hong Kong."

"You don't have a birth certificate?"

I shook my head.

"How do you get bank accounts and mortgages?"

"Mortgages? God Adam I am twenty-five and living on a minimum wage."

He grinned back, "Fair point."

"I was left with a passport and that covers me for most things."

I rubbed some residual mud off my knee and looked out of the window to see a man carrying his young daughter on his shoulders.

"Have you tried looking for information in the National Archives?"

"The where?"

"The National Archives in Kew. They have thousands of documents and articles available. I even have a friend who works there. He could probably help you out."

"Oh, god no. Promise me you won't do that!"

"It was just an idea."

"I know but if I do this, I have to do it alone."

Adam walked me across to my flat once he had found a parking space and it felt nice to be strolling along as a couple.

I remembered Max's warning that he shouldn't be trusted. It wasn't as if I would ever be able to dive into a "reveal all" relationship, so Max had nothing to worry about from my end. But I still puzzled over Adam. The cold and callous ice man was a long way from showing his cards.

I asked brightly, "How is Gabrielle by the way, has she recovered from all that publicity?"

"Hell, she doesn't care. She's the paparazzi wild child. A few midnight antics won't stop her working."

I laughed.

"You seem to have a strange relationship with her."

He shrugged and leant on the wall by my front door, "She reminds me I'm human sometimes."

I rummaged around for my keys, "You know she said you couldn't ever love anyone."

"Gabi?"

I nodded and he looked down at the ground.

"And is that a prerequisite for another date?"

"No, I didn't mean…" I blushed.

"I am the way I am, Alice. Perhaps you have to accept that I have weaknesses too."

I shifted my shoulders, feeling awkward, "I haven't seen any weaknesses."

He said, "Not yet perhaps," and put his fingers out to touch my electrostatic hydrogen bomb of an arm.

I jerked backwards and he drew his eyebrows together. "Do you want me to give up trying Alice?"

"No."

He closed the space between us until I felt the door hard against my back and could hardly breathe, crippled by the fear of my own power.

"Promise me something then."

His arm was so close to mine I could feel an electrical charge tingling under my skin.

"What?"

"That you won't always be this terrified of me."

I whispered, "I'm not."

"Alice…"

"No, I mean it."

"What are you terrified of then?"

"Nothing," I said but my voice sounded weak.

"Let me touch you then."

He tipped his head slightly, hesitated for a second and then his lips moved to the brink of touching mine.

The urge to shock him ached inside me.

I wanted to connect, to let him into the secret, to finally release all the tension that fired like acid in my skin, but the bonds that had tied me for so long, tightened and I pulled back, jamming my eyes shut.

I whispered, "I can't."

A frustrated tear escaped down my cheek.

He stopped, his lips millimetres away from a violent static discharge, his breath warm across my mouth.

After a few seconds I was aware of him stepping back and saying desperately, "Alice, you are ruining me."

I gave a wretched nod, "I ruin everything."

"You have no idea how alike we are…"

I turned away to face the door, ashamed that I couldn't let myself relax, not for even one moment.

"I can't do this Adam."

I pushed my head against the inert wood in frustration. The feeling of the cool oak under my skin calming the fire in my brain. I let my thoughts settle for a few seconds and then drew a breath, turning back to him.

"Perhaps you're right. Understanding my history will explain why I'm like this."

He gave a frustrated laugh, "It might be a start."

I made an internal resolution and said, "I am going to look around the archives."

"Alice you don't need to just because…"

"No, I have to do it. I have the afternoon off on Wednesday, so I'll go over then."

"Well, if you're sure… Do you want my friend Andrew to help? He can pull documents in from deep storage and can even access the vault if necessary."

"What's deep storage?"

"It's the place where they keep all the documents they can't store on site and the vault is where they keep the high security documents."

"Why would I need high security documents?"

"I'm not saying you do…it's just…he could if you needed to."

"Oh, I see." I wiped my clammy hands on my dress, "Well, I'll make a start by myself and see where I get to, perhaps."

"And perhaps, I can come over to celebrate with you in the evening?"

I shrugged.

"Maybe. I'll let you know how it goes."

I waited for him to walk away and then faced the unpleasant splatter of electricity that smacked my fingers every time my keys slid in the front door.

As I pushed the heavy panel open, the familiar, stale air of the corridor hit me, and two things crossed my mind. Number one; I didn't want Adam to see the inside of my miniature, electrician-adapted, shock-proof flat and two; it was unlikely that I would ever want to tell him anything about my mass murderer of a father.

I never turn on the downstairs light at night to save the building's fuses. Therefore, I clunked the door shut and leant against it, breathing in the cool dark air and thought about what had just happened.

Why was Adam still interested in me when I was obviously a crack pot? And why was I still going back for more misery when every second with him was painfully, cripplingly tantalising...

I stopped and peered into the darkness.

At the far end of the corridor a shape was materialising and moving towards me. I drew in a deep breath, tensed to defend myself and scuffed my feet on the floor, ready to discharge my fingers against the intruder.

Hackles raised, I poised to strike but stood down when I recognised the familiar sloping outline of the man's shoulders.

"Paul?"

Paul gave a soft whimper and answered desperately, "Alice, I've lost Hope!"

"You've what?"

"I've lost her, she was there this morning and then, when I looked in the cage after I came home from work, it was completely empty."

"Oh God, not the hamster."

"What am I going to do? Parker is going to kill me!"

Parker was our landlord.

"Only if he finds out."

"Of course, he will find out. I've got Betty who complains about everything and Sergent bloody Mack, who is the biggest stickler for law and order I have ever come across, on my floor."

"Have you checked in your room really thoroughly?"

"Yes, like sixteen times."

"Let's go upstairs and check again. She must be in there."

I led the way like an old-time detective in a murder investigation, grappling under the bed and shocking myself on its dusty frame, emptying out cupboards and even checking in his shoes.

We tracked along all of his high shelves looking for animal droppings and sat listening in silence for ten minutes waiting for the slightest hint of a rustle. There was nothing.

"She is probably asleep. When is she most active?"

"I normally hear her at about 1.30 every night in her wheel."

I sighed; dog tired after my stressful day.

"I don't think I can keep going that long, Paul. I've been out startling horses all afternoon."

"Oh, I wondered why you looked so smart."

I pulled my dress down to cover a hole in my tights. "Well, I looked smart when I got dressed this morning."

My once neat hair was now hanging in ragged strands around my face, "You are just going to have to do a midnight vigil and hope she comes back."

"I'll leave some cheese out, oh and some raisins. She loves them."

I left him to it, showered, changed and collapsed, exhausted, onto my bed.

I lay on my back, looking up at the familiar swirls on my ceiling and worried about tracing my father.

Then I sighed, turned over and plumped up the pillow. What kind of paranoia and violence would I find in him? What if I saw the same traits in my own character? What if I hated him? What if he wanted to kill me too?

The thoughts trickled through my head like a familiar piano tune. I reached out and took a drink from the glass of water by my bed, remembering the muddy wet ground in the members enclosure, the horse's bottom, the fall on top of Adam, the shocks I had given Zara and the reappearance of the nosy bouncer.

The nosy bouncer...

He was an uncomfortable spectator who kept appearing and knew too much. He couldn't have seen me shock the horse, could he? Not from that distance, besides why would anyone expect me to pack a punching static shock?

If I stayed with Adam, I would have to tell him soon. There was no way he would put up with me behaving like this, I was surprised he had even put up with me for this long.

But then again, a second little voice argued, how could I have a relationship where I hurt him with every touch?

Sometimes my static was so painful that I would sit sobbing with the spasms and burns it gave me, why would anyone else choose to put up with it?

He would probably just walk away once the novelty had worn off, back into the arms of his models. Perhaps I had to find a sadomasochist to love me, some people like a bit of pain, after all, some men get a kick out of...

I heard a rustle.

I lifted my head and listened carefully.

After about thirty seconds a gnawing sound grated in the room. The animal was behind my radiator.

I pulled my light switch on and yanked my bed away from the wall, trying to peer down the back of the panel, knowing I couldn't touch the metal because I could potentially electrocute the little creature. Just like I had electrocuted my poor hamster, Mootie when I was ten.

I tugged on a pair of fluffy socks and tiptoed down to Paul's room where a blue light shone from under the door frame. I knocked but, as there was no reply, I had to bite the bullet and shock myself on the door handle.

Paul's anxious eyes peered around the frame and I whispered, "I think I've found her, bring some cheese."

Paul joined me back in my room about five minutes later, carrying a Tesco's bag full of vegetables.

"I think she is behind the radiator," I whispered and then wondered why I was whispering.

"Did you hear her?"

"Yes," I was still whispering.

"How did she get up to your room though?" Paul asked in a more normal voice as he squinted down the back of the panel.

"I think she shimmied up the pipe," I signalled over to the pipework in the far corner.

"I can't see her back there," he said, craning his head.

"Well I definitely heard her. Put some cheese down on the floor and see what happens."

We both sat on my bed as if it was a ship on a carpet ocean and waited, looking down at my floor for any sign of re-emergence.

"Perhaps we need to turn the light off," Paul whispered, and I reached over to pull the light switch. "Why are all your lights on strings, by the way?"

I lied, "It was like that when I got here."

"I bet it was someone with some crazy kind of OCD shit who couldn't cope with germs or something," he laughed.

"Yes, probably. Something like that."

We waited in silence and then he said, "My mates will never believe I'm sitting here like this."

"Don't get any ideas Paul, or I'll ship you to the landlord."

"Of course I wouldn't. But still. It is midnight."

I didn't say anything.

"And I am on your bed."

"You're about to get kicked in the balls."

He chuckled and made a loud crunching sound.

"What are you eating?" I asked.

"A carrot. It'll help me see better." He finished his mouthful and then said, "You know, I've been working on that idea of yours."

"What idea?"

"The one about us all having a mini superpower of our own."

"Oh?"

"I think I've found mine."

"Really?"

"Yes, do you want to see it?"

"It doesn't involve taking your clothes off, does it?"

"No, but I will have to switch the torch on to show you."

He turned to me and knelt, wedging the torch between his knees which made his face take on macabre shadows as he spoke.

"Well, I was inspired by my hamster storing nuts in its cheek and I wondered whether I could do something similar."

He pulled the shopping bag towards him.

"Anyway, I started experimenting with small things and realised my cheeks are, in fact, really stretchy."

He pulled one cheek out sideways to demonstrate and then plucked something out of the bag. "Look what I can fit in there."

He held a small courgette up and I gasped, "No way."

He nodded proudly, "And not just one either. I can fit one in each cheek."

"Go on then."

Paul grinned, opened his mouth very wide and posted two courgettes into his cheeks. "I can ewen tawk wif them in."

"That is pretty impressive!"

He delivered his long babies and slid them back into the bag, grinning. "I'm planning to get even bigger things in there in the future. Just imagine, I could be on an MI5 mission and the agent could be stuck in a lethal trap with no hope of escape and he could turn to me and say, "It's no good we're done for, Gabble," (that was Paul's surname), "And I would unexpectedly produce the two guns I had cunningly stored in my mouth when the gangsters weren't looking." He shone the light back into my face and asked, "What do you think?"

"It's certainly original."

"Does it fit your criteria for a mini superpower?"

"It would definitely impress people." I stopped short of mentioning that the porn industry would also love it and we fell into silence, Paul scanning the base of the radiator like a search light during World War Two.

I took a breath, decided that, if I told anyone, surely, I could tell Paul and bravely said, "What if I told you I had a mini power too."

"You do?"

I nodded and braced myself as he asked, "What is it? What can you do?"

"Well, it's a bit strange but I can..."

Paul cut me off with a gasp and his flashlight spun sideways, pinpointing a little fawn blob by the lump of cheese. He jumped forwards and fumbled, dropping his torch on the floor and scrabbled under the bed to find it.

I lunged for the light switch and pulled it as Paul shouted, "Quick Alice, catch her!"

I bent down, cupping my hands and then hesitated as I remembered my static charge. The hamster scuttled back towards the pipes and I squealed, "I can't touch it! I can't touch it, Paul! You have to do it!"

"Move!" Paul ordered and hit into my legs like a bowling ball, bringing me sparking and crashing down on top of him as he grabbed hold of the hamster.

We both lay in a heap, groaning.

I pushed Paul off me, sparks pin pricking through my pyjamas as he gasped, "Oh my God, have you got nylon carpets up here or something?

Talk about static shocks! I feel like I've just been..." he struggled for a word, "...Galvinised."

"That is what I was about to explain..." I began, but stopped as he opened his hands and revealed a rigid little bundle.

He nudged the ball of fluff, but she lay unresponsive under his giant, prodding finger.

"Oh Paul, I'm so sorry."

"I must have squashed her," he sobbed with a sniff. "I was so worried about my stupid landlord and neighbour finding out that I panicked and squashed her."

"You didn't, it was me. I did it."

Giant tears were now coursing down his cheeks. "No, you tried to be gentle, tried not to hurt her. I'm such an idiot."

"You aren't Paul, I..."

"No, I think I am some stupid, fake hero, but I can't even save a missing hamster without killing it." He wiped his nose with a sleeve.

"Paul..."

"I'm going to take her upstairs. I'll bury her tomorrow."

"Paul, wait..."

But he turned and walked away, his head bent over the tiny form.

I sat back on my bed, stared blankly at my wall for a minute and then flopped down into a heap and cried into my wretched pillow.

Not just for the two hamsters I had maimed and killed but for my sad existence, for everything I had hidden from, for my entire life.

I had to find my father and I had to find out what happened to him. I couldn't go on like this. My mentality had to change.

Eventually weariness swamped my brain and I fell into a nightmare filled sleep.

There was a loud rapping at my door at five forty-five the next morning and I tried to orientate myself. My bed was in the middle of my room and I was freezing cold with no sheets over me at all.

I scrabbled to the door and opened it a crack to see the tiny whiskered nose of a hamster lunge towards me and sniff my face. I gasped with surprised and then realised I was looking at Hope.

"She's alive!" Paul cheered from the hallway.

"How?" I asked, pulling my door open.

"She must have gone into shock or something because she was as dead as a door nail when I put her into her nest last night."

He lifted the little creature up and gave her a nuzzle. "Then, at about five, I heard this little rustling noise and there she was, stuffing bits of carrot into her cheeks."

"Oh Paul. I'm so relieved. I thought I had killed her."

He blew micro kisses at her little pink nose, "You didn't do anything, Alice. It was my heavy-handedness that smushed her."

"Is she back to normal?"

"Well she's a little wobbly in her back legs but she seems alright."

I recognised the symptoms and gave a weak smile, "Well thank heavens for small miracles then."

"And I still have Hope in my world," Paul cheered as he span out into the corridor and then poked his head back in through my door again. "By the way, do you have lots of nylon in here?"

"What?"

"That static kick I got last night was awesome! It kind of hurt but was like being in a sci-fi torture chamber. Do you think I could do it again?"

He began rubbing his foot on the carpet.

"Not when you're holding a sick hamster, Paul," I warned and pushed the door shut on him.

He called back through the wood, "Another time perhaps?"

Chapter 15

"I've come to look at some documents."

An elderly woman, perched behind a curved reception desk peered at me over her spectacles.

"Are you registered with us?"

She had tiny bones and a long neck that sat, way too small in her collar.

"Yes. I did it online."

"Name?"

"Alice Carter."

"Can you write your details down in our entry book please? Any documents in the public domain have to remain in this building but may be photocopied at a small cost in our media room over there."

She pointed out a room with blinking computers and various machines and I nodded.

"Our main files are through the double doors to your left. Is there a specific field you are interested in?"

"I am looking for information about Hong Kong in the 1990s."

"Did you research the files you needed before you got here?"

"No."

She raised her eyebrows disparagingly and I felt like a naughty schoolchild.

"Our foreign territories section is along the corridor and down the stairs at the end of it. You will be looking for series code FCO 40, columns 1130 to 1211 HK."

She looked at my blank face.

"Do you want to write it down?"

"Er...no...I'm fine."

"1130 to 1211 HK," she repeated, "Come back to me if you can't find your information."

Heading off, I kept repeating the letters and numbers to myself, conscious that the lino floor was charging me with every step. I paused and pushed the swing door open with my bum, trying to spread the unusually painful shocks evenly around my body.

Well-worn stairs took me down to a musty basement that was filled with dense filing racks. These stood like long lines of soldiers, grey and regimented under the flat strip-lighting.

I brushed my hand against one of them and had such a big shock I could see the blue spark jump out of my fingers.

The lino flooring was exaggerating my static really badly. I braced myself for hard hits and began to wander along the long corridor.

Each line of storage was labelled with three alphabetical letters. I found the racks with FCO at the beginning of them and, to save myself from repeated shocks, kept my hand pressed against the metal of the shelving as I walked along it.

Halfway down I found the files 1130-1211 and reached up to pull a random cardboard file out. It was entitled Environmental Agencies. Further down I found Government Funded Agencies and, later Policy and Administrative Processes. Of course, FCO stood for The Foreign and Commonwealth Office. This wasn't what I needed at all.

I realised why the receptionist had given me such a withering look earlier and stood, feeling pessimistic about my chances of spotting anything useful. Then I heard a woman say a sharp, "Ow!" And then, "Did you just get a shock Harry?"

An old school, army voice rattled back, "Like a bloody viper bite. There's an electrical short out down here. Probably damp shafts or mice in the flashing. Typical ruddy bureaucracy, no safety regulations, it could have killed you."

I yanked my hand off the shelving, realizing that I had altered the charge on the entire unit and dismally sank to my knees. This was impossible. Adam was right. How was I ever going to find my way through this lot?

"Excuse me, are you Alice Carter?"

A flabby man with a northern accent and a chin that had lost its edges was looking down at me.

I nodded and he stuck out a limp hand.

"I'm Andrew Spade. But all my friends call me Andy."

"Oh."

I scrabbled to my feet and used the excuse of dusting myself off to avoid shaking the pudgy fingers.

"I hope you don't mind me seeking you out, but I was talking to Adam Warner about your history the other day and he said you might need help with some research on your parents."

I gaped at him in outrage, Adam had stepped in when I had specifically said no.

Andrew wondered away, seemingly oblivious to my fury, so I stomped after him, ordering him to stop.

"Wait! I'm not going with you. I don't want your help. I don't want Adam's help."

He shrugged, "Adam isn't helping you, I am, and I could save you hours of work."

"How did you know I was here?"

"My software told me you had signed in."

"You were looking out for me?"

"No," he waved the idea away, "Well, not really. You just pinged up on the system, and I thought, I know I'll just go and see if she needs anything."

He held one of the swing doors open for me, "Shall we go?"

Bulldozed into following, I squeezed past, almost touching his overflowing belly.

"I'm not happy."

"You will be soon," he said, grinning smugly and beckoned me to follow him back up the stairs. I trailed behind him, brooding about the blunt arrogance of Adam's actions.

Andrew rambled on, talking about the architecture, age, storage capacity and security of the elegant, enormous building.

"...And when I heard that Maggie had sent you through to FC40, I thought, FC40? What is the poor girl doing there? You won't find anything by rummaging down in the bowels of the National Archives, I'll go and give her a hand."

"I appreciate that, but..."

"No, don't mention it. Warner explained your case to me, and I have to confess, I was a little bit curious to find out more. Keep up, I can't wait to show you my little surprise."

"A surprise?"

"A really exciting one!" He pressed his hand against his lips, "I have found a long-lost file for you."

"You have?"

"It's taken me forever. I had to treck all around the houses to find it. I've gone through census documents, visa entry forms and travel passenger lists. Not to mention births, deaths and marriages, but you don't appear anywhere. You're blocked in every direction. So, I decided to contact deep storage in Cheshire."

"Deep storage?"

"Yes, it's an old, unused salt mine where they keep outdated files."

"Did they have something there?"

"Well, yes and no. They had a file on you, but it was empty."

"What does that mean?"

"Exactly. Who has empty public files? I began to think sideways and looked into our high security vaults and there you were."

"High security vaults?" I heard alarm in my voice, "What did the files say?"

"Oh, the documents are for your interest and digestion only. I just locate information for other people. After all, that's my job."

He led me back to the main entrance desk where Maggie still sat as expressionless as ever.

Andrew gave her a special code number for my case. She studied it and then said bluntly, "Two different forms of identification please."

I slid my passport and electricity bill on the side and wondered what I was getting myself into.

She pulled the documents towards her and scrutinized them before typing into her computer.

"These are restricted access files I need your signature here," I signed, "here," she flipped the paper, "and here."

As I gathered everything back into my bag, Andrew wandered off to fill up a plastic cup from the water tank and I asked anxiously.

"What does restricted access mean?"

"That the documents have been recovered from our high security storage vault and only pre-approved individuals are allowed to view them."

"And why would I have access to this information?"

She shrugged without interest.

"It must be relevant to you."

"What sort of information is it?"

"I would have to be a computer to know everything about everybody walking into this place, Miss Carter."

"Oh, of course. I was just a bit anxious, that's all."

My angst must have mined a faint seam of pity in her because the woman sighed, placed a small key in front of me and explained in a hushed voice, "These security measures are often taken because the information is politically or socially sensitive."

"And socially sensitive means…"

"That there is a need to protect a person's activity or identity."

"Ahh, I see."

She sat back and said in a louder voice, "This key will give you access to the secured box in reading room seventeen. Andrew will take you across and show you where it is."

I nodded, went to walk off and then reversed again to ask, "And does that mean I can't reproduce or photocopy the information inside it?"

"No, because you've signed for the documents they've become your own property Miss Carter. You can take them with you, flush them down the toilet or write your shopping list on them for all I care."

She sniffed and typed some details into her computer. Then pressed a button on her phone and said into it, "National Archives, main reception."

"So how do you know Adam?" I asked as we headed off down a hallway to the right.

"Adam?"

"Yes, you know, Adam. Adam Warner. He asked you to give me a hand."

The man's flaccid cheeks were shaking with each step.

"Oh, Adam. Yes, Adam, of course." He pushed open a heavy door, "I tend to remember the documents more than the people."

"Oh."

"And of course, I love a challenge! I'm just like a terrier, I won't give up until I've found my prey," he did a little scurrying movement with is hands and became worryingly out of breath.

I raised my eyebrows. A pig searching for truffles perhaps but never a terrier.

Eventually we stopped by a yellow, heavy duty door and Andrew swiped a security card through a reader on the wall.

Slipping the card back into his top pocket, he waited for the panel to slide open and held an arm out, guiding me in.

"Welcome to reading room seventeen."

A large metal table stood in the middle of the room with a wooden case about the size of a shoebox, placed perfectly at its centre. I inspected the locked container and held up the key.

"Do I use this to open the box?"

"Yes, that's the general idea with keys."

Andrew retreated, taking a step back from me to rest against the far wall and pat his face with a hanky.

I would have been happier if he wasn't there but as long as he stayed where he was, there was no way he could see inside my box.

Reaching forwards and being careful not to touch the metal table, I twisted the stiff little lock and lifted the container's lid.

A large brown envelope lay inside it. I reached in and, with shaking fingers, picked it up, sliding my finger under its flap.

Inside were three thick documents.

The first was a birth certificate that I scanned slowly, studying the detail that was written in oblong boxes with spider writing.

The top name was my mother's, Sophia Cooper and my father (I held my breath as I took him in...) my father was called Christopher Cooper and there was me underneath, described as Alice Cooper.

That meant I was a Cooper, not a Carter.

I stroked my thumb over the aged ink and imagined them both signing it whilst holding me in their arms.

With clammy hands, I flicked to the second of the three pages. This was a solicitor's letter confirming my name change from Alice Cooper to Alice Carter when I was a baby.

I heard a shuffle and realised that Andrew had drifted across the room to stand right behind me.

Twisting away, I hugged the documents to my chest but he leant his hip against the alloy table and tried to peer around my shoulder.

"And the other one, you have to read the other certificate too, what does that say?"

Alarm bells fired off inside my head. This was my information, my secret and there was no way any sweating archivist was going to scoop it from me.

Anger driving my actions, I let my hand drift down towards one of his bulging thighs. Then I jabbed a swift finger sideways and stabbed a very painful, high-voltage prod.

Instantly he leapt from the table, shrieking.

"My leg!"

"What's the matter?"

"My leg!"

"Did something bite you?"

"I don't know."

"Like a spider?"

"A spider?" he started slapping himself on the legs. "How would a spider get in here?"

"These documents come from all around the world don't they? It must have fallen out and hidden under the table."

I shocked him again, further down his leg and Andrew jumped like a frog.

"I think it's in my trousers!"

I watched panic spread across his face as he started to unbutton his fly, pulling down his trousers to see the wounds.

Simultaneously I reached out to snatch the pass card from his top pocket, shoved the papers into my bag and took three steps towards the door, swiping at the reader.

As the metal panel slid open, I glanced backwards to see him grappling with his trousers and said, "Actually, on second thoughts Andy, I think I'll take this with me."

"No, wait! You have to look at it here."

I gave him a wave.

"Got to go."

"But you're meant to read it while I'm..."

I didn't wait for the end of the sentence and set off at a sprint, hearing Andrew's belt drag on the floor as he staggered up the corridor after me. Still holding his trousers around his thighs, he shouted, "...Just the last page... please!"

I clutched my handbag tightly to my chest on the bus back into London, desperate to get the documents out and reread the names on it but public transport probably wasn't the best place for examining my criminal heritage.

I looked at a woman who sat opposite me with a snub-nosed little girl clutched on her lap. She sat calm and quiet, murmuring details into the child's ear and pointing out a man on a bicycle, a stray dog and an old orange and white police car and I felt sadly envious.

The writing on the birth certificate inside my bag would be the closest I would ever come to knowing my mother. I gazed out at the busy hubbub of London streets. Every person out there had someone to reach out for, blood ties that anchored them to each other.

I remembered Christopher Cooper's name written above mine. He had given me up to the safest home he could think of when his crisis had hit, hadn't he? Perhaps he did love me once. Perhaps he wasn't out of control now and would want to know me if I found him.

The bus had slowed and swung its doors open with a swish of pistons. I looked up to see a fibreglass bride wearing a frilly lace dress in a shop window and leapt up.

I was already at the wedding shop!

I slalomed out, almost getting trapped by the closing doors and stumbled on a cracked paving stone. Then I clicked my handbag tightly closed and tucked it under my armpit. The documents would have to wait until I had faced the nightmare of Lola's bridesmaid fitting.

Chapter 16

I had never been in a bridal shop before and pushed its door open with an apprehensive elbow, revealing a puffball, plastic-wrapped haven of pure white dreams.

Only, to me, the dresses looked as if they were being suffocated in clear, zipped up body bags.

I felt out of place in my shabby jeans and old shirt and hovered by the entrance until a thin woman in a green, tight fitting trouser suit beckoned me in,

"Don't worry, we don't bite."

She was resting her palms on a white counter with both elbows sticking out, perching like a praying mantis.

I raised one eyebrow, "Bite?"

The room smelt hot, perfumed and dry like a sterile orchid farm and the woman didn't move from her predatory position.

"You know, bite your head off," she gnashed her teeth at me and then smiled, dropping the pose and walking around her counter, "Not if you're a woman anyhow. Are you here to buy a wedding dress?"

"No, I'm one of the flowers. I mean bridesmaids."

"Ahhh, you must be part of my Rose party."

I nodded and she continued, "I have to say I love Lola's floral approach, but she has stretched me to snapping point with her time-table. I am her dress consultant, Persephone, and you are?"

"Alice."

"Ah, the famous, Alice!"

I frowned, why did people keep saying that?

She led me to the back of the shop, asking, "Have you got a good, supportive strapless bra on?"

"I...err...no." I hadn't thought about wearing different underwear this morning and looked down my shirt to check, "Just my normal one."

She sucked air in with a low hiss and shook her head, "You'll regret that in a minute. You will need to put this chapeau over your head once you are in the cubicle."

Persephone held up the type of hessian bag used by an executioner. I took it, looking dubious.

"You aren't going to hang me or something?"

She paused for a few seconds and then laughed, making a high-pitched stuttering noise and fanning herself, "Oh, hang you, I get it. That's so funny."

The smile fell away, and she explained abruptly, "You have makeup on, and I can't risk blood red lipstick stains on my dresses, people would think I had been murdering my brides."

"Alice!" Lola's head poked out from behind a curtain, "I'm so excited about these dresses. Yours is in the fourth changing room down."

Persephone lifted a pastel curtain and held an arm out to direct me in.

"Keep all underwear on, please."

"What shall…" she swiped the curtain across my face, and I grabbed a corner to stick my head out, "What shall I do about my old bra?"

"It's better on than off, we can't have anything drooping today. Besides we are all girls here."

"Except me," Vinny said

"You don't count," Donna chipped back.

I grimaced and pulled my head in.

Then I regretted it.

"Lola?"

"Yes?"

"Am I in the right cubicle?"

I heard the curtain rings rattle as she said, "Yes. Why?"

"It's…what is my dress meant to be exactly?"

"You are a peony. Isn't it beautiful? You must put the tights and shoes on too so we can get the full effect."

"Er…" I pulled a green pair of tights out of a bag on the chair and spotted the matching shoes underneath it. Good god, what was I going to look like?

After a few minutes of bending and wriggling, I managed to pop all my necessary body parts into a white frilled boob tube of a dress which had a ball-shaped, leaf-layered white tutu hanging off it.

"My bottom looks huge," I called out and Donna's deep voice boomed back, saying, "You think you've got problems."

"You are all going to look wonderful. I can't wait to see my flower garden."

Oh god, Lola what have you done to us all, I thought and shut my eyes. I was going to have to spend the entire day looking like an oversized exclamation mark.

"My shoes are on the small side," I called out again as huffs and grunts emerged from the cubicles around me and a green arm shoved through the curtain, handing me another, identical pair.

"Try these on."

I did and they were bigger but no more comfortable.

"Are you ready?" Vinny's distinctive voice asked.

"Hang on a minute," I said as I tried to wriggle the tube a bit higher over my chest. "Where did you find these dresses at such short notice, Lola?"

"They are from the children's range but I've had a special order on hold for the last few months, just in case."

"Mine's a little tight around my midriff," said Donna from the middle cubicle.

"What are you?"

"A golden tulip."

A curtain scraped and Persephone said confidently, "Don't worry, I can put an extra panel in. You need them in three weeks, don't you?"

I whistled."Three weeks, Lola, you're moving fast."

"Why not? I don't have any venues to book because I'm holding it in a field close to my flat."

I tugged at my preposterous dress and sighed. Well, as I had never been to a wedding before, it might as well be the flower-laden wedding of the rose-obsessed bride with a vagina on her back.

"I'm ready," Lola sang, "Come on out and join me once you're dressed."

I pulled at the bodice again, regretting not thinking about my bra and shifted the grey straps in the hope they would magically disappear.

"Oh, and I have some matching hair clips for each of you, hang on."

A hair clip with small green and white roses was posted through my curtain and I crowned myself, faintly horrified.

"Come on out, come on out," Lola cried. "I'm waiting by the mirror."

I emerged to see Lola standing dressed as a pink rose. She had large fuchsia petals that draped across a calf length skirt and short, puffed sleeves decorated with dozens of tiny buds on each shoulder. A tight bodice pulled in her mid-section, emphasising her voluptuous bust.

She looked radiant.

Lola was flanked by her other two bridesmaids, Donna looking like a rugby player in a knee-length, yellow tulip costume (although, I have to be honest, it was the ideal flower shape to fit Donna's unusual dimensions) and Vinny who was dressed as a…a strange lilac creation. He had a tight, tubular dress with a few longer petals hanging down behind him and a scooped front panel.

I walked up to join them and formed the most absurd bridal group I could imagine. However, Lola could see none of it. Instead she clasped her hands and did a little hop and paddle of her feet on the ground.

"Oooh, you all look wonderful!"

"I think my boobs are going to pop out when I dance though," Donna did some karate moves to check, letting out a liquid wobbling sound and Vinny raised his eyebrows.

"Armpits Donna?"

"I'm not shaving them for you."

"They look like two hamsters."

"At least I have some body hair."

"I have body hair; I just don't flaunt it." Vinny straightened his fringe indignantly and I realised she had a point. After all, I had never seen him with a five o'clock shadow on is chin and he definitely had no hairs on his arms.

He changed the subject, "Oh, and Lola, I tried the tights on but they ripped in the crotch. You'll have to get me a larger pair or something."

"I can see that she's a tulip but what are you?" I asked Vinny as Lola and tulip went off to discuss alterations.

"I think I am an orchid, but I could also be a snapdragon." He put a hand inside his front pouch and flapped the large metal ring running around its top edge.

"You're meant to be a pitcher plant," Lola called over to him, "You are going to have confetti in your trap."

He looked back at me and quirked his bottom lip sideways, asking, "What's a pitcher plant when it's at home?"

"It's one of those plants that drowns flies," I said undiplomatically but Vinny covered his mouth, suddenly rapt with joy.

"That is genius!" He cupped his hand, shouted back, "You're a genius, Lola!" and then twiddled in front of the mirror, "I love it! Love it! Love it! Do you think they'll have high heels in my size?"

I was about to warn him off the heels, when I become aware of an increasing clamour coming from the front of the shop.

A few seconds later, Persephone came flustering back towards us, "There is a man here and he has asked to see Alice Carter."

I put my hand up like a nervous volunteer, "I think that's me."

"I don't like men here during my fittings," she snapped.

"Did you ask his name?"

"No, but he's tall, dark and so handsome that he'd be perfect in one of my bridal magazines. However, handsome faces do not work in my shop. Virile men put my ladies on edge!"

My eyes opened wide, "That sounds like Adam."

"Whoever he is, please get rid of him!" Persephone urged.

I looked down at my dress, "But I look like a powder puff."

"With grey bra straps," she added unhelpfully. "Go quickly, before he scares off all my clients." She flicked her fingers and I walked out obediently, tugging my dress up to make sure it covered my chest.

"Alice, I need to speak to you," Adam went to grab hold of my elbow, but I circled it away.

"About what?"

"Your father. You found some information about him didn't you."

"That I have to talk about in a bridal shop?"

"Do you have the documents from The National Archives here?"

"Yes, they're in my bag."

"Can I see them?"

I frowned and called out, "Vinny can you grab my bag for me?"

My tubular friend waddled over to the changing rooms and collected my bag.

"Why are you all dressed so strangely?" Adam had unfortunately noticed our wedding costumes.

"It's a long story that I am quite happy to discuss tonight. I haven't even had a chance to look at the thing properly yet. Plus, I'm really cross with you, pulling Andrew in on my case was out of line."

Persephone was still watching me as she heaved the material tight around Donna's bust, pins sticking out of her mouth.

"Don't puncture me!" Donna shrieked with alarm.

"Do you have it there?" Adam asked, his focus on my bag.

I nodded, began to pull the envelope out and then realised Adam had snapped the demand at me. His eyes were also darting to the window of the shop and then to my bag.

"Are you alright?"

"Yes, I just need the envelope with the certificates in it."

I hesitated.

"Hang on, why did you say certificates and not certificate? How did you know there's more than…"

He put his hand down to snatch the envelope from me and my instinct, as all good toddlers learn, was to fix my hold and tug backwards in the opposite direction until a very painful, loud crack flicked out from my hand.

He dropped the paper and I immediately panicked, saying, "Oh god, I'm sorry, I'm so sorry. It's just, well you...you don't seem yourself this afternoon."

"I'm not. I just need the documents."

This was not like him and I backed away, shoving the envelope deep inside my bag.

"What are you playing at Adam?"

He changed his approach and said suddenly, "Come with me," snatching at my elbow.

Snatching at my elbow twice actually, because the first time his hand recoiled with an angry, Ow!

The second grasp caught, and, through gritted teeth, he said dryly, "I didn't want this to be the way that I finally touched you, Alice."

Before I had a chance to reply, he tugged hard and pulled me out of the shop, zapping himself again as he pushed the door open.

Then, strong-arming me down the high street, I tottered beside him, feeling like a circus act/ballet dancer who could barely stay on her feet.

A woman stopped with heavy bags in her hands and a little girl tugged at her mother's arm pointing at the man dragging a dandelion behind him. I tried to give her a smile of reassurance but tripped and fell head long on the filthy pavement.

Adam turned to help me up and the woman with the little girl reached out a hand to me.

"No don't touch her!" Adam almost shouted and the woman stopped and looked from him to me. "She...she's dangerous."

I groaned with despair and shook my head as I lay on the ground.

"I'm dressed as a dandelion Adam. I'm not exactly a terror threat."

"She's infectious. I'm taking her to the hospital," he warned, and the woman pulled back.

"Don't worry, the illness only affects two-faced unpredictable men!" I added sarcastically and had the satisfaction of giving Adam a fourth painful shock as he pulled me to my feet.

He scooped me up using one, very strong arm around my waist and carried me until we reached the end of a closed alley.

Then, with me still in the air, he set my back against the wall and asked, "How the hell do you cope with this electrocution thing all the time?"

He was extremely close.

"Why the hell aren't you surprised by it?"

"Surprised by it?" he grinned, "I love it, despite the fact that it bloody hurts."

"What are you talking about? How do you know all this?"

"Alice...I don't have time to explain."

He brushed my hair out of my eyes, and I would have felt my knees wilt underneath me if my feet were actually touching the ground, "I need to know the name of your father, it's really important."

"Adam, what is going on? How can I trust...?"

But even as I spoke, the light from the open end of the ally dimmed and I looked towards it.

There, the outline of three flowers stood like a posse of outlaws about to draw weapons on my abductor.

Adam had seen them too and laughed to himself.

"I can't stay and explain, Alice, it looks like your flowers are here to save you."

He looked down at me, hesitated and then dropped a kiss on my mouth.

It was completely unexpected and so intimate I forgot how to breath. His arms tightened and pressed even closer until every part of his body was touching mine. Time stretched out as my heart melted in my chest and the contact between us swamped my senses.

This unravelling, this dissolving into Adam was so delicious and satisfying I wanted to fix the memory, to freeze all my sensations in that one moment. But seconds later he pulled back and I struggled to stand as he set me gently down on the floor.

For a long moment I fought for balance, my senses blurred by surging hormones. Then, as the spinning world settled, I blinked twice and realised that Adam had walked away.

Walked away and taken my bag from my shoulder.

I should have shouted and ran after him, but my ridiculous brain had switched to slow motion. Instead my legs folded in on me until my rear end hit the ground and I simply watched him sprint to the end of the ally and jump over a high, corrugated fence.

Lola reached me first, "He stole your bag."

Then Donna and Vinny, "He's ruined your dress."

"Oh and look at your poor tights."

My pink knees showed up like mountains above the green pastures below and I stared vacantly at them.

"Did he hurt you?"

"She isn't speaking. Is she in shock?"

"When is Max getting here?"

A deeper voice cut in.

"I'm here already."

Large hands moved the women away.

"Is she alright?"

"My bag," I said, coming back to myself, "He took my bag. My keys. Oh god, my money...," my chest hollowed out and then I whispered ominously, "My birth certificate. He took my birth certificate."

Looks were exchanged above my head and Lola said with an uneasy wince, "I think we're going to have to tell her."

Max brushed them away, "Don't try to touch her, I'll do it."

His solid hand came down to slip coolly under my shoulder with the smoothness of a comfy pillow, no shock, no pain.

I let myself be supported and managed to find my feet as my colourful posse made their way across to the nearest communal seating area, Fred's Fry Up Breakfast Café.

The café had blue and yellow stripes covering every wall and was steeped in the smell of bacon and chip oil but at least it was empty.

Max and Donna pulled two plastic tables together, their sunflower tablecloths sticky and not particularly clean.

Then gormless Zac appeared from nowhere, mousing his way in to sit by Lola. He looked pale and wispy next to her fuchsia petals and I wondered if he had arrived with Max.

Max broke through my thoughts, standing awkwardly in front of me as he announced,

"Alice, we have a confession to make."

"You do?"

"Yes, we haven't exactly been straight with you."

"Well I realise that! You're not meant to be here, you're a bouncer."

"There's a lot you don't understand," Lola explained, with a grim set to her eyebrows. "None of us are what we seem to be."

I looked at the ridiculous flowers around my table and shook my head.

"That really doesn't surprise me."

"And we know about your static problem."

My heart froze. "My static problem?"

"That's why we've never tried to touch you."

"What do you mean?" my lips were numb.

"Haven't you noticed?" Vinny popped a sugar cube in his mouth.

"I think I'm going to faint."

The world span and Max shoved my head between my knees as Lola fetched a glass of water.

"It's alright Alice, you don't have to pretend anymore."

I stared at the ground, dragging air into my chest.

"We've known about you all along. We all work for a special police force that's been assigned to protect you."

Suddenly my friends, friends I had known for over six months were fragmenting.

They were all police officers doing a job?

Did that mean that everything they had said and done was an act? If so, how could I have been so gullible?

I sat back up, took a slow gulp of water, and asked calmly, "Assigned by who?"

They all looked across at Max who shrugged and lifted a hand.

"Don't blame me. It was Chief Inspector Nightly who set this up. I'm just a tail ender."

"Who's Nightly? What do you mean 'set this up'?" My voice was tight with tension.

"Me, Donna and Vinny began working at TSI to keep an eye on you," Lola confessed.

I looked around in horror as I worked out why. "You thought I might electrocute someone. You thought that I might suddenly go berserk and murder the whole department."

Vinny reined me in, "No, wait, it was nothing like that, Alice. We were assigned to protect you."

"Protect me? From who?"

"Your dad, of course. We were posted there when you started receiving letters from him," Lola explained.

"How did you know? Have you've been reading my post?"

She nodded forlornly, "We've been reading everything, but was in your own interest. Chief Inspector Nightly was so sure that your father would make contact that he set up a whole network to watch you."

"And you've spent the last six months staking me out?"

Donna gave me a sympathetic pat on the shoulder and received a sharp jolt of static.

"Sorry Alice. At least you don't have to hide your 'shock' problem anymore."

Lola added, "Plus you aren't alone with a strange problem."

"Not alone?"

"Yes," she squirmed in her seat, "We are all a little bit…odd."

I took in the grave faces around me and said nothing as Lola began to explain.

"You know how you have grown up hiding your unusual power?"

I nodded.

"Well, we have also been born with strange abilities and have to keep them hidden."

"Like what?"

Lola lifted her shoulders, "Oh, small things, things that most humans can't do."

"Like what?" I repeated.

Lola looked uncomfortable and passed the buck, "Perhaps you should explain first, Vinny,"

Vinny grinned. "I have a lizard's tongue; sticky fingers and I eat flies."

He reached sideways, stuck one finger into the side of Zac's cheek and pulled back. Zac's skin stretched towards him and then released with a gentle plop.

"No way. This has to be a wind-up."

"Do you want to see me in action?"

I watched in astonishment as a sticky, pink tongue strung out of his mouth towards the sugar bowl, latched a cube and pulled it back into his open mouth again.

"How did you do that?" I turned to Max and said, "Did I hit my head earlier?"

"Think about the boy crossing the road the other day, how do you think I reached him?" Vinny challenged.

"You reached…? You mean you saved that boy with your tongue?"

I tried to recall the scene and drew in a breath as I remembered the boy's words… 'mummy, that man stuck his tongue out at me.'

He nodded.

I began to understand, saying, "And is that why you were upset when that tattooed man took the video on his phone?"

"God yes, you saved me from complete global meltdown. If my tongue had gone viral…"

"We try to keep under the radar as far as possible," Max explained. "Do you remember that supermodel getting stuck when you went to the BFAs?"

"Gabrielle Hall?" I replied cautiously,

Donna raised a victory fist in the air.

"That was my work."

"Your work?"

"She bet me that I couldn't fit through the toilet window and I said 'you've got a deal'. I slithered through easily and she tried to follow."

"How?"

"Because I have bendable bones."

"Bendable?"

"Yup, my whole body contorts. I'm like a huge water balloon, if you squeeze me tightly I just kind of squash in."

She demonstrated by pushing both hands in on either side of her waist and releasing them rapidly to set off a wobbling, hot water bottle resonance, "I call it morphability."

"That's not possible."

"I'll show you if you want."

Donna stood up and looked around the café for inspiration but not seeing anything big to 'morph' through, she dived for the small gap in the back of her plastic chair.

Her head, shoulders and back squeezed through the watermelon sized hole like toothpaste from a tube, her bottom needed an extra push from Lola and then she popped out the other side, holding her hands up triumphantly.

I rubbed my forehead, "This can't be happening."

Then I had a thought and looked up at Max the mysterious, turn-up-everywhere bouncer and asked, "Is that the reason you can touch me?"

"Err...yes."

"But what's weird about you?"

"Well..."

"You seem normal."

"...well..."

I waited.

"I'm kind of wood-based."

"Which makes him very slow at running," explained Donna, "That's why he always gets everywhere last."

"Wood?" I repeated, "How does that work?"

"Oh, I am mostly human but my muscles are quite pulpy, you can feel them if you want."

I squashed a rock solid bicep and whispered, "But you look normal."

"I thought I was when I was younger, apart from my problems with food, remaining permanently cold and being useless at any sport."

Vinny's tongue popped out to fix onto another cube and Donna reached forwards to smack it.

"Vinny, that's gross. People have to eat those,"

Vinny crunched on the sugar and explained, "Zachary can download online data into his head."

Lola gave a coy smile and her dress fluttered as she clasped Zac's arm, "Yes, my gorgeous fiancé is able to access WiFi through his brain." She affectionately tucked his fringe behind his ear, "It's just one of his amazing gifts."

Donna added, "Get real, Lola, it bloody drives everyone around the bend."

"It might drive you mad, Donna, but I love him for it."

"He spends his whole life playing crappy games like Casino rush or Grand Theft Auto."

"At least I know where he is and, so what if he plays games all the time, lots of people do the same," Lola said defensively.

I drew my eyebrows together, trying to normalise the situation.

"So, let's imagine that I believe all of this, which I don't by the way."

"But you just saw everything that we can…"

"Wait," Max held his hand up, "Slow it down Donna, she's got a lot to take in."

I thanked Max and started again, "Let's imagine I believe all of this. Why have you developed these weird abilities?

Vinny shrugged, "We have no idea, most of us were just born with unusual plant and animal traits. Some people inherit them from their parents though, like Lola, she is *identical* to her mother."

I sighed and looked across at the only person who hadn't spoken yet and said resignedly, "And what are you going to throw at me Lola?"

She flapped her hands. "Oh, you know, flower stuff."

"Flower stuff?"

"Go for it, Lola," Donna encouraged.

"Fine...I smell very strongly of roses and can attract almost any man I want with my heady bouquet."

"Which is how you controlled those men in the office," I said with understanding.

"Tell her the other thing hon...you can't miss that bit out," Vinny prompted with a mischievous grin.

"Alright, I'm getting there, let me put it in my own words," Lola shifted in her chair.

I waited and she said slowly, "I have to have a man in my bed every night or I run the risk that I can...self-pollinate."

Well if there were ever words to leave you speechless, they would have to be it. My mouth hung uselessly as I watched Lola blush scarlet.

Stupefied, I asked, "What the hell does that mean?"

"It means that if I ever find myself...you know...bored during the night and get a bit carried away, I can..." she wobbled her head slightly, "Self-pollinate."

I gawped in silence until the Australian waitress walked up behind us and said, "Do you guys want to order any drinks yet? Coffees, teas or anything?"

None of us replied and she looked at Lola's shoulder.

"Nice tattoo by the way." She twisted her head sideways, "What is it?"

Chapter 17

"Alice, we need to talk about what is happening to *you* at the moment."

Max had pulled out a small book and looked down at his scribbled notes.

"Me?" I took a sip of tea from a utilitarian white mug, relieved to talk about something that I could actually understand.

"You've figured out that Adam has been trying to manipulate you?"

"Of course I have, and, to my credit I fought him off in the shop."

"It wasn't just the shop, he's been following you for the past six months."

"That's not possible."

"Why?"

"I've only known him for a few weeks."

"He's been priming you from a distance."

"How?"

"All those cards from your 'father' were actually sent from Adam."

An empty chasm opened up inside.

"My dad didn't send them?"

Max shook his head and I sank in my chair. Adam's cold blooded intervention, felt like a metal knife sliding into my ribs.

"Why would he do that?"

"To make you open the strong box in the archives."

"I don't understand."

"He needed to know the information inside it. Were there two other sheets of paper with your birth certificate?"

"Yes."

"Did you look at them?"

"Only one of them."

"Which one?"

The entire group sat forwards, suspended as they waited for my next words.

"My name change certificate."

All the shoulders around me slumped.

"You didn't see the other piece of paper?"

"No, the man in the archives was trying to read it over my shoulder, so I zapped him and decided to look at it later."

"Which man?"

"Andrew, he was...he was Adam's friend."

I felt the stab of betrayal deepen as I realised how far Adam's set up had gone.

Max sighed, looked across at Zac and ordered, "See if we can trace Warner's movements."

Zac nodded and fixed his eyes back up to the ceiling.

I asked tentatively, "What did the other piece of paper have on it?"

"Your father's alias. The one he re-entered the country with. It's the key piece of information that we need to begin searching for him."

Lola asked, "What are we going to do next, Max?"

"Adam will use one of his contacts to trace the name. We need to work out where he's driving to and pick his trail up from there."

"But I don't understand. Why did he need my dad's alias?"

"Your father forged two new identities for himself. The Carter one, in order to bring you safely back into the country, and another to go into hiding with. He then left both certificates at the registry office under high security so you, and only you would ever be able to find out his second alias. A piece of information that Adam's been desperate to get hold of."

"Why."

"Because Adam wants to kill your father."

Zac brought his eyes down from the ceiling. "Ok, he's just used the sat nav on his phone and plugged in Dexter's address, which is out toward the docks."

"Damn! That's a bloody grim place to have to visit. Still, we have to move quickly to stay on Adam's tracks."

"And it's already five-o-clock," added Donna.

"Five-o-clock. Oh crap, the dresses. Persephone is going to eat us alive!" Lola leapt from her chair and said, like a captain leading her soldiers to war, "Flowers with me!"

"No, I need Alice to come with me," Max ordered.

"What, now?"

"I have a lead, Lola. I need to get to Dexter and Alice could be useful."

"Well, she can't go like that."

I looked down at my skirt, feeling like a ping pong ball in the middle of a match.

"She can grab her clothes while you bring your car round," Lola bargained. "Alice, this way."

She disappeared through the doorway and I promised Max, "I can get changed really quickly."

"Plus we can help," Vinny chipped in with a grin, his tongue darting out for an extra sugar cube as we headed for the door.

I heard Max shout back, "No you can't!" just before the door closed and I had to agree with him. Anyone helping me get dressed faced a barrage of harsh shocks and sore fingers.

I had three flowers swearing five minutes later as they tried to undo the zip at the back of my dress.

Fortune would have it that the hook of my bra-strap had caught in the zip and the damn thing would not release.

In order to shift the problem, each one of my helpers stepped forwards like boxers braving for the fight, zapping and stinging their fingers as they forced the metal zip.

"Can't you ground yourself or something?" Lola asked, swearing under her breath.

"It won't help. Every time you move the zip even slightly, the friction will give you another shock."

"Then you'll have to get Max to do it."

The car was honking outside, and I slouched my shoulders.

"Do I have to get in his car dressed like this?"

"Well I think you look beautiful," Lola said defensively.

"Oh...I agree, beautiful in a garden, wedding sense," I backtracked, trying to save her feelings. "I mean, it's a lovely dress but I'm worried I might ruin it."

"Honey bun, you've already ruined it," Lola said with a resigned sigh.

I looked down at my grey, ripped lace and torn tights.

"Lola I'm so sorry. I promise I'll pay for a new one."

She waved my anxiety away.

"Don't worry. Once I've married Zac, I'll be loaded."

"Why? Is he rich?"

"Of course he is. That's half the reason I'm marrying him. I never did mention his short stay in the clink, did I?"

I shook my head.

"Nine months ago, he accessed the Bank of England's central reserve and made a huge donation to the earthquake fund in Indonesia." She folded up my jeans and handed them to me.

"The British government were embarrassed into honouring the payment and there was a massive scandal about the whole thing. MI6 were desperate to nail Zac for it and arrested him, but of course, found no evidence on any mainframe anywhere."

"Because it was all in his head?"

She nodded and I smiled as I took my shirt.

"So they had to release him?"

"Eventually. The case fell through and somehow he ended up with lots of money sitting in his bank account." She shrugged, "It's amazing the way life works out sometimes."

"And the scam was almost worth doing time for?"

"It was a no-brainer. Donna's family are always on the edge of the law. Her other brother has just been sent to jail too and it doesn't look quite so promising for him."

"What did he get put away for?"

"Bank robbery."

Chapter 18

"I think I put Donna's brother away in prison," I confessed to Max as I climbed into the front seat of a clapped-out old police car.

"Who, Lash?"

I nodded and he chuckled, "Didn't you realise? He was in that bank robbery you thwarted."

"No! Oh god, now I feel really bad about it."

"He held you up at gunpoint in a bank, Alice, he got what he deserved. Besides Donna doesn't care, Lash's always in and out of prison. Do up your seatbelt."

I struggled to get the buckle to click in and said, "Hang on, I think I saw this car when I was on the bus earlier."

I looked around it as Max set off, "It's pretty run down for a police car isn't it?"

"What do you expect? Luxury in the arms of the law? It drives alright. Besides, it passed its MOT last year."

The seat I was sitting on had a gash in it and yellow foam was bulging out of one corner, the carpet under my feet had warn through to the metal frame and the gear leaver was so heavily used that its black plastic shone like a polished snooker ball.

"Do you have to drive this because you are quite junior, do all the captains get the new ones?"

"We don't have captains, Alice. And this car is not a reflection of my rank."

I had obviously hit a sore spot going by Max's tight-mouthed irritation and grinned.

The complex unfurling of events wasn't all bad. At least I would get to know the man in the wooden apartment.

We sunk into silence as the car pulled up to some traffic lights. A cyclist drew up beside us and looked in the window. I gave a little wave as he did a double take and tried to keep his attention on the road, setting off to a wobbly start.

"I bet he thinks you've arrested me, and I am a prostitute."

"Well, going by the fact that you are still dressed as a... what are you dressed as by the way?"

"A peony."

He looked sceptical.

"A peony?"

I nodded and looked down at my ripped skirt.

"A well-trodden one."

He bunched his lips together to stop a smile and shook his head.

"Still beautiful though, despite the crumpled edges."

I blushed at the unexpected compliment, remembering my grey bra straps and opted to change the subject.

"So, what are we going to do now?"

"We are going to try and find your father, Chris, before Adam does."

"Are you going to put my father in prison?"

"If necessary."

"But he hasn't done anything wrong! He's been living, quietly under the radar all these years!"

"I understand that, but we also have to keep the public safe. What else can we do when he is such a liability?"

I looked down at my hands and pressed my thumbnail into my palm. I had caused this to happen.

Max softened his voice and asked, "How much do you know about your dad?"

I plucked at the white netting of my skirt. "That he killed my mum and some other people in Hong Kong."

"Among them Adam's father."

"Adam's dad?"

"Yes. Steven Metal. He was a multimillionaire who inherited the giant steel production company Metacob. He was famous for being incredibly rich and incredibly strong. So strong apparently that he lifted the front of a tank to free a man's legs when he served in the army."

"Do you know why my dad killed him?"

"No, but we do know that he left behind a five-year-old son called Benedict Metal. A son who disappeared during a gap year in Thailand eleven years ago and then reappeared again posing as Adam Warner."

"How did you know Adam was Benedict?"

"We didn't. We only became suspicious when Adam kept asking you out."

I huffed, "Why, because I wasn't a six-foot tall, beautiful supermodel?"

Max ignored me.

"Gabrielle Hall then referred to Adam as "Benny Boy" when you were talking to her in the toilet."

"Oh my god!" I said, "Does that mean Donna was doing surveillance at the BFAs? Did she give the pot to Gabrielle deliberately?"

He frowned, "Well, I wouldn't go that far. You know what Donna's like, Alice."

"But all the time she was sitting there, quietly listening into my conversation with Gabrielle, she was looking for evidence?" I let the scene turn over in my mind, "I thought she was a bit subdued in the toilets."

"We began to scan our databases, trying to work out whether Adam was actually Benedict and tightened our security."

"And you watched me every time I went out with him?"

"Which is why Vinny was in the Lupo restaurant."

I began to understand, "That's why he was so flustered when I saw him!"

"Yes, Vinny didn't have much time to think up a back story and he isn't great at improvising on the spot."

"And then you spied on me at the races!"

"We were trying to…"

"Jesus, everyone must have thought I was so stupid. Why didn't you just tell me?"

"Because you would change your behaviour."

"Is that all?"

"Plus, we would lose your trust, it would have blown our set up, and you would probably have sided with your father. Hell, you may even have run off with Adam. How many more reasons do you want?"

Although I disliked his assumptions, he was probably right, I would have been a loose gun.

Despite the fact that I resented my father, I still believed he wasn't a monster. He was a 'good man' once, according to my aunt and I held onto my childish dream that, one day, the mass murderer would be proved innocent.

And then there was Adam, he had manipulated me, no, not just manipulated me, he had broken every defence I had.

He had been so convincing that I would have done anything for him, the man that had saved me in the thunderstorm, the man that had struggled to hold onto me in Lupo, the man that had just smashed my senses to pieces with a snog in a grubby side alley. How could everything have been an act?

"Why didn't you arrest Adam?"

"Because Adam hadn't done anything wrong. At that stage we had no idea what he was planning. We just knew that he was talking to you."

"And now I've ballsed everything up?"

Max raised his eyebrows hopefully, "On the up side you did use Adam's phone to ring Lola once, which means we picked up his mobile number."

"Did that help?"

"Not with his conversations, his phone's encrypted, but we did pick up his satnav coordinates. Which is why we're heading to Dexter's."

"Can't we set up a massive police raid at Dexter's house then?"

Max drew air in through his teeth.

"Dexter can't be manipulated like that, he's...he's in a fragile state."

"Fragile state?" I heard exasperation in my voice, "He's about to give Adam a vital lead about my father."

"Don't snap at me Alice, you opened the vault."

"Well if you had the sense to talk to me rather than being a wooden headed, pompous ass maybe I would have acted differently."

"I was following orders, Alice."

"What stupid bloody orders. He's got a huge advantage now!"

"Then we have to fire-fight."

"What will he do with the information he picks up?" I tried to calm down.

"Trace Chris' name changes over the last twenty-five years and track him down."

I slumped in the chair, "I was an idiot to imagine he would actually be interested in me."

Max twisted his mouth sideways and said, "Oh, I don't know. In a get up like that you could probably turn the most illustrious of heads."

"For all the wrong reasons!" I huffed. "Here can you tug on this?"

I twisted sideways and noticed the car slur to the left as Max's large hand tugged my zip down firmly. It took three hard yanks before giving way with an alarming rip.

"Was that my bra or my dress ripping?"

"I don't know!" Max took his eyes off the road for a second to peer across at my back. "The bra, I think, it doesn't look quite right."

I put my hand behind me to find the lower of the two hooks had bent completely out of shape. "That's fine, at least it wasn't the peony outfit."

Wriggling the thing down and off my body was hard work while still keeping my seatbelt done up. I didn't spark off static as I was in a car, which made life easier, but I might as well have been firing lightning bolts by the erratic nature of Max's driving.

"Do you always drive this badly?" I asked as I heaved up my trousers.

"No! I don't normally have this kind of distraction next to me."

I finally did up my zip, tucked my shirt in and looked down at my feet, saying, "Damn, I left my trainers in the fitting room."

I looked at the green wedding shoes and rolled my eyes. It was either them or bare feet. I kicked them to one side, hoping I wouldn't have to walk far before wriggling back to sit comfortably in my seat.

"Ok, tree man, now you have to tell me everything about everything."

Max raised his eyebrows and blew out his cheeks.

"Where to start?"

He changed gear and then said, "Ok, well I work for a police arm called 'Ploid Operations', it is one of the Met's Criminal Investigation Departments."

"Ploid Operations. That's a mouthful?"

"It's often shortened to PlOps."

"You're kidding me? PlOps?"

"Enough of the judgements, I didn't come up with it, alright? We were already called that when I joined."

"What are Ploids?"

"Ploids are people who, for some reason, have been born with plant or animal genes mixed into their DNA."

"So I'm one of these Ploids? I could be related to an animal?"

"You don't have to say it so negatively, and yes you are one. Now can I keep explaining?"

"Hang on, can I ask another question?"

He waited; eyebrows raised.

"How many Ploids are there?"

"Several thousand, probably more. I don't know, I've never counted."

"Several thousand? How can so many people exist, and nobody know about them?"

"We can't exactly shout about our abnormalities from the roof tops. Most of us are societal misfits who struggle to be accepted."

He stared at me and his jaw clenched with anger. "Hell, don't look so surprised, Alice. You've been living as one for twenty-five years and never told a soul."

"Don't get so het up! I'm learning all this for the first time," I said defensively.

"Also you have to take this information and lock it inside your head, everything you have heard today has to remain confidential."

The tone of his voice had changed, and I looked at him quizzically.

"But surely I can talk to my aun…"

"No, nobody Alice. You have to swear to me that you will keep everything you have seen and everything I tell you under wraps." He knitted his thick brows together and added bluntly, "Officially PlOps doesn't exist and neither do Ploids."

"Why?"

"Imagine how hard life would become if the public found out about us, there would be prejudice on every corner."

I thought about the weird traits they were dealing with and sighed, "Fine. No one would ever believe me anyway."

I stared out of the window and realised we had turned off the motorway and were now heading down a desolate junkyard of a road. After traveling at five miles an hour and bumping down several potholes for ten minutes, I asked, "How much further do we have to go?"

"Not much. The harbour is where those lights are in the distance. We're currently driving down 'the graveyard'. It's an unmade road where metal work and old boat hulls get dumped before being broken down into scrap."

The last remnants of twilight were rapidly fading, and I shivered as the dark shapes beside us drifted past looking like the bones of dinosaurs destined for extinction.

"How many people work with you in PlOps?"

"In my division there are 20 full time staff, but you will never see all of us, because we split into various shifts. Then we are backed up with sleeping agents in the community and, of course, we have uniformed PCs posted in most major cities throughout the U.K."

"Is this thing country-wide then?"

He nodded, "And people are beginning to interbreed, creating even more complications. Zac is an example of that, he is a strange anomaly."

"But he's Donna's brother."

"Half-brother, god knows who his father was. I've never come across a Ploid who can interface before. He is a complete liability by himself but, if controlled, he could be a real asset to the branch."

"So you're a senior detective then, despite the clapped-out old car?" But I got no further as the said car choked and like the boats around us, came to a slow death.

Max tutted and turned the key hoping the sick engine would restart but there was only a dull whine each time.

"Did you put any petrol in it?"

"Yes of course I put bloody petrol in it."

"It's not like you to bite my head off. I was just checking."

He gave a cross sigh, released the bonnet with a handle down by his feet and loped around to peer at the engine. I undid my seatbelt and went to join him.

"What's the problem?"

He shook his head, "I have no idea. I really don't know my elbow from my arse when it comes to cars."

"You should still put your hands in and fiddle with something, so you at least look knowledgeable."

My attempt at humour obviously didn't help, so I said brightly, "I could try and jump start the engine."

"Jump start it? How?"

"By touching the battery with my hands as you turn the key."

"That is the most preposterous, dangerous, idiotic suggestion I have ever heard you utter."

"Well, it might work."

"Or kill you. But hey, don't let me be the spoilsport. You are welcome to sacrifice yourself if you want. You're just part of our inferior race after all."

I didn't say anything, and he put his hands on his hips, thinking for a moment.

Then he scrubbed his fingers across his cheek and said, "I think we're going to have to phone for another car. Have you got a mobile on you?"

I tilted my head, "Dur...no. Haven't you noticed I short out everything electrical? Don't you have one?"

He sighed, "No, my old one broke and the new one they've just given me is a touch screen which wasn't even worth me picking up."

I didn't get it and he held his hands up.

"Dur...wooden fingers. I don't conduct electricity."

"Great."

"Great" he echoed and went back to get his jacket out of the car.

"What are we going to do?"

"We'll have to walk."

"I can't walk in these, they're wedding shoes, they'll kill me."

He grunted, "It's safer than stroking a car battery back to life."

We set off down the damp, deserted road which was strewn with potholes and corroded lumps of metal.

The sea, or an inlet of it, ran along one side of us and played in the background with a rhythmic plop and suck on the rusting riveted siding. I wobbled along beside Max, the click and scrape of my shoes on the ground lost to the constant tap tapping of halyards on distant masts.

"Is Adam a Ploid too?"

Max kept his eyes fixed on the road.

"We think so. His father was incredibly strong. We haven't seen any evidence of it since we have been monitoring him, but we suspect he will have inherited some kind of anomaly."

"This whole Ploid thing is so weird. Just think, if you and I interbred we could cancel each other out. My static would be insulated by your wood." He still stayed quiet as I figured something else out, "Also if you and Lola married each other, you could give birth to a full English country garden."

"Do you have to be so insulting?"

"Come on, give me a break, Max. You have just laid so much on my plate. I have about a zillion things I don't understand."

"Fine, yes we are all defective, useless mutants. Ask me another question."

"Are you going to take it personally and jump down my throat?"

"No."

"Right." I thought for a moment, "Did you get your tree thing from your parents."

"No... Next question."

"How did you come about then?"

Silence.

"I don't know."

"You were just born a tree?"

"Yes."

"With no reason?"

"Some people just occur from spontaneous mutations and then have to grow up completely isolated and miserable because there is nobody else to help. Others have Ploid parents but spin off in unpredictable directions."

"How do you function? I mean, do you eat and drink everything that we do?"

"Mostly, like I said, I thought I was almost normal till I was 14."

"Almost?"

"I would wake up each morning feeling rigid and stiff and I was never any good at athletics as I can't run."

"Sports lessons must have been a bummer then!"

My chirpy comment didn't help because his mouth tightened, "Plus I couldn't move properly if I became cold and was very sick every time I ate any kind of meat."

That did sound pretty grim, I said more sympathetically, "Didn't your parents suspect anything?"

"Oh, I was the biggest disappointment in the world to my father. He was a rugby playing thug of a butcher and would make me prepare meat in the shop and then every evening he would force me to sit down and eat it. And every time I did I...I would spend the next two hours throwing up."

He fell into silence and I limped beside him. Eventually he added, "It was hard, every day was hard. I never thought it would end."

I saw him as a little boy and imagined the nightly misery he must have gone through. I swallowed a lump in my throat before I could talk again.

"How long did that go on for?"

He gave a dry huff of a laugh.

"Oh, years. I tried running away a few times, but I never got very far."

"How did you finally escape?"

"He hit me so hard with frustration when I couldn't run for the bus one day that I fell on a concrete curb and broke my arm. I had to be taken to the hospital where I was X-rayed and had a blood test. My X-ray came back as unreadable and my blood had a chlorophyll-based derivative in it. That's when a consultant realised I was a ploid and sat us all down to explain my problems. My father blew up saying he knew something was wrong with me, shouted that he didn't want a crippled, subhuman for a son, claimed my mother must have had an affair and told me not to bother coming home again."

I gasped. "What happened then?"

"I was taken into care."

My feet were so squashed into the pointed heels that every step was agony.

"Was that better?"

"In some ways."

He stopped, obviously frustrated with my slow progress and pushed his hand through his hair. "Look, do you want me to carry you for a while? It's only another couple of miles up this road."

Couple of miles? I was going to be a cripple!

"No, you can't carry me!"

I would just end up in a fireman's lift with my bottom by his face!

I remembered back to our first meeting and realised that he had probably lifted me like that after the awards party.

My cheeks burnt.

Then I remembered Adam's romantic, one-armed scoop earlier and felt my bones soften…hang on…that wasn't a lift that most ordinary men could do so easily.

"I think Adam might be stronger than normal."

"Why?"

"It's the way he lifted me earlier."

"Oh?"

"Yes, as if I weighed nothing."

"So he can lift you then but I can't?"

"Well that was different, you're nothing like Adam. His was kind of romantic."

"What? While he was mugging you?"

I ignored him and walked in silence for the next 10 minutes, then I slipped on a large screw that had been left on the road and went over on my ankle, falling onto the gritty track. Yet again, Max tried to pull me up.

"Are you alright?"

"Yes, fine," I snapped back and forced myself on in an ever-slowing hobble. "Do you think I can walk in bare feet?"

"Not with this much rubble on the road."

I grumbled but he had a point, the last rays of sunlight had almost faded, and any jagged debris was practically invisible.

Eventually I said, "I think I need to sit down," and limped to the edge of the bank. Where I slipped my sorest shoe off and let out an unguarded sob as my entire day crashed into me.

"Are you alri…?

"Don't be nice to me or I'll cry."

"Oh."

In fact, I was too far gone with morose self-pity to stop.

"I can't do this," my chin buckled.

"You can, it's not that far."

"No, no, it's not just that. Your story from when you were young is so grim and I've done nothing but think about myself and how uncomfortable these shoes are. You've walked calmly along, knowing that you might seize up at any second and I've been ponsing beside you, complaining about my blisters. Everything has gone wrong and I've caused it."

I slammed my agonizing shoe on the ground. "And now I have to get to those bloody lights in a green pair of torture shoes."

"I'll carry you."

I waved a heel in the air and shook my head.

"And that's not even the half of it. I've also messed up Lola's bridesmaid's dress, thrown my dad into danger, let everybody down and thought a handsome man would actually have been interested in me!"

"It's not your fault. We hadn't told you anything, Alice."

He sat down beside me and reached across to brush my hair back from my miserable face, hooking it behind my ear.

"Yes, but when Adam kissed me, I let him take my bag, because I thought he liked me. That's what really hurts."

My nose was running, and I wiped it with the back of my sleeve.

"I didn't know he kissed you."

I nodded. "Down the alley, but only to manipulate me. And there's me with a big arrow above my head saying, 'gullible virgin, desperate for a shag, give her a kiss and she will give you her life savings, plus anything else you want while you at it'."

"It hurts more than the shoes then?"

I slumped and said, "That's debatable at the moment."

We stared out at the ragged skeletons of ships as I regained control of my jerking breath. Max cleared his throat.

"I bet he enjoyed it though."

"What?"

"The kiss."

I looked at him and mustered the edge of a smile.

"Do you think so?"

"Perk of the job. He could have easily taken your bag without lip contact."

I shoved my elbow into his arm.

"You say the best and the worst things to me, Max Greenstick."

"Good, does that mean you'll let me carry you now?"

"How? Not with my bum in the air?"

"I only do that when you're unconscious. This time you can hitch a lift on my back."

I sighed.

"Fine then, but I warn you, I'm heavy!"

"Not as heavy as me," he muttered and prepared to hitch me up.

Chapter 19

Our destination turned out to be an old ship-manufacturing warehouse that we entered via a broken sliding door, hanging lopsidedly on its hinges.

Max hauled it sideways with a loud scrape of metal against metal.

"You had better put your shoes back on. There's a lot of rubbish inside."

I bent down and slipped my raw feet back into the shoes that now felt about two sizes too small and followed Max into the dark interior.

The building smelt of tar and ink and had just six, high-up, bare light bulbs shedding light into its dim interior. A relentless tap dripped into an industrial metal sink and an old teak table was propped against one wall, its surface hidden in a mound of food wrappers, broken bottles and carrier bags,

A faint scratching came from my right and I turned to see that someone had built a bank of newspapers halfway across the building, creating a fifteen-foot-high wall.

"Welcome to the paper warren."

Max pointed to a low opening carved into the bank like a rabbit hole and motioned with his hand, "He's in there. Follow me and don't touch anything."

"Paper is an insulator Max; I think I can risk it."

The tunnel was surfaced with a smooth carpet of Daily Mirrors, so I yanked my shoes off and followed Max into the burrow, my tights crackling on the warm floor that was ironed flat with repeated footfall.

After about fifteen feet the tunnel opened up into a sloping crater, a massive moonscape pockmarking the middle of the fortification where grey printed sheets rose, layer upon layer from the center of it.

I tucked my hands under my armpits, I may have been low risk, but the incandescently dry tabloids would catch like kindling. Then a movement caught my eye and I fixed on a small, camouflaged figure of a man, sitting halfway up a bluff bank, scrabbling amongst the printed pages.

His whole body and face had become blackened by grey ink and he would have been invisible if he hadn't scuttled from one sheet to the next in staccato movements, behaving like a rat scavenging for scraps among the paper debris.

"Dexter," Max called out.

The beast stopped and sniffed the air, shocked by the intrusion.

"Dexter, I need to talk to you."

"Greenstick, is that you?"

Max nodded and the creature flapped him away, "Get out, I don't want you here."

"Have you just had a different visitor?"

"It's no business of yours."

"Do you remember that demolition order on this place?" Max's voice had taken on a sharper edge.

"It was cancelled," the inky man snuffled.

"Only on my say so, if I change my mind…"

The figure paused and then sighed, climbing down from his high pile.

"What do you want?" He had very small, dark eyes and a long nose that poked up slightly at the end.

"I want to know what you told Adam Warner."

"Adam Warner? No, no Adam Warner here."

"You know who I'm talking about."

"Well let me look at my busy diary to see if it jogs my memory." He scavenged around amongst the sheets on the floor and picked up a completely grey notebook, holding it so close to his eyes it was actually touching his nose.

"You need to get your vision checked, Dexter."

"It does me well enough as long as I can see my writing." He tapped the open page, dropped the book and turned to rub his hands over the paper slope.

"Weren't you supposed to be asking for Benedict Metal instead?"

"Is that the name he gave you?" Max rubbed his spiky chin, "Interesting. What did he ask you to look up?"

"What's it worth?"

"Dexter," Max warned.

"Let me take a look at this pretty pink girl first. Now why would you have brought her with you?"

"She's a friend."

The man gave a sniffy laugh and Max warned, "Focus Dexter. I need information."

"What a beautiful alabaster she is, skin like newly bleached parchment."

"Don't even think about it."

"But she's so clean, if I could just get a little bit of ink on her, it would make me so happy."

The filthy little man walked up to us and put a grubby hand out to touch my cheek, but Max clicked his tongue.

"Well, don't say I haven't warned you."

The hand hovered and I tried not to back away. His little moist eyes blinked and then switched back to Max.

"Warned me?"

"This place is a tinderbox Dex, if you move that hand any closer you will create a spark and then..." He shrugged, "Who knows what might happen?"

"She can spark?" His voice held wonderment and fascination. He licked his lips and looked at me like a prize chocolate éclair, "She's the daughter, isn't she?"

Max nodded and his hands hovered for a moment, longing to make contact, "If I could only just…" but then his fingers shook and withdrew into reluctant fists.

He nodded and took a step backwards, "No, you're right, I can't risk my papers."

He wiped his hands down his trousers and turned agitatedly to Max instead, "Let me do you then."

"Dexter, do you have to?"

"I'll do it quickly."

"It is a sick habit."

"I know but I don't have many pleasures for all my work and effort, and you won't let me do it to the girl."

Max sighed and angled his chin forwards as the man's boney hands came up to daub dark lines of print down each side of the detective's face, smearing his mouth, nose and forehead. Then, in an almost tribal ritual, the inky man splayed his fingers and slathered them indulgently over Max's arms, dragging black smudges all the way down to the ends of his fingertips.

This was followed by a close, almost dancing shimmy, rubbing Dexters blackened body against the entire, wooden man's torso.

Dexter finally stepped away, quivering with satisfaction. Then he shut his eyes and had to stagger off to lean against a paper wall for a couple of minutes before he was able to speak again.

Max and I exchanged glances and I mouthed, "That was gross."

He shrugged his shoulders and mouthed back, "What else was I meant to do?" before looking at his blackened palms and trying to find a cleaner part of his body to wipe them off with.

Finally, Dexter calmed down enough to talk again.

"Getting back to business?" Max prompted.

"Back to business, yes." Dexter's little eyes glinted in the dim light, "The metal man showed me the girl's birth certificate with Chris Cooper written on it but the other document, the one you would be interested in, that had the important name on it."

"Which was?"

"Which was Colin Colt."

The man started shifting newspapers everywhere and talked animatedly. "Now I managed to find out that Colin Colt had changed his name every two years since then. I was able to trace his path in the homeless community for about ten years but then lost the trail."

He pointed at one sheet and then another. "He was a Devon Dawlish the last I heard."

Dexter dumped the papers and scrambled back up his pile to retrieve a small pamphlet and pawed at it with a grubby finger. "Here he is on the list of residents in the Liverpool home for the homeless."

He gave the booklet to Max and I looked over his shoulder at a long list of names, surprised that any book would have information like that in it. Then I read the title and began to understand.

It was called Home to Home and held a census of all the homeless people in 2007.

"I can't give you the next location after that because filthy technology cuts in to take the words away from me. You need things to be printed. Need them solid, something to hold in your hand. You need to smell the ink."

He put the book by his nose and rubbed it around his face before holding it out to me. "Do you want a smell? This one's still fresh."

I shook my head and he turned away, picking up other documents and rubbing them against his cheeks, his arms, his legs.

Max tugged my elbow.

"We've got everything we need, come on."

I tiptoed out after him and allowed myself to drink in a great gasp of fresh air as I left the building.

"Sorry about that," Max mumbled, "Blackening clean skin is a bit like dope to him and he doesn't get a fix very often."

"So I saw. That was fairly disturbing to watch."

He nodded and walked beside me before saying grimly, "This job puts you right down with some of the strangest perversions you can imagine. It was tough when I first started but I have to do it in order to get these people on my side."

He stopped for a moment and stood looking down at the ground with his hands on his hips, his breath held, and eyes closed.

"Are you alright?"

He nodded and began walking again. "I'm sorry you had to see that."

I shrugged, "I admired you for doing it, actually."

I saw a slight lifting in his face.

"You did?"

"He wanted to do it to me Max, and you stepped in to take my place."

He gave a half smile and ran his hand through his hair.

"You know what?"

"What?"

"You say the best and the worst things, Alice Carter."

We had begun making our way down the road which would eventually lead back to the distant, twinkling town and I, still walking bare-footed asked, "So what do we do now?"

He grimaced and looked down at my feet. "I'm not sure, you can't go far like that."

He thought for a moment and then clicked his fingers, "I've got an idea. Can you wait here for twenty minutes while I sort some transport out? It won't be ideal, but it will get us back to London."

I shrugged and said. "Hey, if I don't have to walk anywhere, I'll be happy."

I sat looking down at my feet, still covered in the remnants of the green tights I had pulled on earlier that afternoon, one big toe now sticking out like a white worm in the rapidly darkening evening.

The eerie isolation of the ship's graveyard seemed to complete the unreality that had settled over me in the past twelve hours.

This morning my life had seemed utterly normal, but all these cracks had been rumbling like seismic activity below the surface.

The players were all in position and I was the linchpin, an innocent bystander who had been bobbing along unaware that everything was about to explode.

I remembered Max's comment when I first met him, "You still don't know anything?"

Well now I knew everything and it made my head throb. I felt as if I had been trapped down a convoluted rabbit warren where the laws of humanity had been ripped to shreds.

I reached out to write Adam's name in the dirt with the heel of my shoe and was enjoying the satisfaction of scrawling "bastard" after it, followed by three big exclamation marks, when a man spoke beside me.

"So you followed me?"

The sound made me jump and I scuffed over my scribbles.

"Adam?"

"Did you get what you wanted out of Dexter?"

"You mustn't go near my father."

"And I thought I was the one manipulating you."

"I know what he did. I know you must be angry but my dad's dangerous."

"How long have you known?"

"That's irrelevant." I wasn't going to tell him I had only found out four hours ago. "Why did you have to manipulate me like that Adam? Why not talk to me? Why couldn't you have just bloody talked to me about this? I'm not stupid!"

I picked my shoe up in anger and threw it down the bank, groaning as I heard it plop into the water.

"This is an appropriate place, don't you think?" Adam sat down beside me, "A graveyard for once healthy ships."

"You've got to stay away from him."

"I doubt that either of us ever remember being healthy."

"I liked you. I really liked you! I think I was even falling in love with you."

He looked down and kicked the loose pebbles that peppered the barren bank we were sitting on. "Then you fell in love with a lie."

"No, I don't believe that."

"My whole life is a lie, Alice. I've manipulated you from the first day that we met."

The night chill fell densely around us, thick tendrils of sea salted air etching through my shirt as I whispered, "Adam?"

"Yes?"

"Why are you here talking to me?"

He hung his head, "I wanted you to understand."

The last stain of light left the water and the aching ships rocked in their silted beds as we sat quiet and alone on the rusting plateau.

"He didn't just kill those people in Hong Kong, you know."

"My father?"

He nodded and reached out to take my hand. I felt the sharp click of electricity shoot between us, causing him to pause and then try again.

"He killed the rest of my family too."

"What?"

Adam nodded and I stammered, "I...I never knew they were involved."

"Oh, they didn't die on that day, they died afterwards." He traced his fingertips across the bones in the back of my hand, my skin prickling with static as he talked. "No, my dad was the lucky one, he didn't have to cope with the fall out."

"I don't understand."

"When my mother heard the news of his death, she tried to kill herself. She was admitted to a psychiatric ward where they discovered she was pregnant. After a very long stay she returned home with severe depression and was barely functioning but then everything changed in the house because Annabel arrived. A tiny vulnerable human who needed my help. She was my lifeline. The house became happy again and I adored her. But all that time my mother's moods became blacker and blacker until, one July afternoon, just after Annabel turned five, I was dropped home from school to find a silent house. I walked upstairs to discover my mother lying with her wrists cut, dead in the bath."

I swallowed, not knowing what to say as he brushed his fingers over my knuckles, his eyes distant.

"She left me a note which said she had only ever loved my father and had never been able to love anyone again after he had gone. It wasn't fair to bring Annabel up in a heartbroken house and it was better that the child died than grew up in a world without love."

The night air seemed to smother me as I imagined the scene.

"I searched frantically, pulling the house apart looking for any sign of Annabel. Eventually I ran out into the garden and found her body floating, face down in the pond."

"No."

"She was so cold and so blue. I had found her too late. Everything I ever valued died in my arms as I held her."

He picked up a stone and threw it miles until I heard a distant splash in the water beyond and I shivered in the cold night air.

"Then I phoned for an ambulance and watched them take my heart away, wrapped in a red blanket."

He stared into the distance and I choked, "Adam..."

Surprisingly Adam gave a dry laugh and shook his head.

"Oh, it doesn't end there, no. I lost control after that. Did I ever tell you that I am stronger than normal people?"

I shook my head and he huffed.

"I seemed to power up that afternoon. I went berserk, smashed everything in the house, ripped doors from their hangings, tore the sink from the wall and destroyed every item of furniture we owned. Then I hit out at the officers who tried to restrain me and left them both unconscious. After that I was admitted to a high-risk unit where my uncle had me locked in a reinforced metal cell and spent the next five years forcing cognitive therapy down my throat. He punished me every time I used my strength against him. To begin with, I fought it and remained in isolation, but it began to get to me."

He looked into the distance, lost in his memories.

"Do you know what that does to your brain, Alice? When you are locked up for months on end and you can think of nothing but revenge and blame? They become part of you."

They also carved him into an ice king.

"So I played his game, learnt how to control my temper and strength and vowed never to use them in anger on another person. I learnt how to manipulate the world around me and eventually became my uncle's perfect reformer. I was finally deemed safe enough for release when I turned eighteen. Then I inherited all the money my grandfather left me, made myself disappear, changed my identity and started up various companies, with one aim."

"To find my father."

He laughed and shook his head, "To find you. I knew you would eventually lead me to him."

"And you sent me emotional, paternal notes to push me into action?" I pulled my hand back and he released his hold.

"I initially planned to keep you out of it. I was simply going to break in and steal the documents after you picked them up, but you didn't take the bait." He huffed a laugh and shook his head. "So I moved my entire company in an attempt to seduce you. It would have worked on any other woman, but you were so scared that you couldn't cope with me coming anywhere close."

"I couldn't...I couldn't risk shocking you."

"You were unreachable."

"I had spent most of my life locking away secrets too, Adam."

"It threw me."

I challenged him, "Why? Because you felt sorry for me?"

He shook his head, "I can't feel emotion. Everyone that I care for dies, Alice."

"It doesn't have to be like that."

He twisted and pushed me back to lie on the bank.

"It does. Look at me. There's nothing positive about my life. I am the monster that has been hunting you all these years. I am the reason you have had to hide. I have lived to find your father and I have to take revenge for my family."

"But you don't have to kill him. You can still change that part of the plan."

"I can't."

"Then I will stop you."

"You?" he huffed with surprise, "How could you ever stop me?"

"Well, not just myself, there are others."

He frowned and became still.

"Like?"

"The police."

"PlOps?"

I nodded and he laughed, shaking his head.

"Does Max work for PlOps?"

"Max?" I asked cautiously.

"Max, the hero who keeps stealing my thunder."

"I wouldn't exactly call him a hero."

"You went home with him that evening, didn't you?"

"Adam, it wasn't like…"

"I was frantic with worry."

"For me or for your plan?"

"What do you think?"

"Nothing happened."

"Really?"

I nodded, "I smoked pot in the toilets and then passed out in the taxi on the way home. Max just scooped me up and let me sleep it off."

He rolled his eyes, "I thought you were stuck, dying in a gutter somewhere."

"Perhaps I should have died, it would have made everybody's life easier."

"Don't say that."

He stroked a sparking finger across my cheek and then brushed his mouth over mine and I forgot how to breath.

Strength ran through his body as he tipped me into a rollercoaster of sensations. I had never been so close, so warm, so vital and so encompassed and suddenly, desperately, I wanted more.

Illicit shocks jabbed into my hands as I traced the powerful muscles in his back making me sick and giddy with a strange mix of elation and guilt.

This was the contact I had craved all my adult life, the sensations I never let myself feel. This was the man that had broken my safe world and filled it with danger and desire, the man I couldn't resist any longer.

His fingers slid up under my shirt, dancing with sparks as they brushed against my ribs. His breath juddered as prickles of static lightning flicked through the dark air. Then he hesitated as a larger shock juddered from my skin and I whispered, "You can stop if it hurts."

He shook his head and crackled kisses across my collarbone, "You set me on fire Alice."

This was the most dangerous man I had ever met, my nemesis, my anathema. This man had manipulated me and wanted to destroy my father, but I was helpless in his hands, guiltily enraptured by his caresses and craved him more than oxygen.

Adam shifted his full weight and lifted his shirt to expose the skin of his stomach to mine, his body moved, heavy, drugging and slowly generating sparks that stung us, needlepoint sharp and painfully exquisite. Adam was pushing me to give him more, his fingers bruising into my flesh, his lips so demanding that I tasted blood in my mouth

I was losing control. This man was too powerful for me to mess with. I had to hold onto my senses and try to rein him in.

I sucked in a breath and shook my head, pressing my hands against his shoulders but he ignored me, still demanding more. Then I pressed harder and whispered a muffled, "No, Adam, stop!"

He paused then, breathing heavily.

"Jesus Alice, you don't really mean that?"

"I do. You have to stop, this is wrong," I said bluntly and pushed his shoulders a second time.

Adam groaned and rested his forehead against mine, "You are killing me, Alice."

He lifted his head and huffed a puzzled laugh. "What is it with you?"

"What do you mean?"

"This isn't how you were meant to be."

"What was I meant to be?"

"Predictable? Compliant? God, every other woman I've met has been."

"Well they probably weren't as screwed up as me, were they?"

I looked away from him and he pulled my chin back, saying, with a hint of admiration, "You made me waver in my plan."

"Waver but not stop?"

"I can't, I have to see this through."

He brushed some dust off my face, tracing the line of my cheek with a sparking finger. Then he stopped suddenly, staring back over his shoulder.

"It looks like Max has come back to rescue you again." He screwed up his eyes, "Is he driving a three-wheeler?"

I squinted and could just make out the narrow and unstable shape of one of those tiny local delivery vans chugging in our direction.

"Oh God," I said, "probably."

Adam turned back to me and laughed.

"Don't go falling for the wrong man."

I said gravely, "My father is a dangerous opponent, Adam."

He pressed his thumb against my lips and said, "He and I are well matched then."

Then he pushed up and away, pausing to say, "Oh and Alice."

"Yes?"

"I have lived my entire life to do this, don't get in my way."

"Or I'll end up dead too?"

He looked at me gravely, "I have to do whatever it takes."

"I might be a lowly pawn in this hideous chess game of yours, but I will fight you if I have to."

"Not a pawn, Alice," he laughed, "don't underestimate your role. A pawn couldn't force me into checkmate."

And, with that, he turned away, disappearing into the complex shadows beyond. Adam was still devastatingly attractive, even when he was threatening to kill me.

Chapter 20

Well, there is transport and there is "transport."

The van looked as if a strong gust of wind or a sharp turn would have it over on its side and it was driven by, yes, you guessed it, a doughy faced man with fat, Pillsbury fingers.

I didn't even have the energy to find out where Max had got it from.

"Do I have to?" I asked as Max pointed to the rear of the van.

"There are only two seats at the front, and I need to direct Dale," he replied with a smug grin.

Dale, the yeasty smelling driver, reached into his glove compartment to retrieve the rear door keys and I noticed a thick book inside it. A book that I had seen before called 'The Beginning of Life's Secret.'

"Didn't I see that at your house?" I asked and Max stuck his bottom lip out as he picked it up.

"It's a new book about the history of the Ploids. I tried reading it but it's very heavy going. There's barely any of these published, how did you get it Dale?"

Dale grinned and tapped the side of his nose, "I make friends in high places. You know what they say: A good baker will always 'rise' above the rest."

"How far have you got?"

"Second chapter." Dale's cheeks dimpled, "I'm determined to get through it, even though it sends my brain to sleep every time I try."

Max laughed and swung the back door open for me, "Perhaps your first challenge will be to find a spare book and read up on us, Alice."

As I went to climb up, Max brushed dirt and gravel off my back, "What have you been doing? Rolling along the street or something?"

I didn't think my answer would go down well and sat back quietly so they could manoeuvre the bread crates to fit in around me.

Max's humour bubbled up as he wedged the last crate into position and he chuckled, "If we have an accident in this thing, you'll be toast."

I rolled my eyes and he closed the door, locking me into a pitch black, yeasty coffin. Then the van set off along the potholed road, its bouncy suspension toppling the squashy packets of bread all over me.

What kind of a mess had I got myself into? I had just snogged Adam. Not only that, I had thoroughly enjoyed it!

Resting my head in my hands I realised that I had developed Stockholm Syndrome for a man whose main purpose in life was manipulation and revenge.

Adam was a lethal assassin who was programmed to kill my father. I should have abhorred him, should have been sickened, repulsed and terrified of him, but instead I had just stuck my tongue down his bloody throat!

I felt ashamed and kicked my foot out hard into the packets of bread.

I had fallen for a man who's whole life was a lie. A man had threatened to kill me if I got in the way. A man who had spent the last six months pulling my strings like a puppet master and yet my sodding hormones raged every time I was around him. What kind of freak was I?

I put my tongue against my lip and still tasted blood. Adam was dangerous, this was real life and if I didn't sodding we'll grow up, my dad was about to be murdered.

I had set Adam on this trail and now I had to stop him.

Pushing my palms hard against my eyes, I slid myself into a reclined position and grabbed a soft packet to wedge under my ear.

Then I relaxed back into my padded van and let its unstable suspension rock me like a cradle.

I woke up with a start to find Max shifting crates off my legs. Yawning, I moved gingerly and stretched my cramped muscles out straight, throwing off the eight loaves of bread that had fallen on my chest during the journey.

"Did you enjoy the kip?"

I blinked him into focus and grinned, refreshed by my quick kip. "Do you know what? Despite the fact that I was so 'sandwiched in', I feel better."

"Your sense of humour's deteriorated."

"Where are we?"

He stepped back and revealed the distinctive sign outside Scotland Yard.

"Is that sign really so small? It looks gigantic when you see it on the T.V."

"How are you through metal detector machines?"

"I've never done one."

"You've...?" He blinked at me, "Blimey you must have had a sheltered life. Come on, we'll give it a go."

He waved at the dough man and called out, "Thanks Dale, I owe you one."

"Send me the recipe that uses those root rhysomes to flavour the dough."

Max laughed. "I'll do that."

"Root what?"

Max cleared his throat and spoke artificially deeply.

"Oh...It's man-talk Alice."

Well, the machine beeped, of course but it didn't short out or shock me, unlike the strange metal device the policewoman scanned me with.

After three shocks, she tried to frisk me and leapt away like a cat on hot coals with every pat. Giving up finally, she had to write a note saying that I was not search compatible in future visits and waved me through.

Max led me down a flight of stairs where I found a large, bare bones basement with a concrete floor.

Water and heating pipes ran across every wall, a generator hummed in one corner and a cleaning cupboard smell hovered in the hot, dry air.

Nine desks were spaced out on the gritty floor and strip-lighting gave everything a yellow tinge. However, Lola and Donna softened the daunting room and jumped up as we walked in.

Lola went to hug me, hesitated and air-kissed a greeting instead.

"How did it go? Have you picked up any information to work with?"

Max shrugged, "We've traced Cooper's name up till ten years ago, but we need to push further in order to find him. Where's Zac?"

Donna directed Max over to a door in the far wall and Lola smiled back at me.

"It's so good that you know all about us now, we can finally discuss things properly. Do you know how hard it was hiding everything from you?"

I began to answer but she cut me off with a concerned look. "Why are you only holding one of your bridesmaids' shoes?"

"Oh, my shoes! I'm really, really sorry Lola, but I lost one of them in the Thames Estuary."

We both looked down at my feet and my grubby white toes waved a cheerful hello where the material split into wide ladders.

"Your tights are ruined too."

"I know."

She sighed forlornly and then said, "It doesn't matter anyway, you might not need them. The wedding will probably be off. Follow me."

She led me back to a group of desks as Donna caught up with me and whispered, "Zac's in her bad books" and made a cutting action across her throat.

I gaped silently and mouthed, "What happened?"

Lola turned around. "I know exactly what you are talking about, Donna."

We stood like unruly children as Lola pushed the hair out of her eyes. "I love you to pieces,

Donna but your youngest brother is a little shit. Do you know what he has been up to, Alice?"

I shook my head.

"I've been carrying out a mini investigation to find out what Zac has been doing for hours here every day. I thought he was helping with police enquiries most of the time, but no, he has been sneaking out the back and watching the massive stash of porn films that Larry confiscated from an illegal knocking shop three weeks ago."

"Ohhh."

Disgruntled, she wriggled her shoulders. "It's not as if I ever left him needing more at the end of each night. I mean, what does it take to satisfy some people?"

She took off her jacket and hooked it onto the back of a chair and almost instantly a man's voice rang out, "Nice tattoo Lola."

Lola held a sarcastic finger up and then introduced me to him.

"This is Larry, believe it or not he's one of our senior officers."

The pasty faced man had large, outward facing eyeballs, one of which looked at me.

He said, "Larry Borry, at your service."

"The same Larry that raided the knocking shop?"

He grinned and pointed at his eyes, "Nothing gets past these peepers, Alice."

I smiled back and said, "I'm sure."

"No really, I'm serious. I have divergent vision. I can study a menu and lip read at the same time! How's your hamster 'Mootie' by the way?"

I gasped, "Were you in Lopo, listening to my conversation?"

But Larry didn't reply, instead an angry voice broke across us.

"Did you bring her in, Lola?"

I turned to see a man with wide, hunched up shoulders and a brick red face.

"No Rufus," Lola snapped back, "You know I don't have that kind of authority."

He swore under his breath, his head jutting forwards, "She's a complete liability! What the fuck is she doing in here?"

"Drop the foul language."

"It was bloody Max wasn't it?"

"It doesn't matter who it was. She needs our protection."

"No, *we* need protection from *her*! You have no idea what she can do."

Then he turned to walk away from us, asking the whole room loudly, "Has anyone even bothered to think about MET security recently?"

He slammed his hand into the door at the far end of the room and raged, "You are a fucking idiot Greenstick. You've put this entire station at risk by dragging her in here."

A deep, American voice replied, "Before you jump down his throat Rufus, Max has assured me that she..." then the door was kicked shut behind him and the conversation was cut off.

I looked around the room to see that everybody had stopped working to stare at me.

Lola sighed, "That was Rufus Bull and he isn't great with anyone new. But don't worry, he'll be fine once he realises you aren't going to kill us."

I bit the side of my lip. Did all these people simply see me as a security risk?

"Come and meet Sam Tickle instead. You'll like him."

Lola swanned towards a man that I recognised. I paused and said, "Hang on, weren't you the handsome barman at the BFAs who put out my fire?"

Vinny, who was sitting on Sam's desk reading a document, tutted, "Oh God, don't call him handsome, Alice, his ego's big enough already."

Sam laughed.

"I wasn't the one wearing a gold lame suit."

"I think I looked rather good in it actually," Vinny flicked his fringe.

Lola said, "Why aren't you at your own desk, Vinny?"

"Sam has asked me to help with his research," Vinny replied smugly, pointing at Sam's computer screen.

I looked over Sam's shoulder, it showed a map of Watford with a dot flashing on it.

"Isn't that my aunt's house?"

"Yes. I checked the land registry and it looks like the property has been in your family for over sixty years."

"Well she's definitely lived there all her life. I think she was born in Watford General hospital."

"Did your parents grow up around there too?"

"I don't know, she's never talked about them."

He frowned and clicked the mouse several times as Vinny reached out towards a tall stack of papers. "We've been searching school attendance records but...," his fingers stuck to the top sheet and the whole pile wobbled.

Sam slammed his palm down to stabilise the papers beneath and finished, "But we haven't found anything yet. What school did you go to?"

"Haydon Comprehensive, although I think it changed to be an institute or something like that."

Sam nodded and squinted back at the computer as Lola led me away.

I asked her quietly, "Why is Sam a Ploid?"

She raised an eyebrow, "He has two very interesting appendages that he keeps hidden, you should ask him to show you them later."

Putting her finger on her chin, Lola looked around the room, "Now, who else will you recognize? Ah yes," she pointed to a far corner, "Jack Cable."

Tucked quietly away was a man with distinctive red headphones. I had seen him sitting with Vinny in the restaurant and at the award ceremony.

Lola whispered, "He has extremely sensitive ears and can hear absolutely everything."

I whispered back, "Everything?" and watched him give a shy wave.

"That's why he has to wear headphones all the time," Lola explained.

"And you put him in Lupo to listen to my conversation, that's why he was sitting next to Vinny." I shook my head, feeling like a fool as Jack gave an apologetic shrug.

Lola dimpled and blew him a kiss, "Don't hold it against him, Jack's a sweetie, plus he barely ever talks because his voice is really loud in his own head. It's unbearably painful apparently."

Pointing at a woman with a short pony-tail, who was concentrating on a thick report, Lola explained. "The officer sitting to his left is Beth, she's new here, but I think you'll like her."

Jack nudged Beth on the shoulder, and she looked up, pushing a thick fringe out of her eyes and gave us both a bright smile.

"She's just been transferred here from Cardiff." Lola popped a honey and lemon lozenge into her mouth and offered me one, "Beth is quite a mild Ploid as far as I can tell, she has webbed feet and if you look closely at the hair on her arms, they are actually tiny feathers but you can barely notice."

The door to the main office opened again and Max came out looking like thunder. He was followed by a tall black man in full fatigues with an eye patch over one eye.

Zac scuttled out next, giving a sheepish glance in Lola's direction and Rufus Bull hung behind them, looking obdurate and angry.

The man with the eye patch spoke with a deep, commanding American accent, catching the attention of the entire room.

"Ok, we're making great progress, team. It's good to have you here Miss Cooper. My name is Nightly. Chief Inspector Nightly."

He strode over to me and held out a muscular hand.

"Don't forget she shocks men, Nightly," Vinny called out and a ripple of subdued laughter rolled around the room.

"Yes, it's probably best not to shake hands then," he said earnestly. "Anyways, welcome to our division. We are an unusual squad, but we get results."

"Not always the right ones though," Rufus added as he paced the back of the room.

"Can you follow me across to the board please, Miss Cooper?"

"Carter," I corrected.

"...err yes, of course, Carter, after your aunt."

I nodded and everyone except Beth followed him over to the right of the room.

Gathering for an impromptu conference, they sat on various desks and chairs in front of a white board where Nightly began jotting notes.

Max came to stand beside me.

"Am I upsetting people by being here, Max?" I whispered.

Max shook his head, grinning, "Only one and he's all hot air."

Nightly raised his voice, "So this is what we know about Chris Cooper."

He pointed at the board.

"Thanks to Max, we have a fix on his identity ten years back. Sam has then extended this and traced him through to the Duty Halls centre for homeless six years ago. At that time, we pick him up as Derick Drayton. We even have an image of 'Derick' at Leeds station."

"Good enough for a facial I.D.?" Larry asked

Nightly shook his head, "I doubt it, this is a pretty low-grade capture."

The screen lit up to show a photo of a tall, thin man by a turnstile.

He was hunched over with a beige raincoat and a wide hat on. Dark, lank hair straggled down over his shoulders and, although his head was deeply shadowed, I could still make out dark, sunken eyes in a gaunt, ashen face.

"Is that my father?"

This was the first time I had ever seen him, it made me feel strangely moved and slightly sick.

"Bear in mind that this was taken six years ago, he will probably have aged since then," Nightly cautioned.

"But he already looks so…haggard," I said, mainly to myself.

"Life on the edge is tough. That kind of existence would drain anyone, Alice," Lola cooed.

"Drained perhaps, but still lethal," Rufus warned, "Just like his daughter."

"Alice hasn't shown any signs of psychosis or instability while we've been monitoring her," Nightly countered as if I was some kind of clinical study.

"Give her a criminal psychology assessment then, I bet that'll give you a different answer. Like breeds like."

"Drop the beef, Bull," Max warned and tension filled the room.

Nightly tapped his pen, "Can we continue?"

He shot Max a warning stare and then said, "Right, let's move on. Larry and Jack, you need to scan all the homeless databases to pick up Cooper's identity changes in the last five years. He has shown a trend towards alliterative names up till now which could narrow the field."

We watched as Nightly drew a diagram with circles and arrows showing the previous names and locations that my father had lived in.

"I want you to identify any other patterns that might link his change of destination, accommodation choices or contact points. Every eighteen months to two years he has moved on to a new place and picked up a new identity."

He pointed at the arrows on the board, the last arrow taking us to the railway station in Leeds six years ago.

"How can you be certain that image was my father?"

"We also have him on video at that time. It was taken in the same station. Could you run the security camera footage, Sam?"

A grainy image appeared on the whiteboard and showed the tall figure placing his hand on the centre of the turn-style. A bright spark jumped out and the metal unit juddered open, allowing the man through the gate without a ticket.

Nightly explained, "He shorted out the mechanism. The station only kept the tape because they had a spate of broken turn-styles around that time. They never managed to trace the perpetrator, of course, probably because he had moved on."

I looked down at my own hands knowing I could potentially do the same thing. After all I had paralleled it during the bank robbery and fused almost every piece of machinery in the office.

I suddenly felt afraid of myself, if I was the same as him, did that mean that I could also murder people? I pushed my dangerous fingers under my thighs and knew Max had seen me do it.

Nightly turned to address me.

"Miss Cooper, I want you to go back and talk to your aunt with Max tomorrow morning. Find out anything you can about your father, ask where he grew up, went to school, who his friends were and how he met you mother."

"It's Carter."

"What?"

"You called me Miss Cooper."

"Yeh, Carter. I said Carter, didn't I?"

Rufus smirked and I shrugged, "It doesn't matter."

"Where was I? Ah, yes. Do you think your Aunt will cooperate?"

"We might struggle, Aunty Phyl never wants to talk about Chris."

"She will if she realises that he is in danger. This doesn't all begin and end with the Hong Kong incident, Alice. Tell her Chris' life is now on the line, tell her *your* life is on the line. Drop in trigger words like that and she'll open up like a parachute."

I frowned anxiously as the briefing disbanded around me. I was about to delve deep into my terrifying past and could end up hating myself by the end of it.

Nightly walked me down to Lola's car later that evening after she offered to take me back to my flat.
"What if my aunt doesn't have any extra information to tell us?" I asked as my single green shoe clicked on the uneven pavement.
"Pump her for any tiny crumb that she can remember. You'll be surprised what she'll come up with. We need to find your father before Adam Warner does."
Although it was almost midnight, the dark sky was lit by a clear moon and I looked up to see Nightly's profile hovering above me.
His face seemed different somehow and I puzzled, unable to understand why.
"What if we can't? What will happen if Adam finds him first?"
"If Adam Warner confronts Cooper they could end up killing each other, and anybody else in their way. This is a very high-risk situation, Carter, we can't afford to balls the whole thing up."

I felt sick and drained of energy but the smell of roses in Lola's car acted like a comfort blanket.

Resting my head back against the headrest, I let my numb mind fold in on itself, spiraling the day out behind me like a black hole. My tired body desperately needed a bath and some sleep.

Lola hadn't stopped talking since she had turned the engine on and I found her chatter a soothing distraction as she honed in on my flat.

"Of course, my mum has already said she would come to the wedding, as did three of my sisters but I don't know what to tell them now."

"How many sisters have you got?"

"There are 8 of us altogether. My mum pollinated herself twice before she realised what had triggered the whole thing off."

"And you are all Identical?"

"Exactly the same."

"And every one of you runs the risk of...?"

"A night-time mishap. Yes."

"But how do you...what happens if you...?" I scratched my head, the questions were too numerous and too complex to face.

Fortunately Lola was saved from explaining because she pulled up outside my front door.

Reaching for the car's handle, I stopped, noticing that Lola was putting on lipstick and checking her appearance in the rear-view mirror.

"Are you…are you going out somewhere?"

She nodded and pressed her rosebud lips together.

"I need a man."

"But it's midnight, surely just one night…"

Lola shivered.

"Alice, if I'm half asleep and I don't have a man beside me, who knows what I could do?"

I wanted to help Lola and keep her company on the pitiful, nightly quest, but I also knew that I was too exhausted to go on.

Instead I asked if she could find it in her heart to forgive Zac, after all most of the men I knew would have taken a sneak peek given half the chance.

She shrugged, told me she would think about it and then drove off, my heart breaking as I understood, for the first time, why Lola held such a devastating fear of her own, lonely bed.

Paul was in the main foyer collecting his post when I opened the front door and waved as I kicked it shut behind me.

"You're up late." I said, making him look at his Darth Vader watch.

"It's only twelve thirty. Besides it's D and D night."

He looked comfortable and normal in his trainers and old sweater.

"Jesus, have I had a weird day Paul," I said wearily, and he perked up looking interested.

"Weird is good."

"No," I said definitively, "Weird is not good. Everything is wrong... I discovered that loads of people have..." But I trailed off remembering Max's warning not to reveal the existence of Ploids.

"Loads of people have what?" Paul asked.

"Loads of people... have an addiction to those role-play computer games you love."

"Oh," he threw back over his shoulder as he led the way up the stairs, "I could have told you that, I've probably know most of them."

"I met someone called Zac Lee who said he plays on-line with you."

"You don't mean Zac Lee, The Grand Theft Auto master?"

"Yup."

"Alice you have to introduce me, that man is a legend. He holds a god-like status in my gaming circles, I've been struggling to get in a chat-room with him for months."

"I'll see what I can do. You'll have to give me a few days though. I've got a lot of other stuff to get through. How's Hope?"

"She's still shaky, but seems a little better. Ooh, and talking of hamsters, I've been refining my powers."

"How?"

"Watch."

Opening his mouth, he flamboyantly produced a set of door keys from one of his cheeks and waved them in front of my face.

The impressive trick was sadly dented when Paul tossed them up in the air and missed the catch, splattering saliva down his trousers.

"I had those in my mouth all evening and nobody noticed."

Impressed, I opened my eyes wide, but he held a finger up.

"That's not all, I also have...." he reached into his other cheek, "these."

He drew out a plastic bag with a small notebook and pencil sealed inside it.

"What do you think of that then?"

"Impressive and you could always be a great drugs smuggler."

"Drugs?"

"Yes, you know, little white bags of stuff. Customs would never think of checking your hidden pouches."

His eyes went glassy with imagination.

"I could even write to Marvel about that. Just imagine a penniless guy on holiday who gets caught up with an evil drug baron and then, when he goes to visit the criminals in their house, he...."

"Do you know what Paul; I'll leave you to write it. I have to hit the sack."

"No, you're right, I'll jot down some ideas. I wonder what to call him? What about 'Pouch Man'...no, no, no, perhaps 'Deep Cheek'."

I blinked at the pornographic connotations and laughed.

"You'll think of something! Goodnight Paul."

I closed the door to my flat and sighed in the calm air of my room. Preparing for bed seemed ridiculously normal after my ground-breaking day.

Hearing the kettle spouting a low whistle twenty minutes later, I climbed out of my half-sized bath and picked up the towel, only to feel it was still slightly damp from the shower that I had taken that morning.

The last time I had used the thing, I had no idea Ploids could even exist in this world.

Irrationally I yearned to rewind time, to wake and discover that this had all been a nightmare, to find that Adam was truly the perfect man I had always dreamed of.

I got dressed in my pajamas and felt as if my heart was dragging on the floor behind me as I walked across to my kitchen.

Pulling on my light, I spooned a comforting dose of cocoa into my mug, filled it with hot water and finally let myself relax.

It was only later, when I sat with my feet under the covers drinking the hot chocolate, that I felt my bottom lip burn as it hit the raw cut where Adam had pressed his mouth too hard against mine.

The unexpected pain pushed me over the edge and despair surged across me.

My whole life had been shoved into a whirling tumble dryer. Humans were mixing with nature; all my friends were lying to me and the man that I fancied more than anybody else in the world, had turned out to be my sodding nemesis.

I put the cup down and curled up under my sheets, too tired to even cry and let the cooling cotton of my pillow take the weight of my overheated thoughts.

Chapter 21

Max turned up with his old police car fixed and back in action the next morning.

I drew my brows together as the passenger door squeaked opened, "Is your old banger going to get us there this time?"

"Just climb in and trust my mechanic. He's cleared this jam sandwich for another six months at least."

"Jam sandwich?"

"It's the nickname for these cars," he said, slamming his own door, "She has the old orange and white police markings. I've put my name down for one of the newer blue and yellow 'Batenburgs' but God knows when it will come through."

I wriggled back on the seat, conscious that I was wearing very bright lipstick.

This was a vain and probably useless attempt to disguise the angry bruise darkening under my bottom lip.

Opening the sun visor to examine my hasty camouflage, I found that the mirror was missing and a torn flap of plastic dangled down in its place.

"Why the hell are you driving around in such a defunct car, Max? This thing has been hammered to pieces."

He scratched behind his ear.

"It's because I work for PlOps. Our branch is allocated a very small budget. So small that we can only afford decommissioned cars. The vehicles are roadworthy, they just aren't police worthy."

"I don't understand though. Surely you are doing the same job as anyone else in the force."

"Not quite, we're seen as a Cinderella department."

"Do you get paid the same?"

"Well, we get paid something. That's an achievement. I used to get called in on a voluntary basis."

"What, like one of those part time community officers?"

"Yes, except I was dealing with serious crime."

"Impressive," I said, cheekily. "I like a man who can handle dangerous criminals."

"Dangerous Ploids," he amended.

"Ploids. I forgot that I have to talk about Ploids and not humans from now on."

The corners of his mouth tipped up, "Is it beginning to sink in yet?"

"I don't think it'll ever sink in."

The plastic from the sun visor fell off and plopped on my lap.

I folded it in half, wedged it into a dusty cup holder and asked, "How are you different from the normal police force then?"

"We have the same principals, but we make up our own rules and punishments."

"You make your own rules?"

"Of course. You can't judge people for following their natural traits. We have to find a way to manage their unusual conditions and keep everything hidden from the public. Take some of the superstars at the BFAs, famous Ploids really struggle to hide their problems."

I gaped, "Some of those superstars were ploids?"

He laughed, "Ploids exist in every walk of life. Sometimes the ploid trait is the thing that actually makes them famous."

I opened my eyes wide.

"Like who?"

"I shouldn't say."

"Come on Max, I give you my word that it stops here."

It didn't take much for him to crumble and he licked his lips tentatively, "Did you know that Zara Capaldi works for us?"

I put my hand on my chest, "No way? Zara Capaldi? The Zara Capaldi with long blond hair and endless legs?"

He nodded and I processed the information, "Hold on…Does that mean she was at the BFAs because of me?"

"Partially."

I gasped, "And is that the reason she went out with George Canther?"

Max nodded again and I sighed.

"Poor George."

"Don't look at it like that. George was our only route through to Adam Warner."

"But Zara looks completely normal. What's wrong with her?"

"Did you ever notice how small her feet were?"

"Small feet?"

I stared blankly back at him and he explained, "She has to have her shoes especially designed because she walks on her toes. If you look very carefully you will see an extra joint that bends backwards halfway up her shin, like a horse or a dog. She hides it well normally, but I've seen Zara take her shoes off at the end of a party once. She dropped back onto her whole foot, looked as if she had flippers on, and became a full 30 centimeters shorter."

"No way? That's freaky."

Max was so smugly pleased with himself that I pushed him further. "Anyone else hiding a body malfunction?"

He wavered, saying, "If I tell you this next one, you have to keep it under wraps."

I zipped my mouth and nodded eagerly as he confided, "What if I told you that Milo Topen has an extra...How do I put this? An extra piece of male anatomy."

"What?"

"An extra willy."

"You're joking."

He laughed and shook his head.

"How? where?"

"One on the front and one on the back."

"You're having me on. There is no possible way you would know that."

He stuck his tongue in his cheek and nodded.

"Do you want to know how I know?"

"I can't believe this."

"He got caught up in an extremely tanked-up party once and, after a heavy night on the gin, ended up playing strip poker and sprinting around a nearby football pitch, naked. I was the one who received a phone call from his agent the following morning, asking to have all the security cameras overhauled before the story got out."

"And you saw the double tackle?"

He nodded.

"But how does he...? How does everything...? Does Vinny know?"

"I've been asking myself the same questions, Alice. I have no more idea than you have."

Sitting back in my seat, I tried to envisage Max's description and failed.

Directors of films couldn't have two peni. (What was the plural for that word anyway)? Supermodels couldn't have extendable legs? How did Max get wood inside his body? How was Donna so bendy? I was too new to this secret society to understand anything.

It made me wonder if everyone was hiding strange abilities and I remembered Adam talking at the BFAs. He had kissed my neck and said, "aren't we all hiding something in this place?"

The memory left me hot and flustered and I tried to refocus, asking, "Were you also guarding celebrities when you worked as a bouncer at the races?"

"No, I was posted there to keep an eye on you."

"On me?" I laughed, "You must have been in agony watching me electrocuting horses."

"The electrocution part was fine, it was way harder watching you before-hand."

"Why?"

"Because I knew Adam was drawing you in."

He didn't look at me as he spoke, but the simple sentence rested on my chest like a lead weight.

I wondered how Max would react if he knew what had happened last night on the graveyard's stony embankment.

Pressing my teeth into my sore lip, I fell silent and stared at the early morning lampposts, their shadows as regular as a concrete metronome through Max's steamy windows.

Some time later, I forced myself to brighten up and asked Max, "Did you always want to be a police detective?"

"I'm glad you said detective finally and not bouncer."

I grinned, "If you act like one, then I'll call you one, Max."

"I'm actually a Detective Inspector. And no, I never planned to do this. I was originally studying for a degree in arboreal science, but felling trees is hard work when you've a body like mine. Then, by chance, I met Nightly and he asked me to help with his most challenging cases. I enjoyed police investigations far more than lugging timber, so I put in a request to join the team, the rest is history."

"Is Nightly a Ploid too?"

"Nightly was born with nocturnal vision in one eye and normal in the other, hence the eye patch."

"So both eyes work?"

Max shrugged. "Yes, but never at the same time."

I slapped my leg, "That's why he looked different by Lola's car, he'd swapped his patch over."

I thought about it for a few seconds and said, "That must be a really useful trait."

"Yes and no. His day eye is unusable at night and vice-versa. He's effectively blind if the wrong eye is uncovered. The US military realised as much and kicked him out. That's how he came to live in the UK."

I sat back in reflection as the early breeze ramped up into a squally wind. Then increasingly heavy raindrops made Max turn on his juddering windscreen wipers and I regretted leaving my raincoat at home.

Eventually houses began to replace high-rise buildings and the roads became wide tree lined avenues. The familiar red bricked semi's of suburbia hunched beneath the concrete sky, wet roofs emptying their damp loads into overflowing drainpipes.

My aunty Phyl answered the door after a couple of loud knocks, her eyebrows shooting up when she saw the two unexpected figures on her doorstep.

"Alice, what are you doing here? You look so wet."

The rain had coalesced into a thick deluge of water that cascaded off her porch and onto our shoulders. Despite Max's best efforts to hold his raincoat over both of us, we were still soaked. I pushed my wet hair out of my eyes and grinned at her.

"Can we come in?"

She threw the door open and waved us through, "Of course you can. You should have phoned; I would have got the house ready!"

"Sorry, we're going to drip everywhere." I shivered slightly as I shook my wet hair out.

"I'll get you a towel. Why don't you have a waterproof on? The weatherman said it was going to rain."

She disappeared into the kitchen and I shouted, "It was dry when we left home."

Phyl came back with two towels and handed them out, looking expectantly at Max.

He said politely, "Can I hang my coat somewhere? It's very wet."

"Oh, don't worry about this old floor, it's had all sorts on it over the years hasn't it Alice?"

I nodded remembering the string of peculiar strangers that had trailed through our hallway and hung Max's coat on the bannister.

Phyl lifted an arm to guide us into the living room and, as Max went through, she whispered, "Well he looks nice, dear."

I hissed sharply back, "He's not my boyfriend."

"Any man-friend is progress, Alice. Does he know about 'your problem'?"

"Yes, he knows all about 'my problem'."

She gasped "You told a stranger about 'your problem'?"

"He's not a stranger, Phyl. I'll explain why when we sit down."

"I'll make some tea first, you must be parched, and hungry, I've got all sorts of goodies on offer."

She disappeared into the kitchen and began clunking plates around. I gave up calming Phyl down and let her mother me, after all, she was on a mission to impress.

The cloud-darkened sitting room still held its comfortable smell of bee's wax and shake-and-vac. I pulled at a cotton cord to turn on the main bulb and it's yellow light softened the shabby edges of her furniture.

Phyl had static-proofed our house when I was younger and the fixtures, along with the room, had become stuck in time.

As well as a thread bare settee, a lopsided pouffe and drooping armchair, there was a teak dining table covered in a kaleidoscope of bright photos, each one charting my gawky progress through childhood.

I warned, "Don't eat the cake and don't look at my school pictures."

"What's wrong with the cake?" he said and smirked at a picture of me with wonky bunches, missing two front teeth.

"They're happy bakes."

"Happy bakes?"

"Ones with pot in them. Phyl cooks batches for our neighbours, so you better look the other way and pretend they don't exist."

He said, "You mean your aunt's a drugs dealer?"

"No, they are purely medicinal."

My aunt bustled into the room with a tray of teapots, biscuits and cups, setting them down on a low coffee table as Max raised a curious eyebrow.

"Oh, I forgot the milk," Phyl said, "I'll be back in a second."

"Medicinal?" Max continued.

"Yes, for old ladies, now stop talking about it."

My aunt came back in again and put the milk jug down.

"Would you like a biscuit?" she asked, holding the plate out to Max.

He lifted a hand, "I think I'll pass Miss Carter, but I would love a cup of tea."

"When did you start making biscuits, Phyl? I thought you preferred cakes," I said, disconcerted by the change in offering.

"It's a new recipe," she boasted, "I find them more portable than the cakes."

After a period of bracelet clunking, milk pouring and checking that we were all comfortably seated, Phyl flicked her long, grey hair behind her shoulders and settled back to begin her inquisition.

"Now Alice, am I finally going to get an introduction?"

"This is Max, he's a police detective."

"A policeman? Well that's a very noble profession."

Her hand began to shake as she lifted the biscuits off her wonky pouffe, hiding them on the floor.

"He doesn't care about the hash cakes Phyl. He's here to ask some questions about my dad."

"They are just herbal biscuits, Alice," she chided and then realised what else I had said, "To find out more about...?"

"Dad," I finished.

"But...?" Her shaky hands pressed against her chest. "Alice, after all these years? How could you?"

"It's alright Phyl, he isn't a normal policeman. He wants to protect dad."

"No one can protect him, Alice. They want to lock him away. I've told you that again and again."

Phyl reached over the edge of her chair to take a biscuit and then, hiding it behind her bottom, mumbled, "I have to go back to the kitchen, I need more sugar."

Max pleaded, "Please Miss Carter, I'm here from a special branch of...," but she didn't stop to listen and bolted out of the door.

I held up a hand, "Don't worry, I'll go and have a word. She'll be fine in a minute."

I walked into the kitchen to find Phyl standing over the sink, stuffing half a dry biscuit into her mouth.

She looked around guiltily as I closed the door and then blew out dry crumbs as she snapped, "You shouldn't have brought him here."

"Aunty Phyl, I had to. There is a very dangerous man out there who is looking for Dad and we have to find a way to stop him."

"I tried to keep you safe for so many years, Alice and now you come back to me like this."

"It's not me I'm worried about. These policemen know all about Dad and I think that's a good thing. They've been looking after me and keeping me out of trouble. Phyl, I trust them, and I need your help now."

"You trust that man?"

I nodded.

"He doesn't *look* very much like a police officer."

"He's a detective, so he doesn't have a uniform."

"And he doesn't care about my happy biscuits?"

"He'd probably eat them if he wasn't on duty," I grinned, "Come back in and see if you can help."

She sighed but hung back by the sink, "You go through and I'll bring the sugar."

I walked out of the door and heard another muffled crunch behind me. The second half of the cookie had just disappeared.

Phyl had only ever eaten her hash bakes twice in my life and I had been the cause both times.

I returned to find Max examining the pictures on the table, the worst one showing me as an adolescent teenager with an artificial smile, spots and my hair parted in the middle.

"I told you not to look at them."

He shook his head, "Why have you changed your hair? I quite liked this look." Max grinned and then put the photo down, checking, "Is she alright?"

"Yes, yes she's fine, she'll be back in in a minute."

"Do you come and visit often?"

I felt guilty, "Every other week if I can manage it. I know Phyl misses me, but it's really hard to get beck."

"And she never got married?"

I shook my head and thought of the string of unkempt, drunken men that had graced her bed over the years. Uncle Mo was the one and only light that remained constant enough to helped her through.

"There is one man, but she never married him because she was too busy bringing me up. It must have been hard being a single parent to somebody else's child."

He nodded, sticking out his bottom lip, "She did a good job though."

"I brought some spoons," Phyl said abruptly as she put them by the sugar caddy and then turned to Max, "Alice says you know about Chris and that she trusts you."

"I want to help both of them, Miss Carter."

I saw colour rising in her cheeks as she sat down, "I'm not sure that I'll have anything extra to tell you."

"Perhaps you won't but even a tiny piece of information can make a big difference to our investigation."

"Ok, what do you need to know?"

"I need to find out what happened when Alice was left here as a baby."

"All I know is that Chris arrived on my doorstep with her, twenty-five years ago."

"Did he leave any instructions, or a note?"

"No, he said he had done something terrible and killed lots of people, including Sophia."

She rested her teacup on her lap, "He was in a wretched state when he turned up here, stood sobbing on my doorstep and told me I was his last hope."

Her eyes locked onto the carpet, recalling his anguish, "Chris had lost everything, you see, except for Alice and they would have taken her too if he hadn't smuggled her back. He said he couldn't leave his little girl to grow up in care-homes and asked me if I could look after her. He left me some money, a few clothes, nappies and a passport for the baby with my surname on it. Oh, plus a picture of Alice with her mother."

"Do you still have that?" Max asked.

"Yes, of course, it's over here."

She picked up the small silver-plated frame that had been thumbed so much over the years, it had begun to turn brown.

In it, a beautiful, blond-haired woman was smiling at the camera and clutching an extremely round-faced baby in a white dress to her cheek.

I had studied that photo so hard for clues about myself when I was younger that I could see every detail of it with my eyes shut.

Her hair was pulled back into a low ponytail and she had a white, silky shirt on with the top two buttons undone.

The fingers of the hand holding me were slim with a French manicure tipping the ends of her nails. A thin, platinum, wedding ring wrapped snugly around her third finger and she was holding me tight, squashing the material of my dress close to her.

Max studied it carefully and then raised his eyebrows.

"You don't need to say it," I retorted, "I know I don't look anything like her."

"Alice was always the spit of her father, although I never knew him particularly well," Phyl consoled.

"Can you think of any other relative who might be able to tell us more about Chris or Sophia?"

"Well, Sophia's parents are both dead. Chris does have a brother, Tom, but I haven't seen or heard from him for over twenty years now and there aren't any other relatives. That's why he had to leave Alice with me."

"What about a childhood friend, did he grow up or go to school around here?"

She thought about it and twisted her steely hair around her fingers.

"Hmm, I know he went to one of the grammar schools near here and had a friend called Jimmy Malt. I think Jimmy knew Chris quite well when they were younger, and I have a feeling he still lives around here."

"Do you know where to find him?"

She compressed her lips and said, "Down at one of our local pubs I would think. Drank like a fish all his life. I'd hate to be his liver."

"Can you remember what Jimmy looked like, Miss Carter?"

"When I last saw him, he was very thin with sandy brown hair, styled in a pudding bowl cut, but that was about thirty years ago."

"Can we use Zac to find him?" I asked and Max shrugged.

"He used to wear funny tight checked trousers and a hat. You have to have a small head to get away with hats, don't you? I never had a small head."

"Miss Carter...."

"I wonder if the people with tiny heads have the same amount of brain in them as those with big heads."

"I think we had better go. The biscuit is starting to take effect," I said quietly to Max and then added, "I'll come back to see you again properly at the weekend Phyl. Are you off to the nursing home this afternoon?"

She nodded, "Of course I am, dear. I hope this delicious detective is going to take good care of you." She pinched Max's cheek.

"Alice is in safe hands, Miss Carter," he grinned back.

"Perfect, you're perfect for her. Look, Alice, he's handsome, charming and has good manners. Alice needs a good man like you in her life."

"We're off," I grabbed Max by the arm and pulled him towards the door.

"And so polite! Do you want some cookies to take with you? I can wrap them up in cling film." She picked two up and waved them at us.

"I'll catch you later Phyl. Perhaps you should have a lie down before you go on your visits."

"I will," she chimed back, having another mouthful.

"Is she going to be ok?" Max asked as we got in the car.

"She'll be fine," I looked out of the window, "It's the birds I'm worried about."

My aunt had followed us to the front door and was now crumbling her biscuits up for several hungry pigeons to peck at. I sighed, wishing I could stay to make sure she had come back down again before she went out.

Chapter 22

Zac's database took us to a rundown flat with greyed out curtains and peeling paint on its front door. After ten minutes of knocking and walking around to look in grubby windows, a woman with oily brown hair stuck her head out of an upstairs window.

"What's with all the fuckin' noise goin' on down there?"

"We are looking for Jimmy Malt."

"Is he the drunken asshole that lives downstairs?"

"Yes."

"He's down the sodding pub. Now piss off and let me get some sleep."

Max pulled the edges of his mouth down as we walked away and said mildly, "She was polite then."

My knowledge of the local watering holes proved invaluable and, after visiting several pubs, we managed to find Jimmy in The Shipwright's Arms. He was sitting, staring aimlessly at an empty pint glass.

The sandy-haired, tight-trousered look had given way to a beer belly and jogging bottoms, but hints of the bowl haircut still remained.

He was also as yellow as I had ever seen anybody. His face, hands, eyes, in fact everything was a mustard mono-colour.

He sat up with mild alarm as we introduced ourselves.
"Police? Have I done something wrong?"
Max shook his head and put his ID badge away.
"We wanted to talk to you about an old friend."
Jimmy burped, "If I was pissed when I knew him, then I won't remember much."
"You went to school with him."
"You want me to remember back to my school days?" He considered Max's request and then pointed at his empty glass. "I'll tell you what, jog my memory with a jar and I'll see what I can do. Mine's a Brewdog."
Max put in the order and seconds later Jimmy drew his new pint close, his hand shaking a little as he raised the frothy glass to his mouth.
Setting it down, Jimmy smacked his lips together and savored the brew. "Ahh, nectar of the gods. Did you know I was once a weedy little runt who barely had the energy to hold a pint? But look at me now."
Clenching his fist, he tried to form a bicep curl but nothing bulged on his skinny arm.
"I completely changed when I downed my first beer at the grand age of fourteen. Life was a dream after that. I landed a good job taking deliveries

around the local pubs, got a flat and actually had a couple of girlfriends for a while."

He grinned and even his teeth had a saffron tinge to them.

"Then I was done for drunk driving, got in a fight, robbed a shop, went to jail, came out and turned yellow. At that point I decided to give up on all that shit and just drown my sorrows down the pub!"

He hiccuped. "To be honest, you have to take what life throws at you," he hiccuped again, "And for me, that's alcohol." Jimmy scratched his head absently and asked, "What were we talking about?"

"I needed to know if you were friends with a man called Chris Cooper when you were younger," Max prompted.

"Chris Cooper? Oh, now that name takes me back."

He downed half of his new beer and then rapped on the bar for another, "Are you still buying?"

Max nodded and gestured to the barman who was discretely drying wine glasses.

"Chris Cooper was my father," I explained as a second, golden pint slid onto the counter.

"Christ, you're his daughter are you?" Jimmy went to pinch my cheek affectionately but couldn't quite manage to hold his arm still, "I heard a rumour you existed."

He pulled the second pint in and sighed.

"I knew Chris very well when I was young. Chris and Eddie. Very well."

"Who is Eddie?" Max asked.

"Eddie Metal, he was the coolest, most handsome bloke in the school and was stuffed with cash."

I looked across at Max and mouthed, "Adam's Dad?"

He nodded and I turned back, fascinated to hear more.

"We were all in the same class and hung out together. When we finished school Chris and Eddie were…," he tried to cross to fingers, sticking his tongue out with the effort, "Like that."

Another new beer arrived, and Jimmy's eyes reflected the amber liquid.

"But they weren't friends to begin with," he ran his finger down the outside of the glass, "No. Chris and Eddie both hated each other until they were…ooh…let me think…about thirteen or fourteen. Before that, Eddie got into trouble all the time. He came so close to being expelled you wouldn't believe it; I even saw him throw a chair right through a window once and it landed about twenty feet away in the playground."

I remembered Adam's description of rampaging when he was eleven.

"Chris was the only one of us who could stand up to Eddie. He saved my noggin several times in the playground. I don't know why, but Eddie would back off when Chris was around."

Jimmy sank his lips into soft foam and spoke with a white moustache.

"Eddie's parents bribed the governors to keep him on at the school but their money only went so far. When Eddie was on his final warning, he came across a couple of blokes that were roughing up this new girl called Sophia."

Jimmy looked across at me and said, "That would be your mum I think?"

I nodded.

He tilted his head, "I can see the likeness, she was really pretty too."

He scratched his cheek, "Where was I? Oh, yes. Eddie intervened and bashed the boys to a pulp, leaving them completely unconscious. Our headmaster found out and was about to expel Eddie, when Chris knocked on the door and said he had done the bashing. We were all amazed, but when Sophia backed up his story, Eddie had to be let off."

Jimmy looked down into his glass, seeing the scene in the golden bubbles.

"Chris was given a two weeks suspension and no-one ever talked about the fight again. If you ask me, I think Sophia ran off and asked Chris to help them, and Eddie completely adored her for it.

Anyway, after that, the three teenagers became really close. Sophia made a point never to go out with either of them, even though they were both crazy about her."

I stared in amazement. If they had all been friends, how had two of them ended up dead. Max cut in with the same thought.

"Do you know why everything went wrong?"

Jimmy nodded his head mournfully.

"I know the bulk of it. When we left school, old Harry Metal realised his eldest son was becoming obsessed with this girl. He said that Eddie either, had to go and work for the family company up in Sheffield, or join the forces until he was twenty-one. Then, once he had proved himself, Eddie could do as he liked. Eddie agreed to join the army and told Sophia he would work for three years. Then he secretly got engaged to her, promising to come back when he was twenty-one." Jimmy wiped the back of his hand across his mouth and said, "I need a pee."

The next part of the story had to be propped up with yet another glass of beer with a double shot of vodka thrown in and I became seriously worried about Jimmy's liver.

"Eddie was a hero. He was given accolade after accolade until he reached his final three months of duty. Then a report hit home to say he had been killed during an attack on the armored personnel carrier he was traveling in. Sophia didn't believe it and went into shock, not wanting to talk to anyone. We were all in shock, especially my soddingly miserable girlfriend, Cora. Anyway, time stretched out and Sophia struggled to get over it, opting to stay completely away from Chris, a decision that nearly destroyed the poor bloke."

Jimmy pulled his chin back and burped.

"Eventually Sophia agreed to come down to the pub with Cora and me, barely chatted to anyone else. Chris joined us a couple of times, but when he was there Sophia sat like a stone, refusing to say a word to him. After a year she had begun to recover a little and was out shopping one day with her dad when something amazing happened…"

Jimmy Malt nudged Max and asked, "Can you guess what it was?"

"No idea."

"Have a try."

"Tell me or the beers dry up," Max snapped and Jimmy held out his hands.

"Alright, alright, I'm getting there. Imagine the scene as Sophia's father unexpectedly collapses on the pavement clutching his chest in agony. Poor Sophia doesn't know what to do and calls out for help. A crowd forms and someone phones for an ambulance but they all just stand there, watching the fading man die."

He took a long swig.

"Then the hero of the hour strolls by, that's Chris of course, sees what's happening and leaps into action. He drags her dad over to a car, jimmies the bonnet open and takes his shoes and socks off. Then, this is the really freaky part, Chris puts his bare feet onto the dyeing man's chest and touches his hand on the car's battery. The whole crowd watches agog as he repeats this trick three times, adjusting his position each go until the man on the ground eventually spasms with a giant electricity jolt and begins to breathe again. Chris actually shocked Sophia's father back to life."

I gasped, desperate to hear more, "Go on?"

"Sophia collapses on the spot with the stress of the scene and Chris suddenly has two unconscious patients to care for until the ambulance arrives. Sophia revives rapidly though and eventually throws herself, sobbing, into Chris' arms, apologising for treating him so badly. I tell you, that girl didn't have to ask twice because Chris never left her side again and they were married six months later."

Jimmy gave a reminiscent smile and ran a finger around his glass.

"The ceremony was beautiful. Cora was their bridesmaid and I was their best man. Oh, I did look good in a smart set of tails, bearing in mind I wasn't yellow back then. They were both so blissfully happy, it made me cry as they said their vows. But then, someone who was meant to be dead arrived at the after party."

I covered my mouth as Max said, "Eddie?"

Jimmy nodded firmly.

"Yup, he burst in as everyone was listening to the groom's speech and told him to stop, told Sophia that he loved her and she had made a terrible mistake in marrying Chris. Sophia couldn't cope and ran away sobbing as Chris and Eddie faced off in front of the crowd. Eddie accused Chris of taking away the one thing that was precious in his life and poor Chris just shook his head, saying they had thought he was dead."

"What happened next?"

"Sophia recovered enough to talk to Eddie and told him she couldn't break Chris' heart and leave him. She said time had altered everything and she had made her vows. There was nothing that Eddie could say that would change her mind. Then she walked away into Chris' arms and left Eddie a broken man."

Max whistled and Jimmy shook his head, "The disco afterwards was grim, I can tell you. I left early and headed for the Beaver's Last Rest, it was the closest pub down the road. But my girlfriend, Cora, conveniently forgot about me and decided to throw herself at the lamenting Eddie."

He gulped his beer and snorted.

"It turns out that she had obsessed about Eddie for years and consoled him with a very wild night of passion. So wild in fact, that it left her with a broken wrist, bruised ribs and a bun in the oven."

Finally, the puzzle fitted together and I filled in, "She was pregnant with Adam."

"Naa, the baby's name was Benjamin or something like that, I think."

"Benedict," Max corrected.

"Eddie felt guilty and married her out of decency but lived with only one intention. To get Sophia back."

The phrase was hauntingly familiar as I recalled Adam's sole intention.

I asked, "Did my parents move to Hong Kong after that?"

"No, they didn't leave straight away. At first they moved to Cirencester but Eddie kept turning up to talk to Sophia. You know, a chance meeting down the Co-op bread isle or in the romance section of the library. He just couldn't ever drop the tie between them. Finally, when she found she was pregnant with you, Chris took her away completely. That's when they moved abroad and I lost track of them."

"So you don't know why Sophia was killed in Hong Kong?"

The dregs of the glass went down, "Your guess is as good as mine. I think I might…might need to lie down for a minute, excuse me." Jimmy fell off his stool and lay motionless on the floor.

The barman assured us that Jimmy would be fine again in an hour and propped him up against a table leg with a glass of water in his hand.

Max paid his bill and then shoved an extra tenner in Jimmy's top pocket, urging him to have a hot lunch and a coffee once he recovered.

Jimmy grinned, kissed the money and said 'You're a fine man, Max, I'll do exactly that."

Chapter 23

Leaving Jimmy Malt to his hops and jaundice, we drove back to London, shell shocked by the turmoil in my parents' life.

"Does anyone actually know what happened that day in Hong Kong?"

Max shook his head.

"Do you think Eddie and Sophia ran off together and my father killed them both in a fit of rage?"

"You can't jump to conclusions Alice. The only report that reached us from Hong Kong was that your father was wanted for the murder of Sophia, Edward and four other people and an international warrant had been issued for his arrest."

"How old was Adam when all of this happened?"

"He must have been around six."

"And after that his mother died."

"How did you know that?"

I blushed and stammered, "He...er...told me on one of my dates."

Max snorted, "Don't give him any sympathy votes. He inherited one of the richest companies in England from his grandfather."

"But my father still wrecked his life..."

"Again, you don't know the full story, Alice. Who knows what happened back then?"

I chewed at my nail and said, "If Adam is planning to kill Chris, how are we ever going to be able to stop him? He's completely obsessed, Max."

"Your father is the wild card in this equation, Alice. He could be lethal if anyone provokes him. We have to find Chris before Adam does and we have to get someone to talk sense into him. That's where we need you to help."

"I wouldn't be so sure that I'm the silver bullet. Chris doesn't even know who I am, and he hasn't exactly gone out of his way to contact me in the last twenty-five years."

"It may seem like that, but he left a door open. He deliberately set a paper trail for you to follow."

"And I've gone and ruined it." I felt my heart drop, "Do you think Adam has worked out how to find him already?"

"He shouldn't be ahead of us yet. He hasn't had the full power of our hit squad on his side, has he?"

"Your 'hit squad'?" I anxiously bit my whole nail off, "That sounds like you are going to kill him."

Max shook his head, "We'll bring him in alive if we can, Alice. But you have to understand that we are also working to protect the general public."

After a long silence I asked reluctantly.

"I saw how Rufus reacted to me in the office, Max."

He snorted, "Ignore Rufus. He is just a massive thorn in my side."

"He said I was a liability. Do you think I'm as dangerous as my dad?"

Max looked at me incredulously.

"Is that what you're worried about?"

I shrugged and he laughed.

"Believe me, your wimpy shocks are like mosquito bites compared to Chris'. There is no way you could ever pack the same punch that he did."

"Do you think I'm more diluted than him, then?"

"Like lemonade to battery acid."

I sat back and sighed.

It wasn't true but at least he was being kind. I was beginning to like this strange tree man.

Chapter 24

Max checked in with the rest of the team's progress, stopping to phone them at Kilburn police station, a breeze block three-story block that looked like an oversized ice cube tray.

The man behind the front desk greeted Max like an old friend and thanked him for clearing up their recent spate of early morning dustbin raids.

I hovered in the entrance lobby while Max leant in and explained to the duty sergeant that I was helping PlOps with 'covert' enquiries.

The sergeant tapped his nose conspiratorially, peering across to inspect the latest PlOps outlaw and then gave clearance for me to pass security without being searched.

I complained as we walked up a square staircase, "You made me sound like I'm a criminal."

"Tell me how else I'm going to describe you then? The daughter of a murderer and girlfriend of a born psychopath? They'd welcome you in here with open arms and never let you out again."

"Adam isn't a 'born' psychopath," I said defensively, "He's had a crap life."

"Really?"

"Yes, he was just a lonely child who lost his father, mother and his baby sister by the time he was eleven, that kind of thing would screw anyone up."

"It worries me that you're defending him now." He stopped on a penny on the top step and turned back to look at me, one foot returning to my step and bringing him alarmingly close.

"What's happened, Alice?"

"What?" I backed against the wall, a flush rising up my neck.

"That's the second time you've mentioned something from Metal's past you didn't seem to know before."

"I..." A policeman sprinted up the stairs beside us and I waited for the fire door to shut before I opened my mouth again. "I might have spoken to him last night."

"Last night?"

"When you were getting the bread van."

"What do you mean 'you *spoke* to him'?"

I shrugged. "He was watching us come out of the boat shed."

"And you didn't see fit to tell me he was there?"

"What would you do? Chase after him in your tuk tuk?"

"Did he come near you?"

"Max, he didn't do anything..." but Max hit his hand against the wall in unexpected anger.

"Christ, what am I dealing with!"

"I didn't think..."

"This is a police enquiry, Alice. Do you want me to slam you into one of our interview rooms?"

I looked down at my feet in shame.

"He only stayed to tell me about his childhood and warn us not to get in the way."

Max did something so unexpected then it made me catch my breath. He lifted his hand to run his finger over my sore lip.

"Did he do that?"

I pulled his hand away.

"Don't Max."

"How?"

"He kissed me alright? He kissed me and didn't steal my bag this time, just bruised my lip and half electrocuted himself."

Max bit his own bottom lip and then stepped back, shaking his head.

"How could you let him, Alice? Why do you keep falling for his stories?"

"No, it wasn't like that, I just think that he..."

"I don't care what you *think*. Everything about him is a lie. Can't you see how manipulative he has been? Why would he change now?"

"I don't expect him to change."

"He is playing with your mind."

"Max, I'm not forgiving him, I was just saying that his childhood might have..."

"What did he tell you about his sister?"

"His sister?"

"Yes, his 'baby' sister."

"That she was killed when she was five."

"That's exactly it, Alice. She didn't exist. His sister was stillborn. She never survived into childhood."

The words hit me like a shovel around the face and the stairs lurched sideways.

"So everything he told me wasn't true?"

Max turned and walked away, shouting back.

"And finally it sinks in."

Chapter 25

The other teams hadn't got much further along the paper trail, losing Chris in London four years ago. There was a possibility he had been seen in Bromley, but they only had a sketchy description to go on and no name.

Max, although still pissed with me, didn't seem too put out by the slow progress and reassured Nightly over the phone that he could trace Chris anywhere in South East London if he used me as a 'marker'.

This mysterious comment saw us both back in the car five minutes later, where we sat in a loaded silence.

Max followed the road signs to Croydon, turning off along a neglected track that ran behind the giant superstores on the Purley Way.

The road was cracked and strewn with fast-food wrappers.

Car tyres, broken fridges and old settees had been dumped in a deserted wasteland to our left, while a wire fence had netted hundreds of ugly old plastic bags to our right.

Max parked up outside a warehouse the size of an aircraft hanger. This, once vast storage depo was now deserted and grimy with deep fractures running along its concrete struts.

Sparse weeds created desert island tufts in the tarmac and two old IKEA shopping trolleys stood rusting by one wall.

As we walked around to the side of the building, I was surprised to find a small pathway marked out, with white gravel, painted pebbles and several pots of pansies.

This gay little splash of colour led up to a thickly painted green door with "The Croydon Home for Homeless" printed on a small wooden plaque beside it.

Max knocked three times and the door slid back to reveal a bony-faced man with rough, grey stubble on his chin.

He was wearing a drab, grey sweatshirt and had watery blue eyes that lit up once he saw who knocking.

"Max my old mate," he grinned and took ten years off his face, "What brings you our way?"

Max laughed, "I wish it was leisure, Grey. Can we come in?"

"Of course, you're always welcome, PlOps officers are always welcome in this place."

Max walked through and the man's eyes switched to me.

"Max, you're moving up in the world, since when did you saunter around with a beautiful woman in tow?"

Max warned flatly, "Don't touch her, Grey. She's a pain in the arse; she won't listen to advice, and she'll give you a massive static shock if you get too close."

Grey gave me a sympathetic look, "Not in his good books, I gather."

"I'll explain in a minute," Max grunted. "Are you full?"

"Of course. We haven't had a space here for over six months."

Grey stood back and let me in, revealing a panorama of homeless comfort.

The warehouse was split into two halves; one housing a kitchen, a serving counter and dining tables; and the other, set out to accommodate dozens of single camp beds.

"Do you need something to eat? You've missed our lunch service I'm afraid," Grey pointed at a wide serving hatch that was still open beside several long refectory tables.

"I wouldn't want to put you out or anything."

"You know me Max, any excuse to step into my kitchen!"

Max laughed, "We came because we're looking for someone."

"Oh? And you think he's here?"

Grey heaved a huge metal saucepan off one of the tables and passed it through the brightly lit hatch. A white hand grabbed it from the far side and disappeared.

"It's unlikely. We think the man was living rough in Bromley about four years ago."

"What's his name?"

"I don't know. His original name was Chris Cooper."

Grey pushed the middle of his mouth up. "Doesn't ring a bell I'm afraid. What does he look like?"

"That's the problem, we don't have a recent image either."

Grey rubbed his stubbly chin which made a loud rasping sound. "You don't exactly make life easy for me, do you? No name, no face. Age?"

"Early fifties"

"I'm his daughter, Alice Carter," I piped up. "He might look a bit like me."

"His daughter?" Grey looked at Max and then hit him on the back. "Now I understand, you're here because of Joe! He's over in one of the beds by the far wall. None of the other residents will sleep near him these days, I think he's smelling worse and becoming more temperamental as he gets older."

"Joe?" I asked.

Max explained, "Jo can recognise most of the Ploids in London from their scent. I was hoping he might be able to link you to your father. That's if you can get over you're obsession and help me."

"I'm not obsessed."

"Are you're back on my side again, then?"

I put my hands on my hips, "I'm not stupid, Max."

He tucked a smile in one cheek and replied, "I never said you were."

Grey explained, "Smelly Joe loves strong aromas and trades in used items of clothing. He was out all night but will probably wake up if you give him a nudge. Do you want to go and find him while I knock you up some food?"

Max nodded, "Just one meal though Grey, I'm on a diet."

I whispered to Max as we walked away, "Why can't I be on a diet too? I don't want to eat here!"

"What's wrong with eating here?"

"It's a crumbling homeless shelter that's full of scabies and flees."

"The food hygiene is good."

"But these people are filthy, and it stinks."

Max held up a hand. "Enough Alice, it's too late to stop Grey now. You've already said you would eat something."

"I didn't say *I* would eat something. *You* said I would eat something!"

He turned back to me grinning, "Alice, I can guarantee your stomach is in safe hands. Grey is one of the most elite chefs in England. Now follow me."

The beds in the dormitory side of the warehouse were filled with bone-weary bodies, huffing and mumbling from beneath grey, woolen blankets.

I began walking through the sleeping dorm and a grubby toe drew back into its cocoon. Max beckoned me over to the back wall and I wound my way towards him, trying to avoid touching any of the sleeping humps.

I hadn't made it far when an arm flapped out sideways, it's grubby skin brushing against mine.

An untimely click of electricity jumped from my forearm and I froze, the metal bed frame juddering with shock. Then, to my horror the lump surged upwards and a figure threw off his covers like an erupting volcano.

The man saw me, looked at his burnt skin and hissed, "I've been stung by the Devil's spawn!"

Max edged closer to me, reading panic in my face as the man ramped his insults up, his voice becoming louder.

"Demon Harpy! You've infected me, haven't you?"

The shocked tramp stood full upright on his bed, pointing an accusing finger down like Thor.

"You serpent, you harbinger of death. You've injected your poison in me."

"No, I just..."

He lifted his shirt and announced to the room, "Look everyone, this beelzebub is after my liver."

Max shifted to stand in front of me with both hands lifted.

"Lyn..."

"She's going to eat us all alive!"

"No Lyn, get a grip, she's a normal person."

"She's an infiltrator!"

The man jumped down and shot imaginary fire bolts at my face. "You venom-filled hussy. I curse you with all the fire in my belly!"

The comment made Max snap, deciding that he had heard enough. He grabbed the man's hands, circled them outwards, twisted one to arm lock the wild man down to the ground and then jammed a knee into his back.

"Lyn, you need to listen to me, alright?"

"I can't listen, I'm dead!"

"Lyn, if you don't calm down, I am going to have to get you admitted again. Do you want that?"

Lyn struggled and yelled, "She is an alien scout! She's after my flesh!"

"Lyn! Shut the fuck up!"

The man finally relaxed underneath him, although a low growl still rumbled from his mouth.

"Have you been taking your medication, Lyn?"

"I can't, it's poison."

"You need to keep taking it, or you'll have to go back in."

Silence.

"Are you going to calm down?"

"She isn't going to kill me?"

"No, she's a normal woman with electricity issues. Just like we all have issues."

"She hasn't infected me?"

"Nope."

There was a silence and then Max asked.

"Can I release you yet?"

The man mumbled something, and Max tightened his hold again, saying, "Lyn, you're on your last warning."

"Fine, I'm calm."

"What are you going to do when I let you go?"

"I'm going to go to bed."

"No, you're going to go over to Grey and tell him you've been off your meds."

Lyn remained obstinately silent and Max said, "Understand?"

"Yes, yes, off my meds."

Max finally climbed off the man and stood up, releasing the grumbling tramp who knelt suspiciously, his eyes still fixed firmly on my face.

He stood slowly and dusted his filthy clothes off and I stayed absolutely still, terrified of triggering another explosion.

Then, under a stern directive, he turned reluctantly to shuffle away in Grey's direction, wiping his fingers on his trousers.

"Come on Alice, we need to find Joe."

Max planted a solid hand in the middle of my shoulders and pushed me towards the back wall of the room.

I crossed my arms and walked with pigeon steps, being very careful not to touch any of the other sleeping bodies in their beds.

Jo wasn't hard to find.

A hunched figure was lurking under a dark grey woollen blanket on a dimly lit, isolated bed and the rancid body odour emerging from it was wretch-worthy.

"Joe," Max called.

The movement from inside the blanket stopped.

"Joe, I know you're in there. I need to speak to you."

"I'm busy!"

"Well you will have to be busy another time."

"Go away!"

"Joe, it's Max."

The blanket whipped off to reveal a familiar wizened old head with two fowl brown teeth hanging like tombstones in his mouth.

"I know. I could smell you when you bloody walked in 'ere."

"You're the shoe tramp!" I accused.

He opened and closed his mouth, butterflying his fingers as if I was nagging him.

"You took my shoes."

He continued to mouth and then rolled his eyes.

"I found 'em on the pabement."

"You did not!"

"You can't proob anyfing."

"Joe. Fess up or I'll search your revolting bed." Max raised his eyebrows and the tramp caved in, saying a loud "Naaaaa," before diving back under his sheets to rummage around, eventually producing my stiletto and trainer.

He threw them out but I let them clatter to the floor.

"I gave ya' shoes back. Why don't ya' wan'em?"

"Because I've thrown the other half away! What else was I going to do?"

He shrugged, "They weren't worth keepin' if you ask me, didn't smell that strong anyway."

The man went back down into the bed and produced a bottle of vodka in one hand and a disgusting old sock in the other. He took a swig of one, sniffed the other and grinned.

"So why do I habe the honour of a bisit from the forest man?"

"I need your help."

"You always need my 'ewp."

"You'd be bored without me, Joe. Think of all the challenges I've brought you."

Joe's mouth closed so tightly his nose nearly touched his chin.

"You migh' fink dey are chawenges but I fink they are a pain in the buttocks. You say to yourselbes. Oh go and ask smelly Joe when you need somefing. Smell my criminal out for me Joe. Just one more job, Joe."

"I'll nick you for taking her shoes otherwise."

"Proob it."

"Larry Borry's been watching her and has more evidence than you can shake a skunk at."

"Bloody Bug-eyed Borry," Joe growled, "Wait there a minute, I hab to talk to my dog," and with that, he put his head back under his sheet and had a conversation with himself.

"What do you fink?"

"Dey're just crappy coppers, ignore 'em."

"I know but he's got ebidence on dem shoes."

"Dey won't put you away for no shoes! Who's gonna bobber."

"Dis is dat tree man dow. Da' one what can keep me out o' jail…"

I turned and scowled at Max mouthing, "Who's he talking to?"

He shrugged his shoulders and I mouthed, "Did Larry sit and watch me getting mugged?"

He shrugged again, pretending innocence and I gave him a suspicious scowl.

Max turned deliberately away from me and said loudly, "If you help us, I'll buy you a Stinking Bishop next week."

Joe stopped moving and stuck out his hand, rubbing his fingers together, "If you want my 'elp den I need a li'l somfink now too."

"You're not still trading underwear?" Max groaned.

"Dey all go into my bed to sweeten my aromas."

"I'm not giving you my underwear."

I grinned at the idea of Max taking off his pants.

"Wha' abou' ye socks?"

Max sighed. "Fine."

"How long hab' you been wearin' dem?"

"Seven hours."

"Hmmm, weak but dey will do."

Max sat down on the end of the filthy bed and took his shoe off followed by a sock and held it out to Joe. Joe grasped it, rubbed it in his hands and then took a giant inhalation of breath as he pressed it against his nose, his eyes rolling back as if he had taken a hit of glue.

"Ah, mouldy wood and compostin' leabes. How refreshin'." He lifted the counterpane of his bed again and carefully laid it down next to dozens of other filthy pants and socks "Dat can be my garden area."

I took a step backwards as he carefully re-covered them, put the bottle of vodka under his nose, took a huge lungful and turned his attention back to us.

"Right, I'll do one last job for you den. I am finkin' it inbolbes this soap stinkin' woman?"

"I need to find her father."

Joe pouted and toothlessly moved his mouth up and down chewing on his own cheeks.

"Step one, Max, is to get 'em to drop the stenchin' sprays before ye' come 'ere."

Max pulled my arm towards him and sniffed my shoulder.

"She's barely wearing anything."

"It's an Impulse spray called True Lub," the gappy mouth smiled, "Perhaps she's sendin' a message to you, my Maxi boy."

Max dropped my arm.

"We don't have long, Joe, are you going to help?"

"Alright, alright, gib me de details."

"We are looking for Alice's father, he may have stayed here but under a different name."

"'ow long ago?"

"We don't really know."

"Fine, gib me a neck waft then."

Max gestured in smelly Joe's direction and I reluctantly pressed my hand down on the mattress to expose my neck.

"Be careful not to touch her, Jo. She packs a static punch."

Smelly Joe's nose twitched close to my skin and gave a detailed and noisy, sniff of my face and neck while I struggled not to recoil in disgust. He finally sat back and nodded.

"Nylon Lino."

"Is that what I smell of?" I sniffed my arm.

"Doug Decon. 'e stayed 'ere about a year ago."

"Have you smelt him around London recently?"

"Picked 'im up a couple o' times since, an' one ob dem times was only a few weeks back."

"In what area?"

"Dalston."

"You're a star, Joe. I'll give Grey the cheese next week, but you have to eat it outside."

"Yeah, yeah, yeah," Jo agreed.

"And don't hide it in your trousers."

"How much cheese? Ya neber said?"

After further cheese negotiations, Max put his hand on my shoulder as we made our way back to the dinner tables.

I sniffed my arm. "Do you think I smell of nylon Lino?"

"See it as flattery, Alice. I smell of rotting leaves."

I leant over and gave a deep inhalation of his jumper. Maybe there was a slightly woody smell, but it wasn't unpleasant.

"I quite like the way you smell actually, sort of...sandalwoodish." Then I laughed and added,

"Remind me not to have children with you, they'd end up smelling of pine and Lino."

"What's wrong with that?"

"They'd smell like toilet floors all their lives!"

Max didn't see the joke and grumpily changed the subject, "Let's go and get some food."

As we returned to the refectory area, I asked, "Are you sure it's safe to eat here?".

"It's fine. People travel for miles to taste Grey's cooking."

I scowled skeptically, knowing they were homeless tramps whose other alternative was raiding a bin.

Five minutes later, Grey emerged with a meal on a thick white plate and led me to a table that had residents sitting around it. They looked across with interest as Grey placed the overloaded plate in front of me, it looked and smelt delicious.

Smooth potato and celeriac mash were laced with crunchy bacon and layered between thin bands of spinach and pine nuts, while a crispy topping of delicately fried fish strips finished the masterpiece.

After chewing the first mouthful, I was transported into the world of Three Star cuisine.

While I was savoring each sublime morsel, Max wandered off to speak to some people around the room and Grey slid into the seat opposite, looking on and smiling at my enjoyment.

"How can you make food this tasty when you're on a budget?" I asked, clearing the final scraps of potato from my plate, "That was delicious."

He grinned and gestured towards the kitchen. "I trained in Paris when I was younger and opened a restaurant called Le Petit Chou-fleur when I came back to England. After several years of hard work, I was awarded a Michelin Star and my future looked very bright."

"What brought you here then?"

"About a year later I was working in the kitchen, cooking a battered fish dish when I dropped my spoon in a pot of boiling fat and, without thinking, reached in to get it."

I covered my mouth and looked at his perfect hands.

"I leapt back with the shock of what I'd done, of course and the staff immediately wrapped my hand in wet bandages and shipped me off to hospital. When I got there, they pulled everything off to find my hands were barely marked by the burn."

He opened and closed his hand as if to prove it. "The medics began to examine me and found I had no heat sensitivity in my fingers. They sent me for further neurological checks and found out the problem didn't lie in my nerves. It lay here. In my skin."

He rubbed the back of his hand as if it was sandpaper.

"They found my skin was impregnated with asbestos."

"Asbestos?"

He nodded glumly, "No one knows where it came from. I was simply born like that, just like a lot of the other ploids around here."

"And the asbestos stopped you from cooking?"

"The health and safety regulators were so worried about my skin cells contaminating the food that they barred me from all professional kitchens."

I looked uneasily at my empty plate.

"Oh, don't worry, your food is completely safe. I have since proved that I don't shed anything."

"But they still won't let you work?"

"No, the FSA were adamant I should be banned for life. When it first happened, I was devastated. Food was my life. Without it, I was bereft. I fell into a massive depression, lost my house, binged on alcohol and took stronger and stronger drugs until Max found me unconscious on the side of the road early one Sunday morning."

He scuffed a hand against his chin, taking in a deep sniff of air.

"He picked me up, dried me out and, after a few negotiations with the authorities, put me in touch with Ann, who was trying to set up this place."

"Ann?"

"My partner here, she's known affectionately as sweaty Ann by all the residents. Ann has her own set of problems but we both bonded and have loved running this place ever since."

"Is she here now?"

"Yes, hang on." He called back over his shoulder, "Ann, come and say hello."

I heard a clatter from the kitchen and the head of a large woman popped out. Her hair was plastered to her damp forehead and she spoke with a blunt northern accent.

"Am I safe?"

Grey looked back in smelly Joe's direction, "Yep, he's reorganizing his hoard."

"Ann has a bit of a problem with Joe."

Ann skulked out and slid onto a chair, her face almost motionless, "Just for five minutes then."

She wiped her brow with a floury apron and said, "I normally stay in the back kitchen reading my books. I'm not a great one for company."

Trickles of sweat ran down her face and she wiped them away with her tea towel.

Grey explained, "Joe's been alarmingly fixated on Ann recently."

"He's causing problems for everyone it seems, Joe stole my shoes a couple of weeks ago," I commiserated with her.

"Stolen shoes are nothing, this has gone beyond a joke," Grey said gravely. "He got into Ann's bedroom, last week and was found completely rigid in her dirty washing basket. We thought he was dead."

"What happened?"

Ann continued, "I phoned for an ambulance and the medics scooted him off to hospital. They eventually figured out that he had hyper-ventilated and changed the acidity of his blood." She shook her head grimly, "It's becoming dangerous."

Grey grinned and nudged her, "You like it really Ann."

She pressed her lips together, "It's like being loved by a demented bloodhound. I can't get away from him."

"Why don't you send him somewhere else?"

"If we know where Joe is, we can control him," Grey said, but Ann looked dubious.

Flapping the front of her saturated shirt, she added, "Plus, if Joe doesn't stay here, where else would he live? No one would take him."

I admired their generosity and asked, "How long have you been open?"

"Seven years now. It works well for us. Ann feels comfortable and I love my cooking."

Ann nodded, "The people here don't care about a bit of sweat or asbestos. As long as the food tastes good and they have a soft bed to lie in."

"And are the Health and Safety regulators happy with your cooking?"

Grey lifted his shoulders, "I cook good, nutritious food and feed starving, homeless people for pennies. I keep them off the streets and work closely with Max if I ever have any problems, all of which means I get left alone most of the time."

Ann had become engrossed in a damp, well-thumbed book called: Our Inner Ape: The Best and Worst of Human Nature.

Grey nodded in her direction, "Like I said, Ann loves to read. Did I mention that she has a PHD in evolutionary biology?"

"No," I said, surprised, "Any more suppressed geniuses?"

"Actually, we have several!" Grey said and pointed across the room to a man sitting on a neatly made bed, drumming his fingers on a battered suitcase. "Elmer, over there, is a brilliant concert pianist. And that's Amos sitting further down our table, he is the minister for work and pensions."

A few seats away sat a small man with a nut-brown face and an old, green woolly hat on. I studied him, "I thought I recognised him."

"He's also Ann's uncle."

"Surely the work and pensions minister isn't homeless?"

"No, he has a semi in Wapping but doesn't like spending money. He pretends to be 'helping the homeless' but really comes across for the central heating and free meals. Then we also have Yasmine, who used to be a nuclear physicist and Arthur, who was once a brilliant architect."

Grey pointed to a young woman in a blue tracksuit and a thin man with a pencil behind his ear. They were both busy mixing a yellow liquid in a large bowl, on a parallel table.

"They're working out how to save London from a nuclear attack by using custard powder."

"Custard powder?"

"Yes, by pouring it into the Thames in vast quantities, they're calculating how much powder would be needed as an academic challenge."

I watched Arthur scribble some figures on the table and Grey raised his voice, "Arthur don't draw on my tables please!"

As Arthur licked his finger and scrubbed the mark off, I asked, "And who is Max talking to?"

Max was crouched by a tiny old man who was sitting with one leg elevated on a chair and a large bandage across his head.

"Ahh, Ray over there keeps on thinking he can fly. Max has managed to catch him a couple of times, but I think he's going to end up really hurting himself one day."

I saw Max's strong hand fasten over Ray's and decided I would love Max to save me if I was down and out in the gutter.

Then I remembered the first night I met him and realised he had already done exactly that.

Perhaps I owed Max more than the stroppy thank you I had thrown his way, after all, this humble detective seemed to spend his whole life saving vulnerable people.

Chapter 26

After a long day of inquisitions, the team assembled back for a briefing at HQ and I sat, trying to concentrate while Vinny swung his feet next to me, making his fingers pop on the vinyl table.

Rufus Bull and Max were standing to one side of us and I heard Rufus whisper, "If this goes wrong, Nightly could be facing serious casualties."

"Stay out of the kitchen if you can't cope with the fire, Rufus," Max warned.

Rufus grinned sadistically, "You know that I'll take your place for that promotion if you scuff this up?"

"I'm not going to."

"Let's hope that Cooper can keep her fiery hands in her pockets then."

"It's Carter, not Cooper. And I don't plan to hurt anyone!" I snapped.

"You may not *plan* to, perhaps, but time will tell."

Nightly swept in holding a thick file and began speaking as he flicked through its pages.

"Ok, so we have an update on our status. Thank you, Max, for giving us Doug Decon. Donna and Lola have traced him through to someone called Tom Tolkin who, we know for a fact is a resident of the YMCA in Hackney. He is officially domiciled there and is currently being monitored by Jack and Larry."

"Shouldn't we move in now while we have him cornered?" Rufus barked.

"No, if he panics, he could kill everybody in the Y and short out half of London. Our aim is to evacuate the building at dawn tomorrow and then bring Miss cooper, sorry, Miss Carter, in to talk Cooper through this."

"You can just call me Alice, if it's easier."

Nightly fixed his eye on me, "Fine, Alice. Alice will enter with our back up team and warn Cooper about Adam Warner, explaining that we are there to protect him and don't want a confrontation. You need to be clear that we not connecting the Hong Kong murders to him and he can walk away a free man if he is prepared to move to one of our safe houses."

I nodded and he dropped his file on the table.

"The plan is to meet here at 7am tomorrow and transfer, in convoy to the building. All residents will be evacuated at six am by Larry and Sam. I want everyone on standby in the support van. Initially we aim to send Alice and Max in to establish contact and will only back them up with firepower if necessary. Any questions?"

"Do we know anything about Adam Warner's whereabouts?" Donna asked.

"Zac has a trace on him and has tracked him to an address in Berkshire, he hasn't left there in the last twelve hours, so we think we have the advantage over him at the moment."

Donna nodded and Nightly continued, "I repeat, we don't know how dangerous Cooper is, or what he is capable of. He is only to be approached strategically, with care. Are you all clear? Seven am kick off, here."

"Lola, can you do a seven am start?" Vinny checked and she gave a casual swipe with her hand as if to say, no problem.

Chapter 27

I managed to arrive early at the police station the next morning but only because Max came to get me at six fifteen.

At that point I was so tired that I offered him a thousand pounds for an extra ten-minutes in bed, but he just shoved a black coffee into my hand and walked out, waiting in the car.

Nightly met us, anxiously planning the day's manoeuvers as our motley band increased.

At seven forty-five, Nightly was itching to leave but we were still missing Lola and Donna.

"Is Rufus coming along too?" I asked Max.

"No, he is covering H.Q with Beth."

"Was I too high risk for him?" I said sarcastically.

"It isn't you he's mad at," he assured me, a line forming between his eyebrows, "Nightly offered to promote me and Bull got really pissed off about it."

"Does that mean that you're going up in the world if this job goes well?"

"No. I turned it down."

"Why? You deserve it, you're a brilliant detective."

Max grinned "Is that a compliment?"

"It's fact."

"I'm not interested Alice; I need to be out here on patrol. I couldn't stand being locked in an office all day."

Donna rolled up in a car five minutes later with the floppy Miss Rose absolutely out for the count in the passenger seat.

"I'm know we're late, I couldn't get her to move."

Vinny clicked his tongue and flicked Lola's ear, "Flowers that party all night sleep deepest before dawn. You need to use some artificial day light on her."

"Oh, well I'm sorry 'Mr Oracle'," Donna snapped back, "I didn't happen to have an artificial blue light in my backpack!"

Max bent down to lift the sleeping Lola out of the car and sat her, yawning in the back of a rusty green police van as Vinny started the engine.

The Y was an ugly, brick building with small windows and a glass fronted door that didn't open when we pressed the entry button.

A middle-aged woman with bright makeup appeared inside and scowled at our badges as she tried to override the automatic lock. Eventually she had to lean her shoulder against the panel of glass to make it wiggle open.

We squeezed into a well-worn reception area with a faint smell of Detol and vomit.

The warden, Marjorie Phelps, was flustered by the unusual door jam and said, "I'm so sorry, everything has been playing up since we lost power a couple of hours ago."

"A couple of hours ago? Does that mean that this building hasn't been evacuated?"

"Not as far as I know. I just came on shift to find our power banks down."

Max pointed at the fire stairs, ordering, "Lola, Donna check the rooms," then he flashed his PlOps badge, "We are searching for a resident here called Tom Tolkin."

The woman studied it and gasped, one hand splayed on her chest.

"Did that say Max Greenstick?"

Max nodded, unease creeping into his eyes as she leant towards him on her elbows.

"I've heard all about you," she winked at him deliberately, revealing an eyelid covered in bright blue eyeshadow.

Max rocked backwards.

"Oh?"

"Yes," she said with a seductive purr, "My friend Rachel said she had quite an experience with you the other day."

"Rachel?"

"Smithclep. She works for Haringey waterworks."

"Ah," Max blushed, "The woman that was unconscious?"

"Not *quite* unconscious. She said you were amazing. And you stayed up under her for over an hour."

"Is she alright now?"

"Fully recovered thanks to your gallant behaviour."

"Good, well perhaps we can move on to…"

"I think you deserve a medal for endurance like that," Margery said as Max looked a little ill and swallowed.

"Good, well…back to the case?"

"Of course. Anything to help a hero," she pulled the book towards her, licked her finger coquettishly and opened its pages, turning it around for him to see.

"Here, have a browse. I'll always help a hero. If there's anything else I can do, don't hesitate to ask."

She sashayed off and reached up to put some keys away in the back office.

Curiosity was burning inside me, and I asked, "What the hell did you do to Rachel Smithclep?"

"Focus Alice, we're here on an investigation."

I slammed my hand down on the top of the book to force it closed.

"You stayed up under her?"

"Alice…"

I shook my head adamantly, "Spill the beans."

"Fine, I was just doing my job alright…. she fell into something and I had to go in to get her out."

"Fell into what?"

He mumbled and I squashed my hand down on the ledger.

"Alright! It was just a job like any other."

"Details?"

"Rachel fell into a sewage treatment vat."

"Oh god, and you jumped in?"

Max's lips went white as he pressed them together and I linked him to the story in Lola's Speculator.

"That was in the newspaper! You were the policeman that saved her?"

"Yes."

"From a vat full of sewage?"

"From a vat full of sewage. Now can we move on?"

"Well that was either really brave or really stupid."

"She was unconscious and sinking, so I didn't have a choice."

"But you floated?"

"I'm wood, Alice."

I poked a smile at him.

"So that's why you could 'stay up' then."

"The book, please."

"It's good to know that you float to the top, even in the deepest shit, Max."

"Not funny Alice," he said, "Let go of the book."

Max ran his finger along the list of residents and tapped the name Thomas Tolkin.

"He's in room sixty-two."

"No he isn't," a voice corrected from the stairs.

Larry Borry was standing looking out of breath with his hands on his hips.

"Tom Tolkin received a message about two hours ago, making him pack his bags and hotfoot it out of here, fusing the building as he went."

"Where were you?"

"In the room next to his, our door sealed shut when the power failed."

"That's because we go into isolation mode when the panic button's engaged. The Y uses compulsory lockdown to control dangerous situations," Marjorie explained as she returned, "The power cut must have triggered our security system."

"Why the hell didn't you tell us Larry?"

"Because the power surge disabled all of our equipment and we had no way to communicate."

"The landline would still work."

"We only have one landline and that's here," Marjorie said, pointing at her desk.

Max sighed and asked him, "Do you know why Chris left?"

"We found *this* in his room."

Larry held out a crumpled piece of paper and Max snatched it off him.

Dear Chris

I know this will be an unexpected letter, but my name is Alice and I am the daughter you left with Philomena Carter, twenty five years ago. I have wanted to find you for a long time now and have managed to trace your name using the documents that you left me in the high security vault.

I would love to meet up and tell you about my life so far and get to know you a little after all these years.

I am working at the Olympia Conference Centre today and will be waiting in the main hall by the central exhibition stand at nine thirty this morning,

I am keeping everything crossed in the hope that you will come.

Alice Carter

P.S. Here is the picture you left with my aunt when I was a baby and a second photo taken recently to help you recognise me.

P.P.S. I know this might be difficult for you but it would really men the world to me.

The photo was a picture of me in my BFA evening dress, looking white-faced and startled.

"When was that photo taken Alice?"

"At the awards when I first went out with Adam." I frowned, "But I don't understand how he got the photo from my aunt's house, we saw it there yesterday."

"Your Aunt has just phoned to report a break-in that happened at some point last night," Zac announced, squeezing through the foyer door and Larry cursed.

"Shit, we've got to go to Olympia."

"No, I need to phone Aunty Phyl first to check she is alright. He must have been in her house. Max, please?"

Max took a second to deliberate before he called out to the receptionist, "Excuse me? Hello, we need your help over here."

Marjory breezed back to us, smiling at her sewage hero.

"Can I use this phone?"

"Of course, Detective Greenstick. I'll get you an outside line."

A shiny red fingernail pressed the number two twice and the number made her smile, "Two little ducks, they float just like you did, what a coincidence."

Max rolled his eyes and took the receiver, "You have to be quick Alice."

I grounded myself on a water pipe and dialed Phyl's number.

"Aunty Phyl?"

"Alice, why are you calling me so early in the morning? Is everything alright?"

"Yes. Did you have a break in last night?"

"How did you know? I've only just discovered it."

"Max told me."

"Gosh, I only put the phone down two minutes ago, your police detective must be very efficient at his job."

"What happened?"

"I don't really know. I just woke up this morning to find the kitchen window broken and glass everywhere."

"Are you alright? You didn't see or hear anything during the night?"

"No, I must have slept through it. I think they might have got disturbed though, because nothing's missing."

"Can you look for the photo of me and mum in the sitting room?"

"Ok dear..." the phone clunked down and faint shuffles could be heard in the background.

When she came back to the phone, I could hear the distress in her voice, "Alice, I can't find it. Do you think they took it."

"Don't worry Phyl, I know exactly where it is. I'll send it to you. Will you make sure you get that back window repaired for me?"

"Yes dear."

"Oh and Aunty Phyl?"

"Yes?"

"Do you think you can stay with uncle Mo for a couple of days, just until I get this whole mess sorted out?"

Chapter 28

Nightly was pacing outside with his shoulders hunched, heavy rain drenching his jacket. He pulled the back doors of the van open and ordered us all in as Max updated him on our poor performance.

After a deal of swearing and accusations, Nightly set us in motion and asked Zac to look up the website details.

"The exhibition opening at Olympia today is part of a four-day fair based on renewable energy."

"Christ, it would be an *energy* exhibition," I whispered to Max.

"This is an event where the industry's most influential voices will present a series of lectures discussing power solutions for the future. It has a variety of exhibits on display, ranging from home energy management systems to nuclear powered generators. The main sponsors are: Prime Power, Rawnet and an energy derivatives company called…"

He ground to a halt and Nightly finished for him, "Warner and Suma?"

Zac nodded and Nightly hit the side of the van in frustration. "Jesus, we're too late. Metal has set the trap already."

He ran a hand across his mouth and then snapped, "Ok, let's get on top of this. Jack, set the tazer to full capacity."

Jack bent to adjust his tazer, headphones bright against the army-green van.

"Sam, you're fully armed?"

Sam nodded.

"Shoot if you have no other option. If Cooper is looking dangerous, we might have to hit him with both."

Although a piercing siren wailed above our heads, we sat gridlocked in rush hour traffic, the van moving at a grindingly slow speed.

As Max looked at his watch, I asked him quietly, "What will happen if you have to tazer Chris? He isn't like everybody else, is he?"

He shook his head, "We don't know, because Chris conducts electricity strangely, it could be lethal or have no effect at all."

I nodded, looking at the SWAT team around me and then added grimly.

"And if it doesn't work, you'll shoot him?"

Max didn't answer but put his hand across mine as the van hit a pothole and we jolted sideways.

I had caused all this.

It was close to nine fifteen by the time we arrived in Earls Court.

A security guard with a drenched shirt and scuffed shoes waved the van into a car park behind the main building and hobbled as he hurried to catch us up.

"Mckenzie, thanks for coming," Nightly said as he opened the van doors and let the guard in with a squall of rain.

"Anything to help Randy, just tell me what you need." Mckenzie had a strong Scottish accent and steamed up glasses that he wiped with his tie.

Nightly, or should I say *Randy*, adjusted his eye patch, avoiding looking at his team.

"I prefer to be called 'Nightly' on duty."

"Aye, Nightly it is then. Give me the low down."

"Ok, I want guards placed on all the entrances, full Met authority and be ready to evacuate the entire building. Plus Zac needs to access your mainframe and surveillance data."

Mckenzie brushed away a raindrop that had formed on the end of his nose.

"We can try but you do realise there are nine exits from Olympia Grand alone and the building is over 4000 square meters in size, ma' guards canna' cover the whole place."

"I don't have time to call in more support, a violent criminal my be inside already, and another is about to arrive."

"What do they plan to do?"

"I have no idea, but it could jeopardize public safety."

Mckenzie put his glasses back on and shook his head, "I wouldnae want ta be in your shoes, Randy! You're moving into this thing half blind."

Nightly's eye narrowed at the comment, "Half blind? I guess I am, but we have no other option."

Mckenzie nodded, "I'll let security know we have two psychos and lots of PlOps floating around. Oh, and I'll clear ya' access to our software and cameras."

"You must tell your staff that both men are extremely dangerous and must not be confronted."

Mckenzie held a thumb up and began speaking into his walkie-talkie as Nightly called out instructions.

"Jack and Sam, you're inside, the rest of you cover the entrances. Mckenzie can you stay here and guard the van, Alice you wait with Mckenzie until Max comes back to get you. Zac, you're with me. I need to remind everyone again that Alice is the only person who can approach Cooper."

"Zac any evidence of Cooper on CCTV?"

Zac's shook his head, "Nothing yet, boss."

Everyone jumped out of the van except Mckenzie and me. We sat listening to raindrops bouncing like buckshot off the roof until I asked, "Are you a Ploid too then, Mckenzie?"

"I dinnae. I suppose I could be one."

"Oh?"

"I'm n'er like Max or Randy though. I hide ma' secret under ma' trousers."

"You do?" I said warily as Mckenzie pointed at his groin. "What do you mean?"

"I've been different since I was a bairn."

He pulled up his trouser legs, revealing two shoes affixed to shiny metal rods.

"Oh, you have prosthetics?" I said but Mckenzie shook his head.

"Stilts."

"Stilts?"

"Aye," he rapped his knuckles on them and said, "I've had these walkers for a lang time. They're the ol' titanium and aluminum type but I'm gonna get some carbon-fiber shafts next year."

"Stilts?"

"Yes, ya see I was blessed with wee legs, and, when I say wee, I mean *really* wee," he pinched his fingers together to demonstrate how small they were. "The doctors told me that I would ne'r walk on them, but these tubes changed ma' life. Guess where ma' real foot is?"

I pointed at his knee making him laugh, "Na, ma' foot's all the way up here."

He grabbed a small projection, close to his groin, "You can feel it if ya dunna believe me."

"We're clear," Max announced, yanking the door open with a wide umbrella in his hand. "Nightly's waiting for us at the front entrance."

"Thank God."

I grimaced as I climbed out.

"Problems with Mckenzie?"

"I was up close and personal with his groin lumps."

"Oh, you mean his feet? He does well to hide them doesn't he. Come on, Nightly's waiting by the front entrance."

Rain fizzed against my arm and I tried to keep up with Max, saying, "Talking of Nightly."

"Yes?"

"Is his name really Randy?"

Max huffed and stopped, "I knew you would do that."

I tried to keep under the umbrella, "What?"

"Laugh."

"Oh come on, 'Randy Nightly'? What were his parents thinking?"

"His full name is Randal actually."

"Randal Nightly isn't much better. Do you think he has a brother?"

"It's not funny."

"Called Justin?"

"No."

"Roger?"

"No."

I grinned, "How about, Yank?"

"Zip it, or you'll get wet."

Zac was spooling off information like a book as we caught up with Nightly.

"…It opened in 1886, holds up to 10,000 people and has a barrel ceiling with a 1200-ton iron frame carrying 85 tons of glass across ten cast iron columns."

Hundreds of people with lanyards looped around their necks were adding finishing touches to stands set up at one end of the 'Grand Hall'.

These were promoting mini wind turbines, biomass converters, combustion systems, wave action generators and an array of other machines I couldn't even recognise.

My eyes didn't dwell on these exhibits though, something else had caught my attention, something that made my blood run cold.

The exhibition hall had been separated in two by a metal grill which was folded back, revealing a giant pillar that was cemented into a circular concrete platform.

I sucked in a breath as I realised what Adam planned to do.

"What is that machine?" Max asked as he stood beside me.

"It's a Van de Graff generator," I replied faintly and tracked my eyes up the huge structure.

It was made of glass and stretched forty foot into the air with a black belt running all the way up the inside of its shaft, a dull metal ball resting at its peak like the fist of zeus.

"What does it do?"

"It's the most lethal lolly-pop in the world,"

I had learned about the dangers of Van de Graffs the hard way when I was on a school trip to the science museum in Kensington.

We had gone to explore electrical currents and circuits using a child-friendly, extremely safe, hands-on exhibition.

However the 'user friendly' exhibition was anything but safe in my case, every exhibit fizzed with mains electricity and I had to resist button pressing or lever pulling for two hours until we were herded into a room to see the final exhibit.

Each of us stood along a balcony with a wide metal grid running across the front of it. A curator arrived and told us to keep our hands away from the grid and then switched on a machine identical to the one in front of me.

A wide nylon belt began to rotate and create friction. This charged up the metal ball at its peak until it was brimming with negative energy and began to release sparks that jumped to the closest conductive structure around.

This thunderbolt, in normal circumstances, should have danced along the metal grill in front of us, making a thrilling, harmless spectacle, for everybody to admire, but when I went to watch it, the blue bolt stopped firing randomly and focused on the wire directly in front of my face.

I stepped back and then edged to one side, but the white arc followed, belting unceasing power at the crackling grid.

As static built up in the air around me, my teeth began to hurt, my eardrums crackled, blood tingled and muscles soured.

The charge was disrupting all of the circuits in my body and, in an effort to stop the incessant light firing at my face, I lifted my arm to block the beam.

Instantly, charge powered out of my hand, flowing like a stream of white-hot lava towards the grid, my head exploded with pain and my feet left the ground as I was walloped backwards against the wall behind me.

A safety fuse blew, making the machine cut out unexpectedly. This left the curator puzzled, my teacher angry and me with an evil little burn in the palm of my hand that caused a scar so deep I could still feel it today.

I ran my thumb across it, realizing that this machine must be six times the size of my school generator. Six times the height, six times the power and with no grid to protect me, I was a sitting duck.

"This is set to fire up after the opening ceremony, which begins at nine forty-five," Zac explained to Nightly.

"It is twenty feet high and can discharge up to five million volts of electricity. The audience will first assemble around the base of the generator, listen to a speech by a professor Cornelius Stryx about electro-magnetic advances and then be directed back behind the metal grill. Some exhibitors have been issued VIP tickets which allow them to stand in those cages along the side of the hall and be part of the spectacle."

"What would happen if it was switched on now?" Max asked and Zac continued to download information.

"All other machinery must be isolated from the mains during the display and the middle barrier closed. If personnel do not comply with regulations there is a very high risk of electrical damage, fire or death. All suitable precautions must be taken prior to ignition."

"Death?" Max choked.

"It's a minimal risk but the current has the potential to jump to any conductive object."

"Especially people who are highly charged," I reflected solemnly. "This machine will kill my father."

"And you Alice, if we don't get you out of here," Max said but was drowned out by a loud bell.

The exhibitors began filing across into the generator zone, getting ready for the speech on the circular stage at the base of the structure.

"I've got a visual on Warner on the stage and he appears to be holding some kind of trigger or detonator in his hand," Larry Borry shouted as he ran towards us.

He was pointing towards Adam who was fixing duct tape to several thick wires at the base of the generator. "Also, the guest speaker, Stryx is locked in that metal cage over to your left. It looks like the control hub for the generator."

I glanced across to the left and saw Adam's sidekick adjusting dials on a broad dashboard.

"Can we cut the power to that console?" Max asked.

Nightly huffed, "Stryx isn't just going to unlock the door and let us through. Plus, if we approach either of them, Metal could panic and trigger the generator early."

"Can we hack into the software and cut the power that way, Zac?"

Zac screwed his eyes up tight and then shook his head, "They're running off an independent generator and the system is protected by a dozen complex firewalls. I can break them down dude but need more time to work out how."

"I could buy you more time," I said, and Max cut across me.

"Alice, don't even think about it..."

"No, I can talk to Adam, he'll listen to me." I ignored Max and spoke directly to Nightly, "Also, if he knows I am here, he might not set it off, because the generator could kill me too."

Nightly thought for a moment, raised an eyebrow at Max and then turned back to me.

"Fine but if your father gets here your priority is to get him out of the back door and into the van as fast as possible."

"I understand."

Nightly sighed, "Don't look at me like that Max, we have no other option. Alice, keep Warner talking for as long as you can."

I nodded and ran towards the stage, hearing Nightly order, "Larry, all eyes out for Cooper. We hit combustion point once he enters the scene."

I sprinted across the arena, completely brain dead, not knowing what I was going to say to Adam. I knew he wouldn't change his plans, but I might delay him enough to allow Zac to access the mainframe.

A throng of exhibitors had closed in on the generator, hoping to get a better view. I barged recklessly through them, my skin cracking against their shirt-sleeves until I emerged by the base of the platform. Leaning my sweating, static hands on its high cold concrete, I shouted, "Adam."

He didn't hear me at first and I shouted again, drawing his attention.

"Alice? I told you not to come here." He walked across towards me, "You need to get out of this place."

"Did you set this whole exhibition up to draw him in?"

"You can't change this, Alice."

"You're mad."

"I prefer single minded."

"You broke into my aunt's house and stole my photo."

"Oh, come on, that was child's play, Alice."

"You can't turn this machine on early. Not with all these people in the room."

"It's harmless to them and *you* still have time to walk away."

"Why are you doing this? You have no idea what happened in Hong Kong all that time ago."

"I know enough."

"Your mother died due to her depression."

"No, she died because she loved my father."

"But *he* always loved someone else. He only married Cora because she was pregnant."

"Get out."

"Adam," I reached out to touch him, but he drew back, his jaw tense. "Your dad always planned to leave her."

"You're lying."

"*I'm* lying? You have done nothing but lie to me."

"I never *lied*. You just didn't ask the right questions Alice."

"You lied about your sister."

He turned his back and began to walk away as my voice cracked like ice behind him.

"Annabelle was stillborn wasn't she? She didn't die in the water like you said."

When he turned, his face was the colour of chalk.

I snapped, "What the hell was that whole story about Adam? Just another way to manipulate me? To push around the little chess pieces? This isn't a game anymore. This is real. People will die if you set that machine off. *I* will die."

He walked back to me and leant in close, letting his lips brush like needles against my cheek.

"I told you, Alice. Everyone that I care for dies."

He pushed away and I looked frantically back. Jack had translated our conversation and Nightly was shaking his head in despair.

I had lost all bargaining power with Adam and Zac was still standing motionless, his eyes rolled back as he tried to access the power circuit.

I shrugged, mouthing, "What shall I do?" as Larry lifted a hand and pointed to the far exit where a tall, emaciated figure formed a distinctive silhouette.

He was clean shaven, held a small bunch of tulips and was wearing a new shirt, it's crisp folds still package-sharp.

The effort Chris had gone to made him look heart wrenchingly vulnerable, his eyes sunken and anxious in the wide open space.

My father had entered the hall by the far door and was walking towards the deadly device at its centre.

I had to get Chris out of the building.

I began to run, looking back over my shoulder as Adam hopped down from the stage and started walking towards Stryx.

However, he stopped as Lola strode forwards, boldly placing herself between Adam and the caged controls.

I doubted that Lola's curvy form was ever going to stop a man of that strength, but kept watching as Lola planted her feet and lifted her face to the sky. Then she raised her arms and stuck her chest out, the pungent smell of roses filling the air.

Every man in the building stopped and turned to walk in her direction.

Lola was blooming, and this time it was huge. The crowd forming around her piled up so densely that Strix was obscured completely and Adam had to barge his way through to the machinery beyond.

I reached my father, gasping for air and grabbed his elbow as an explosive spark set off between us.

"I'm Alice, Chris. I sent you the letter." I didn't have time to explain about Adam's plan.

"Alice? My Alice?" he held out his flowers.

"They're lovely, but we have to get out of here, we're both in danger from that machine," I shouted and pointed at the generator. "There's a man who wants to kill us. You've got to run!"

I risked another glance back and saw Donna plop out of the crowd. She ran into the caged off compartment, effortlessly squeezing her body through the bars and began kicking and pulling at the console, trying to disable it.

However, her efforts were wasted, the bank of lights kept shining and Adam was rapidly closing in on her.

I took my dad's hand and pulled him towards the distant exit as Adam reached Donna and dumped her out of the control cage.

Then I heard him start the mechanism.

A low hum filled the room as the belt below the ball of metal began to rotate.

We were still in the middle of the concourse as the air thickened with charge. My skin becoming electrified, strands of hair floating away from my head.

Then a small jolt released up into a mesh that covered the ceiling as the belt travelled faster.

My cells began to polarise as the high, crackling whine increased, making my feet give way.

I fell, losing my father's hand as he dropped with a thump behind me.

The air inside my lungs stiffened and my skin felt as if it was being ripped away as the machine reached full capacity.

Then a deadly bolt of lightning shot out of the generator and blasted into the concrete under us. Electricity scorched my skull and I spasmed in agony, the world prickling out of focus as bony fingers reached across to slide around my ankle. With a sudden release, the entire charge drained away from me.

My father had taken all of the voltage. Agony scarred his face as he shouted, "Run, Alice. Please!"

But I had only made it to my knees as the static began to build again.

We couldn't take another hit.

I turned back to see Adam watching us with a set expression on his face, his hand pushing up a lever on the console. But even as he did so a small miracle was happening behind him.

Vinny had thrown his shoes off and was climbing like a lizard up the wall beside the metal cage, his sticky fingers and bare feet helping him to stick to the concrete.

My skin began to burn again, and my muscles ached as I watched his long, thin tongue probe between the bars. It fed behind the paneling and, after a couple of seconds, emerged, wrapped around the bank of plugs that connected the Van de Graff to the power supply.

Unnoticed by Adam, he tugged them through the bars and began yanking each one out of the mother socket. My vision began to white out again as I heard the scream of the belt hitch suddenly and begin slowing. The spasms dropped out of my limbs as the system ground to a halt.

Within another second the air cleared, and my movements became free. I reached across to drag my shaking father upright and began our staggering escape for a second time.

Not daring to turn and see what was happening behind me, I pulled at my father's hand encouraging him to run, however the massive jolt had taken its toll and his legs buckled with the first step.

I lifted his arm across my shoulder and fed another around his waist for balance. Then he closed his eyes, rocking backwards before resting his cheek on my hair.

"The last time I touched anyone was when I held you in my arms all those years ago, Alice."

I tightened my grip.

"I know dad, it's been the same for me."

"I'm so sorry that I haven't been there for you."

"We have to get out of here or he's going to do it again."

He nodded and leant heavily on me as tears rolled down his cheeks and I helped him to walk towards the back exit.

This man I was clinging to was such an essential part of me that it hurt. He knew what it was like to live a life in hiding, starved of contact and alone. Whatever he had done all those years ago, he had paid for through solitude and isolation.

Never to have touched someone for almost twenty-five years wrenched my chest open. I wanted to stand and hug him and forgive him for everything terrible he had ever done but I didn't have the time. If we didn't keep moving, Adam would catch us.

Jack and Sam held the fire doors open and waited as I pushed Chris into a wall of rain.

"This way," Sam shouted, his shirt drenched within seconds as he led us towards the van where Mckenzie was waiting, but my father pulled back.

"What's happening, Alice?"

"They just want to help."

"I'm not getting in that van."

"Dad, we have no choice. Adam is going to kill you."

"Adam? Who is Adam? What is going on?"

"He is Eddie's son. Do you remember?"

"Eddie...?"

"Eddie Metal. The man you killed in Hong Kong. We have to leave. I'll explain it all in the van."

But the hesitation had delayed us too long. The doors banged open and Adam appeared, grabbing the tazer from Jack and throwing the detective away like a rag doll. Sam raised his gun, but Adam punched him in the face and pointed the powerful tazer at Chris.

My father yanked up the bonnet of the van, warning, "If you come anywhere near me, I'll connect to the battery, making the tazer charge double and run straight back to you."

Adam changed his plan and hooked an arm around my wet shoulders, ignoring the gigantic jolt that was set off and shoving the tazer into my cheek.

"Think about it, if you take me out then you take her too."

I watched my father's face crease in pain.

"Don't hurt her."

"Get away from the van."

My father dropped the hand that was hovering over the battery and I could feel Adam's chest dragging in sharp gasps of breath.

"I've been searching for you all these years Chris."

"Please, Adam. Just leave Alice out of this."

The rain was running off us in sheets.

"No, she's tied into everything. And do you know why?" Adam's hold tightened, "You killed everyone that loved us both. Who would miss Alice if she died Chris? You? You've never even spoken to her, never even sent a card. Don't pretend you care."

The door slammed again, and the rest of the squad piled out, all of them juddering to a halt.

Jack dragged himself back to his feet and leveled the gun at Adam who pushed the tazer harder into my face.

My father pleaded, "Stop, I did care, that's why I stayed away. I tried to protect her. I've always tried to protect Alice. It's me that you want Adam, not her."

"Talk then. Tell me what you did. Tell me how you killed them all."

My father licked his lips and leant against the van; his eyes remote as he travelled back in time.

"Thirty-one years ago fate led me to marry Sophia while your father, Eddie, was serving in the army. They had both loved each other once and he was still wildly jealous and determined to win her back."

Chris brushed the rain out of his eyes and the arm around me loosened slightly.

"We tried to live in England for a few years, but Eddie followed Sophia everywhere, turning up in supermarkets, coffee shops and bars. Leaving messages on the answer machine, sending cards, notes and flowers, all of them trying to win her over and all of them pushing to change her mind. I watched Sophia punish herself with guilt every day until she barely left the house and became isolated from the world. When she fell pregnant, I decided she had had enough and took her away to Hong Kong without telling anyone."

He smiled to himself, "It worked. Sophia was finally happy. She gave birth to Alice out there and life was perfect until Alice was about three months old. Then, one day, Eddie turned up at our flat. He must have ordered Sophia to come away with him, but she managed to press the speed dial on the phone to clue me in on what was happening. When I answered she was in mid-sentence saying she didn't want to leave me and wouldn't abandon Alice. Eddie replied that, if she came willingly, he would take the child too and set up a new home for them all, bringing Alice up with his son. I dropped the phone and sprinted back towards our apartment as a huge thunderstorm began cracking in the distance. Sophia must have put the baby into a car seat and prayed that I had heard her message. When I arrived the security-guard told me that no one had left the building, so I made him lock all the ground floor exits and call the police before racing up the stairs. I searched frantically on every floor and eventually found them on the roof. Sophia was standing, soaked by the storm and Eddie was waving to a helicopter that had nearly blown us all off the tarmac. Eddie put the baby carrier to one side as the helicopter dropped a harness down on the end of a wire and he grabbed it."

My father's desolate face became haunted as he begged us to understand.

"You have to see; I was going to lose everything if I let Eddie take them both. I had to act quickly and saw he was standing on a lower area of pitch where a wide puddle had formed, and Sophia and the baby were out of it. I ran to the power shed on the roof, plunged my hand into the emergency generator socket and stretched my foot towards the puddle, planning to shock Eddie and make him drop the harness. I didn't have time to think about the consequences, I just knew that I needed to stop him. Then everything seemed to happen in slow motion. I shifted my foot and just as I dipped it into the puddle, a huge bolt of lightning flashed from the sky and hit the generator like an explosion. My entire charge fed into the water and then channeled across to Eddie and the wire. To my horror, I realised the power surge had done two things. It had knocked Eddie backwards and disabled the electronics in the helicopter."

Tears were mixed with the water dripping off his chin, "I knew what was going to happen and couldn't move, everything teetered in silence, suspended for a desperate second before the horror unfolded."

The tazer slackened beside me.

"Eddie had reached out as he stumbled backwards and grabbed Sophia's hand, dragging her with him as the dying helicopter choked and stalled above me. The metal hulk nose-dived and fell like a stone, taking Eddie, Sophia and the side of the roof with it. When it hit the floor, its fuel tank exploded on the road below. A shockwave pulsed the air and then hollowed out in a ghastly, empty silence. My reason for living had gone. My fragile house of cards collapsed. I was so paper thin that I nearly floated off the edge, diving hopelessly into the devastation below, but one thing remained."

I watched the man before me crumple to his knees, "The only thing that kept me alive, the one person I had left to fix me on this earth was tiny Alice in her car seat."

He put his shaking hands together to pray. "I gave her up for twenty-five years. Please don't take her from me. I have nothing else."

Adams grip tightened, "Oh I know how that feels, Chris. I had everything taken from me too. You took it all. You owe me that life."

Then the tazer arm tensed and began to turn towards Chris. I heard Max shout, "No!" as my father leapt upright to place his hand on the car battery. Adam squeezed the trigger, his arm jerking as the tazer released its darts.

I watched my father's shoulder recoil under the jolt of the electrodes and then a sharp, double crack split the air as Sam fired his gun twice through the curtain of rain.

My father folded forwards when the bullets hit but he kept his hand on the battery, blood blossomed through his shirt, and an arc of blue light pulsed from his shoulder. I tried to knock the tazer from Adam's hand but was too late, the magnified power from my father had already fed through it.

Heat scorched across my skin, pain fed into my bones and blinding light numbed my skull.

Every muscle clenched like a vice and then a sledgehammer crushed my chest. I convulsed, hitting the floor with a deadly spasm.

My body stopped, air stopped, sensation stopped, and the world fell out of time as consciousness spiraled away from me, my heart collapsing in on itself.

I felt arms pull me onto my back and saw Adam's face over mine, white and panicked as his wet, shaking hands brushed the strands of hair from my eyes.

"No, Alice. Don't you dare... You have to come back to me. Stay with me, Alice..."

But the rain bullets descended from an ever-expanding grey sky, the drops falling in divergent lines, their pockets of liquid bursting on my skin until there was no rain at all. Until the whole world became white and numb. Until there was nothing.

Chapter 29

My chest ached as if it had been cranked open with a car jack. Each breath sent daggers into my ribs and my muscles felt as if they had been fed with battery acid.

Life crept back in in small snatches. The crackle of plastic, a rubber glove by my cheek, arms under my shoulders turning me, moisture on my lips.

After many disjointed hours and the constant beep of distant machinery, I finally won the battle against my heavy eyelids and rose back into consciousness.

Focusing my vision on something smooth and pink, I blinked twice and then realised that it was a shoulder with a badly tattooed, pornographic rose on it.

I smiled slightly and closed my eyes, "Lola?"

"Alice, you're awake."

I nodded, "I don't want to be. Everything hurts."

"They can give you some more pain killers. Hang on I'll call the nurses."

She stood up to press a button on the wall and two women came in with thick, rubber gardening gloves. They sat me up slightly and pushed some cold fluid into my arm.

"It's amazing that you're still alive, Alice."

"That doesn't sound good." I tried lifting a hand to brush my dry mouth, but my arm weighed like lead.

"We all thought you were dead after the shock hit you. You turned completely white on us and you had no pulse."

"What saved me?"

"Max, he did CPR for a long time while Donna and I looked on in horror and then silent Jack sprinted back into the building and eventually found a defibi-thing. After that, Max forced us all to stand well back while he gave you a risky zap with the machine."

"It feels like it worked!" I said, rubbing the sore patches on my chest.

"It did but, because of all the water on the ground, the charge knocked Max out too."

"Max? Is he alright?" my weakened voice broke with stress and I coughed painfully.

Lola let me settle and then explained, "It was a bit touch and go. He ended up lying, unconscious over the top of you. But, because my brilliant Zac had called 999, the ambulance arrived within a couple of minutes and treated him straight away. Max was admitted here for observation but he's fine now."

She twisted her hands in her lap and then said quietly, "You need to sleep."

I nodded and closed my heavy eyes, giving into the pain killers.

Waking some time later, I blinked, my mind feeling calmer, my thoughts more organized. I sat up a little and asked Lola for a drink.

She bent a straw so I could reach it with my dry mouth, and I croaked, "Lola?"

"Yes?"

"What happened to my father?"

Her expression told me everything and I put an arm across my eyes.

"Oh god no…"

"He didn't make it, Alice. I'm sorry."

Heavy, painful sobs fell out of me and made my chest cave in with despair.

I couldn't have lost someone that I had only just begun to know. I wanted to talk to Chris and tell him everything about my life, my childhood, my friends, the lengths I had gone to to hide myself. I wanted to make him smile and laugh and more than anything else, I wanted to hug him.

I wanted to reach my arms out and hug the man who hadn't touched a single person for twenty five years.

Lola sat quietly beside me for a long time until I swallowed and stared at the ceiling, finally able to talk again.

"And Adam?"

"Nightly and Larry tried to restrain him while Max was working on you. But Adam was too strong for them. He threw them both off and escaped down one of the alleys. Everybody is out looking for him now."

"So he's on the run?"

She nodded, her voice more confident than her expression, "We'll find him though, Alice. We'll keep you safe, I promise."

I shook my head and sank back into my pillow, "You won't, he's too slick and intelligent to be caught. Plus he has no need of me now, he's achieved his goal. Chris is dead."

The dejection of being a tiny cog in Adam's deadly mechanism of revenge made me feel like a useless piece of trash. I had been used, screwed up and thrown away.

"I thought that Adam had killed you both in the exhibition centre, I can't believe you were still moving after that giant generator hit you."

I remembered the searing pain of it and fought another wave of emotion. It was the only time I had touched my father and his contact had saved me, taking all the charge out of my body.

I sniffed and gave Lola a brave attempt at a smile, "You saved my life, you know."

"Why?"

"You bought us time to escape in there. I watched you bloom."

She laughed and flapped her hand, "Oh, it was nothing. Blooming is a trick I learnt in the nightclubs. How would I end up with someone new every night otherwise?"

"Thank heavens for small miracles, and self-pollination, whatever it involves!" I shut my eyes and asked, "How's Zac?"

If she answered, I didn't remember it because I tipped into a soft-edged dream, my father floating beside me, smiling as he held my hand.

When I opened my eyes again, Max was sitting on a chair by my bed in a dressing gown. I smiled at him and his face lifted with joy.

"Alice, you're back."

"Are you alright, Max? I hear I caused lots of trouble?"

He laughed, "You've fused half the machines in the hospital for a start, so nobody's been able to put any monitors on you. Plus, every time the nurses come in here, they have to wear such thick, rubber gloves that they can't hold any of the instruments or syringes."

I shook my head, "I feel sorry for them, the rubber gloves don't help much."

"Yes, they've realised that, but I gather that the rubber takes the edge off the shock, your aunt recommended them."

"My aunt? Has she been here?"

Max nodded and I gave a soft laugh, "She didn't bring in any cookies, did she?"

Max smiled, "There was a box by your bed, but I think Donna took them, she said they were safer in police custody."

I reached across and swallowed another sip of water.

"I gather that you save my life."

"At the expense of my own heart," he grumbled, and I laughed.

"You brought it on yourself, you idiot. You don't resuscitate a static woman in a puddle of water, no matter how wooden you are."

Someone cleared his throat and I looked across to see Nightly standing at the end of the bed, his face pinched and anxious.

"It's good to see you're recovering, Alice."

"Thank you."

"Did you hear about your father?"

I nodded grimly, "Lola told me what happened."

"I'm sorry we couldn't save him or stop Metal for you. I wish we had a different outcome."

"I assume you haven't found Adam yet?"

"He can't hide forever. I have officers all over the country looking for him, we'll find Metal eventually. In the mean time we can free up some security guards to help get your life back to normal."

I nodded glumly, thinking about my stilted, isolated life.

Max seemed to read my mind and asked, "Will you keep working at your office?"

"I have to pay my rent somehow."

He frowned, "It will be different, you know."

"Why."

"Lola, Donna and Vinny won't be working there anymore."

"Oh." I saw my future flicker into darker shades of grey. How dull would life be without them there? Who would I ever talk to? Big-eared Megan and slimy, tight-trousered Gavin?

"Perhaps I should find a new job somewhere else," I muttered but my options were slim and my voice flat. Finding new people to take on my problem was going to be miserably hard work.

"That's exactly what we were thinking," Nightly said, his eye sparkling, "That's why we'd like you to come and work with us."

"With you?"

He nodded.

"As a detective?"

"Well you would have to start on a very junior level, of course," Nightly explained, "And the pay isn't exactly great."

I shook my head and looked down at my static hands, "But I'm a complete liability!"

Max grinned, "Well no one else that works for PlOps is exactly perfect."

"How can I be a detective if I shock everyone all the time?"

"I think I might have a solution for you," Max said as Nightly opened the door and ushered in a small man with round glasses.

It was Strix, the professor Adam had employed. Not only that, he was followed by my next-door neighbour, Paul who grinned, his cheeks bulging with an unknown stash of objects.

"We have been into the maternity unit," Stryx explained to Nightly.

"Did you find what you were looking for."

Stryx's eyes shone as he nodded.

"Why are they here, together?" I asked, Max, "I thought Stryx was in league with Adam."

Max shook his head and explained, "Stryx was just the physicist that Adam brought in to set up the Van de Graff generator, he had no idea that Adam had an ulterior motive."

"Yes, and I need to pat myself on the back for my calculations," Stryx added, "because neither of you were actually killed, were you? Not by my generator anyway."

"I don't understand. What did Adam ask you to…?"

Paul interrupted with a wave, "And I'm here because I met him by the lifts downstairs. We were both lost and wandered around trying to find you."

A kerfuffle broke out in the corridor beyond and an out of breath security guard pushed into our room and pointed at Paul.

"Are you the man that was just in the maternity unit?"

Paul looked panicked, "I only followed Stryx in there, I didn't steal a baby or anything."

"How did you get past security?"

The professor replied proudly, "Oh, I have a little security scanner in my trouser pocket." He pulled out a small device about the size of a credit card with two wires hanging off it, "I used this on the door."

The security guard shook his head with disgust,

"I am charging you both with illegal entry and theft. We saw you picking something up off the nurses' station on our security cameras."

"Theft?" Asked Stryx.

"Yes sir. Can you both empty out your pockets please?"

Paul looked like a startled rabbit in headlights and turned out his trouser pockets, Stryx doing the same.

The professor pushed his glasses up his nose, "There's nothing illegal about a carrot and a chocolate bar so you must have been mistaken."

The guard wavered uncertainly as Nightly stepped towards him, flashing his badge.

"There is no need for any further action, these men are my responsibility. Can I talk to you for a few moments outside?"

The guard nodded reluctantly and gave Paul a hard look before the door closed.

As soon as it clicked shut Paul high fived the professor and reached into the side of his mouth.

"You see…" Paul produced something that looked like a TV controller from his cheek, "I told you I could fool them."

"That was incredible, I must investigate the elasticity of your skin some time, it could have great potential."

Paul grinned proudly as Max asked, "Why is this strange man with hamster cheeks here, Alice?"

"He's called Paul Gabble and he's my next-door neighbour."

Paul held up strong man arms, still flushed by his success, "Otherwise known as Deep Cheek. Deep Cheek by name Deep Cheek by nature."

The flourish didn't exactly work because none of the others knew what he was on about. He cleared his throat, dropped his arms lamely and put a vegetable onto my lap.

"I brought you this, by the way."

"A carrot?"

"Woops! Sorry. I meant, this." He passed me the Mars bar instead.

"Why did you bring a carrot to the hospital?"

"Ah, it's not for me. Watch…."

He held the carrot up to his mouth and a small head appeared out of his unused cheek, nibbling at it.

I shook my head, "The animal welfare police would have a fit if they saw that, Paul."

"Don't worry, I mouth breathe when she's there and I don't keep her pouched for long."

"I wouldn't complain if I were you, his ample cheeks have proved very useful," Stryx added. "He picked up a Transcutaneous Electrical Nerve Stimulation machine for me."

He admired the damp, black box that Paul had stolen and nodded to himself, "A beautifully simple piece of engineering that sends a pulse of electrical stimulation across the skin at regular intervals."

"What are you going to do with it?" I asked.

"With a few tweaks of this device, I think I can develop something that will allow you to discharge your electrical build up and be portable enough to wear."

I gawped in amazement and Paul asked, "What does that mean?"

"Let's not go into too much detail," Max cut in, "Alice, we have to see you fully recovered before we can begin any experiments."

"You see," Stryx began to explain to Paul, "Alice obviously has electrogenic cells that carry a negative charge and this device can be programmed to…." but he stopped because Nightly opened the door and ordered, "I need a word with you two. Out here."

As the air fell back into silence, I asked Max, "Is Paul going to start asking me lots of questions?"

"No, I'll get Nightly to explain that Stryx is completely off his rocker, you're friend has no idea about what's going on here."

I nodded, reassured.

"Stryx's machine sounds promising. Do you think he can develop something to discharge my static?"

"Who knows."

I nodded and smoothed my sheets across my lap as my thoughts drifted towards the future, I asked, "Does this new job mean that I'm going to have you as my boss, then?"

"Only if you follow my orders."

"Do I have to salute you?"

He grunted, "I can't see that happening."

"What is your first order then?"

He grinned, "Get yourself well enough to go to Lola Rose's wedding."

Chapter 30

The wedding day turned out to be perfect. The whole flower theme coming to life in a poppy-laden meadow under warm autumn sunshine.

Lola's anger with Zac had faded. His valour in the Exhibition Centre outshone his misdemeanors and the man's pasty face had nestled back in the deep pockets of her heart.

"I can't wait to see him," she buzzed as she danced on the spot looking radiant in her rose petal dress.

"What colour suit is Zac wearing Lola?" I asked as Max pinned my peony boob tube to my 'new', white strapless bra. He had been allowed into the girl's tent because I had only left the hospital two days before and my muscles were still weak.

"He's in green of course," Donna answered for her. "By the way are you going to take his surname Lola?"

She shook her head, "I can't drop my heritage, so I've decided to merge our surnames and become Lola Lee Rose. It has a certain ring to it don't you think?"

"Is your other brother coming Donna?" Vinny asked, "I always liked him."

"No, he tried to get a day release permit, but, because he's escaped so many times, the jail wouldn't issue one."

"I'm sorry I got him arrested Donna, if I had known..." I said, still guilt ridden about turning her brother in.

"Don't be stupid. They can never keep Lash in for long. He'll be free and causing havoc again before you blink."

I scowled as Max shoved a hairband on my head, "Ow, Max! You're scalping me!"

"No bloodstains allowed Max," Lola clucked, "Not until after the photos."

"I'm doing my best," Max replied stoically. "I've never had to be a lady in waiting before."

"Perhaps you should be in a dress too," Vinny quipped. Max gave him a lethal stare and put a hair grip in his mouth, trying to twist my hair into a dainty bun.

Eventually, Lola gathered us together in front of the mirror and was overjoyed by the sight.

"Don't we make an impressive bunch?"

"Of Ploids or flowers?" Max asked dryly.

"Of superheroes," Vinny answered inspirationally. "Well, not *quite* superheroes perhaps but we can always dream."

Lola led the way up the grassy aisle, with Donna and Vinny in step behind her and me clinging to Max at the rear.

As we walked up through the middle of the seats I smiled with delight. All the women in the congregation had come as flowers. Surreal pockets of daises, foxgloves, gentians, poppies, violets and fuchsias peppered the crowd, while three identical toddler primroses sat to one side swinging their feet and radiating excitement.

I even saw Stephanie, who had come as a black dahlia, squashed next to leaf green Persephone and the famous Milo Topen.

This time he was wearing a brushed velvet suit and had Persephone's thin arm resting on his thigh, her white hand giving the material a juicy squeeze.

"Don't get jealous but I gather that she is on the lookout for her fourth husband," Donna whispered to Vinny, as Persephone lent across to nibble on Milo's ear. Milo gave a contented grin and I wondered whether the Green Widow had been busy setting him up as her new harvest.

Max led me to my plastic seat, and I collapsed down, utterly exhausted by the short walk.

Nightly, sitting next to me, leant across and said, "You made it girl!"

Then he held out a hand to give me a high-five and I high-fived him back, triggering a spanking great shock that threw Nightly's elbow sharply back into Lola's mother's floral hat.

The petals crumbled, her head shunted sideways and her whole body toppled over like a bowling pin.

I gasped and stood up, trying to help but caught my hand on the line of metal chairs in front of me.

My charge, still stoked from my struggle up the aisle, fed along the row, spreading through every bottom and whipping a sharp punch into all of the plump rumps.

The congregants screamed, I staggered backward, tripped over my chair and collapsed in a tangle of metal and peony fabric.

I lay there, knotted and disgraced, as pandemonium raged around me.

Eventually a large hand extended down towards my shoulder and I reached out to grab it, seeing Max's face grinning down at me.

He stroked his stubbly chin as I extracted myself from the chair's twisted frame and laughed, "You know, we are really going to have to do something about these shocks Alice."

Not Quite A Dective

Preview chapters

With her static under control, Alice discovers a man's body in the Rotherhithe tunnel and embarks on one of the most unusual cases she will ever encounter.

Politicians and civilians are dying in odd circumstances and it leaves Max Greenstick scratching his head.

Why are they being targeted and what links all the deaths?

Max calls on a group of warrior women for help, Alice kisses a hot night-club owner and the two of them battle for their lives in a Masonic Lodge.

Life is never predictable when you work for the world's most unusual police force, however a taxonomist and an underground crypt might help them solve the next, great fun mystery.

Chapter 1

A rusty drip splattered onto Max's cheek and reminded me that we were standing at the centre of the damaged Rotherhithe Tunnel. He looked up at the crack that hair-lined across the ceiling and winced, thinking about the twenty tons of muddy river water that was streaming above our heads.

Brushing the gritty droplet away, he crouched to examine an arm that was sticking out of a crumpled van door.

Turning the flabby wrist over, he studied the white, shapeless limb, its clammy surface resembling one of the unbaked, pre-packaged baguettes that are sold in corner shops all over London.

Then Max dropped the oversized arm and let out a forlorn sigh, asking, "What the hell happened to you Dale?"

The young, uniformed PC beside us cleared her throat and cut in with facts and figures, the strip-lighting in the tunnel so dim that she struggled to read her notebook.

Summing up her findings, she finished, "There doesn't seem to have been a collision. The skid-marks show that he swerved before driving into the tunnel, scraped the van all the way down the wall and ground to a halt in the middle."

Another drip patted onto Max's shoulder and he checked, "I take it that the tunnel's sound?"

"Engineers are checking it now, we think it's safe but our RPU has closed the access route for the next 48 hours, just in case."

"What's an RPU?" I asked quietly.

"Our Road Policing Unit," Max explained.

The constable looked at me as if I was an imbecile and walked off to measure skid marks.

I ignored the insult and hunkered down beside Max, avoided a third drip, and studied the dead man in dismay.

It was hard to believe that Dale, the once cheerful bread delivery man had just become an unexplained fatality, his outsized body wedged tightly into the drivers seat of his van.

No, not outsized, outsized was an understatement, his body had swollen, tripling in volume until his skin had stretched thin, lifting away from his bones like an inflated zeppelin balloon.

Dale's bakery uniform, an outfit he was incredibly proud of, had taken a ragged hit during the expansion. The man's ironed trousers and shirt had ripped into wide gashes, his flesh welling up in pillowy lumps, his stomach had popped every button and was now bulging against the van's steering wheel, its soft indent resembling a giant hot cross bun.

I stared at Dale's swollen face, his eyes barely visible, "Do you think all this puffiness happened to him before or after the crash?"

Prodding his arm with my finger, I left an indent in the white, spongy flesh and Max caught my hand, pulling it away from the body.

He called out to the officer, "Do we need to run a forensic check?"

"No. No other vehicle was involved, and it doesn't look suspect from our point of view. We can hand over to you."

Max reached into his pocket and produced sterile wipes and two sets of gloves. "Clean your hands and put these on."
"Do you think it's something infectious?"
Max scrubbed his own fingers and then rubbed them across his rough chin.

"I have no idea. I've never seen anything like this before." He peered into Dale's poor, pudding face, the rich, yeasty smell mingling with the sweat on the dead man's skin, "Dale seems to have risen. Like a loaf of bread."

I had met Dale Riser four months ago when struggling with my own life crisis. He had picked Max and I up in his tiny bakery delivery van and given us a lift to Scotland Yard. I remembered Dale as being amicable and pleasant and, although slightly on the pudgy side, he was nothing like the overblown body before us.

Max told me to open the passenger door and check the glove compartment while he rummaged through Dale's pockets. Dale's skin deflated with each touch but slowly increased again to fill the space around him.

Eventually Max gave up trying to manhandle the doughy body and shook his head. "His pockets are clear. Any smoking guns in there?"

"I've got a packet of tissues, several bags of browny white powder, a broken comb, a book called 'The Beginning of Life's Secret', some breath freshener and a steamy magazine called 'Bakers' Babes'."

"Bakers' Babes?" he looked at the bloated white face and said affectionately, "Dale, you secret rebel. I thought you just dreamt about chocolate éclairs."

I flicked through it and held up a picture of a well-padded woman with two cinnamon swirls stuck to her chest, "He obviously had an eye for the fuller figure. This page has been really well thumbed. Apparently Didi is the Double D Danish delight this month."

I slid everything into an evidence envelope and held up the small, powder-filled bags, "What do you think these are?"

"It's not heroin, it's too grainy." He stuck a finger in the packet and smelt it, "I think it's yeast."

"How can you tell?"

"Just call me Sherlock," he replied with a grin and then flipped the bag over. The words 'Golden Loaves premium yeast batch A', were printed in bold brown lettering on the other side.

Chapter 2

The Ploid Operation's central office is based in a large converted cellar below New Scotland Yard.

Our address is impressive, but our facilities are very different from those in the shiny public building above.

The PlOps HQ is humbly surrounded by heating pipes, fuse boxes and storage cupboards. It also smells of damp mops and has very little natural lighting.

This claustrophobic, concrete floored, Detol scented basement has become my comfort zone, my training base and my social hub, after all, most of my friends are employed under its reinforced, highly protected walls.

The hotchpotch accommodation came about because our Ploid Police force doesn't officially exist.

It functions on a shoestring and safeguards human Ploids, an unglamorous, secretive population who have been born with tiny snippets of plant or animal DNA in their cells.

This DNA twist does two things; firstly, it gives us hidden abilities, some helpful, some not; and secondly, it makes us worryingly different from the rest of the human race.

Our job is to keep these people safe, under control and, more important than anything else, under the radar.

Everyone that works here is a Ploid, everyone is hiding a small secret that sets them apart, and, in case you're wondering, that includes Max and me.

One of the younger detectives in our squad, Sam Tickle, looked up with a chirpy hello and drew an extra swivel chair across for me to sit on as Max dumped our evidence bags down on his laminated desk.

Max looked keenly at Sam's frozen screen and asked, "Have you pulled anything up yet?"

Sam had apparently been born with two unusual *attachments* on his body.

I had been told about these 'extra' parts but had no idea what or where they were. Sam never spoke about them and the location of stray body parts was a hard subject to bring up in polite conversation.

Running his hands through his blonde hair, Sam said, "I've managed to trace Dale all the way through his bread round this morning, starting in Brompton at five AM and delivering orders through till nine. He travels through Chelsea, Belgravia and Mayfair as normal and then goes on to

Westminster. He drops a final batch off at the Houses of Parliament, hangs around there for about twenty minutes and then drives off. It's only at *that* point that his behaviour becomes really erratic."

Sam clicked on a few buttons and brought up a series of CCTV images showing the little white van backing the wrong way down Old Queen Street, mounting the pavement along Bird Cage Walk and driving six times around Hyde Park Corner.

"After this he branches off and shoots up and over the West Way." Sam switched to show a clip of the unstable vehicle belting along the flyover at about sixty miles an hour.
"Christ, that must be beyond the van's top speed," Max said, leaning both hands on the desk.

"Wait for this though. Dale belts like a bullet back to the Thames, hurtles along the river and is caught doing seventy down Wapping High Street by a speed camera." Sam clicked on to another image which showed a smudged picture of the van and zoomed in on the driver inside.

Dale sat behind his wheel, his whole body ballooned out under him, his cheeks giant and his eyes sunken slits in his distorted face.
"He swerved into the tunnel right after this image was caught."
"So Dale expanded before he crashed? What would make him inflate like that?" I asked.
"Perhaps it was an allergy," Sam suggested, "Or

drugs."

"Not drugs," Max mused, "Not Dale, he was too conformist. He always had a problem with his weight but that wouldn't have made him expand."

"Could it have anything to do with the yeast in his car?" I offered.

"I don't know, but something must have triggered this change. Can you and Jack check out Dale's flat, Sam?"

Sam nodded and brought up a map, zooming in on a high rise in Barking.

"What are we going to do?" I asked as Max picked up his keys.

He lifted his eyebrows, the lure of a challenge brightening his face, "I think a trip to Westminster might be in order."

Chapter 3

We approached The Houses of Parliament through St Stephen's entrance, a large, arched doorway that is flanked on either side by a lion and a unicorn.

These noble creatures, carved by skilled and long forgotten masons, embodied the traditional, regal history of Westminster, hugging elaborately carved coats of arms to their stone chests.

Deferentially passing under them, I followed Max into a high, cathedral ceilinged corridor and squirmed with political ignorance, as he pointed out the statues of Robert Walpole, William Pitt and Charles Fox.

I tried to show interest but watched Max's mouth tighten with frustration as I became distracted by the satisfying echo of my shoes on the ancient, resounding floor and wondered how many people had wanted to tap dance on it.

The Central Lobby itself was even more impressive and I fell behind, turning around in circles, dazed by the octagonal gem at the heart of British politics.

This ornate crossroads between The House of Lords and The House of Commons must have measured 18 metres across and every inch of wall space was decorated with glass mosaics, floral emblems and heraldic badges.

Towering stained glass windows and archways rose up around us, each framed with life sized statues of English and Scottish monarchs, their ermine robes draping off their broad shoulders in limestone ripples.

A pinched nosed woman was talking in a staccato voice to an assorted group of tourists:

"The origin of our current Houses of Parliament, also known as The Palace of Westminster, dates back to the 11th century when a royal residence was built in this location."

They huddled around her, their eyes travelling across the ornate room.

"This was destroyed by fire in 1512 and the site has since housed The Parliament of England. After a subsequent fire in 1834 the building was further damaged and only Westminster Hall, the Cloisters of St Stephen's, and the Jewel Tower were left standing. Reconstruction began in the gothic revival style in 1840 and..."

I edged around the fascinated group of visitors and half wanted to stop and join them as the crowd turned to look at a coat of arms on one wall, but then I caught sight of a tall, dark haired figure beyond them.

A figure with a profile that made my nerves stutter with shock.

Adam?

It couldn't be him.

Why would Adam be here?

Pushing forwards, I wriggled my way through the crowd, elbowing an upset German couple to one side as I wormed out of the densely packed group.

But I emerged to find the bronze figure of Winston Churchill looking down at me with his hands on his hips and, apart from him, the hall was empty.

I looked around me, blinking to recall the silhouette, trying to turn the brief image back into reality, but the tall figure had completely vanished.

Was I going mad?

Why had I just imagined that Adam was standing in parliament's central lobby?

I stood with my hands on my hips and stared back at Churchill, huffing to myself and drawing the attention of two female politicians in tweed suits.

The group of tourists disappeared through a twenty-foot-high archway to my left and Max called out, "Alice, what are you playing at?"

He beckoned me to follow and I nodded, my eyes still scanning each corridor and exit.

It wasn't Adam. Of course.

Why would it be?

Why would Adam Warner be here in the middle of a group of tourists for god's sake? I slapped myself on the forehead, cursing my brain for playing tricks.

Adam Warner, otherwise known as Benedict Metal, had wrecked my life.

I had fallen for him, hook, line and sinker but everything about him was a lie.

The handsome millionaire had manipulated and deceived me, planned to murder my father and left me for dead in a gigantic puddle of rainwater.

I knew that he was on the run, had been registered in the Police 'most wanted' files and would never dare to show up somewhere like this. So why did my warped mind imagine his face in the middle of a tourist attraction?

I huffed, "Get real Alice," focused my mind back on my job and scurried to catch up with Max.

It wasn't hard. Max could never walk anywhere fast because his cells had picked up fragments of a tree's genetic code, a strange quirk of nature that had caused wooden fibres to form throughout his body.

As a result, he had rough, very thick skin, was extremely heavy and had problems moving quickly. In addition, Max couldn't maintain his temperature very well and had to stick to a vegetarian diet.

These may all sound like negative points, but I have also come to realise that Max was the kindest, most level headed, solidly reliable person I had ever met and training to be an officer under him brightened my days beyond measure.

Max led me down a set of long, winding corridors until we found the rear kitchens. Once there, we tracked down Carlos Pulpo, the chef in charge of the morning food delivery.

He was small and balding with a strong Spanish accent.

"I saw Dale on his delivery and he definitely didn't-a look well."

Despite the cool air of the service corridor, Carlos had emerged from the kitchen sweating and lifted his hat to wipe a floury sleeve across his damp forehead, a white smear arched above his eyebrows.

"Can you describe how he looked?"

"His face was white like paper and his eyes, they glittered and were really round like this," he opened his eyes very wide to demonstrate.

Max asked, "Did he say anything to you?"

"Yes, he said that he had something for Lord Canther in his car."

Carlos shrugged and turned down his mouth, "I told him that Lord Canther didn't come in till-a later. So, he said he would wait. But his face, it was-a changing and changing, until it looked like a big golf ball and, his fingers... his fingers were so engorosso that they didn't bend any more. I say to him to go to a doctor and he gives me a couple of plastic packets, saying 'give these to Canther and don't tell nobody'."

"A packet like this?" Max pulled out the yeast.

"Yes, exactly that."

"And you passed them on to Canther?"

"What else was I meant to do? Dale was so sick he needed to go to his home and-a lie down."

As we walked away, I asked, "What would George Canther be doing with premium grade yeast, Max?

"There's an easy solution to that problem Alice." Max held a door open, "We need to go and ask him."

I stopped, "Do I have to?"

"Man up, Alice. Find your police legs and face your fears."

I grumbled, "Thanks for the sympathy vote," and fell in behind him.

George Canther was the inept politician who had been Adam Warner's best friend and, although he didn't have anything to do with Adam's destructive plans to kill my dad, the idea of meeting him face to face again made my insides want to run and hide.

We found George sitting in a small room that overlooked a dingy courtyard. It had dark wood on its walls, a red carpet, a red ceiling and a caramel table at its centre, giving the impression that we had stepped inside an expensive box of fudge.

George's eyes opened wide in surprise as Max and I walked in.

"Alice?" he stood up and brushed croissant crumbs off his chest, his yellow waistcoat tight around a broad midriff.

"George."

"How about that for coincidence? I haven't seen you since you…since you…"

"Since she was left for dead by Adam Warner?" Max answered wryly and George frowned.

"Well, yes, I was going to put it a bit more diplomatically."

"Attempted murder can never be put diplomatically Lord Canther. My name is Detective Inspector Greenstick and this is Alice Carter, my Junior Investigating Officer."

"Investigating Officer? Does that mean that you're a detective now, Alice?"

"Not quite a detective, George, I'm just training to be one."

George grinned, "Well, I've never been interviewed by such a pretty young officer before.

How's that beautiful girlfriend of yours who smells of roses?"

"I'm..." I squared up, trying to look more professional, "I'm here officially George."

"Of course." He put the back of his hand to his mouth and whispered, "By the way, I've always wanted to borrow some real handcuffs. The ones I buy are never strong enough to..."

Max cut in.

"We're here to make enquiries."

"Enquiries about what?" George finally looked at Max and all humour dropped away from his face.

"The movements of a bread delivery driver who called here early this morning."

"Really? A delivery man?" George looked reflective. "Well, if he was here early, I probably missed him. I was in a tad late this morning. But then I'm often late, busy keeping my girlfriends happy." He winked at me and I cringed.

Max remained deadpan. "His name is Dale Riser. I believe he left you some small packets."

"Ahh, you mean the baker? The man who was helping me with my biology lessons?"

"What lessons?"

"I used to be a teacher. I don't turn my hand in so much these days, but, as a special favour, I promised to go back and take a couple of classes on fermentation. You know, beers for the lower sixth form and all that. The boys love it."

"And he was helping you out?"

"Exactly, he dropped some yeast packets off this morning. I think I put them in my desk."

George bent to rummage through his draws and came up with a shining face and a small packet in his hands. "Here's one. Is there a problem with them?"

"Do you mind if I take this to run some tests?"

"Of course not."

"I haven't got him in trouble, have I?"

"He isn't in trouble, he's dead."

George huffed with surprise and flumped down in his seat.

"Well blow me down! What did he die of?"

"It's too early to say."

"Poor chap."

"Just as a formality. Can you give us the name of your girlfriend?"

"Ah, I may have a small problem doing that."

"What?"

"I didn't catch her name."

"Sorry?"

"Yes, more of a call girl than a long termer, but that seems to be the story of my life, more girls than hot meals. You know me, Alice."

"So we can't confirm that you were with her this morning?"

"No, but she had very long eyelashes and a laugh like a donkey. I'm sure that I can find her again if push comes to shove."

Chapter 4

Max and I made our way across to the front entrance and were just about to walk out of its wide doors when Carlos Pulpo, the sweating chef, appeared by my side out of breath, his red face white with shock.

"Carlos, what's the matter?"

"You have to come, there's a woman stealing all of our vegetables."

He tugged my arm, began running and I followed, curious to see what had happened. I took seven steps and then stopped, knowing that Max's stiff, wooden muscles wouldn't keep up.

"Keep going and I'll catch you," he panted, waving me forwards, "But wait for me if it looks dangerous."

Carlos ran all the way through the back corridors to the double kitchen doors we had visited earlier. Outside them, three other chefs were hovering, wide eyed and anxious as they pointed towards their kitchen.

"The mad vegetable woman, she's-a-in there," Carlos explained.

"Is anyone else in the kitchen with her?"

"Yes, Flavia, Morton and Pearl. I think they are hiding."

"Does she have a gun or any weapon?"

"Not a gun, but yes a knife," Carlos mimicked opening a flick knife and I swallowed, my heart racing in my chest. I couldn't wait for Max, I had to protect the kitchen staff.

Evidence of the invasion was strewn everywhere. The fridge door stood open, its salad tray yanked out and smashed to pieces. A sack of potatoes had been thrown across the room, knocking a massive pan off the industrial hob. The tomato and basil soup it once held, now sprayed across several cupboards, leaving a carnage of splatter marks and a puddle of red on the floor.

As I neared the central isle, I passed a severed onion resting, half-sliced on its surface and realised that the soup drops had begun to trail off. Ominous smears of blood took their place and my heart hammered as I inched forwards, tracing the haemorrhage to a woman cowering in one corner. Her head was lacquered with sticky fresh blood that had leaked into her white jacket like a giant red birthmark.

I needed back up, where was Max?

Grabbing a tea towel, I handed it to the woman and ordered her to run out through the main swing doors. She sobbed, nodded and scuttled towards safety.

I crept past more devastation.

Lumps of meat had been thrown across the kitchen and furious knife marks scored the storage cupboards. A chopping board lay at my feet, broken into shards of wood like fragmented bones.

A second woman dressed in a waitress bib was cowering under a service trolley. She looked at me with terrified eyes as I mouthed, "Where is she?"

The woman pointed towards a rear, walk-in refrigerator and I edged silently forwards until I reached its wide metal door.

This was standing ajar with a trail of spinach leaves, squashed tomatoes and smears of blood leading through it.

I hovered outside the crisis zone, uncertain as to whether to go in alone or wait for Max, but a loud shriek hit my ears and spurred me into action, this was not the time to hesitate.

Looking around me for a weapon, I found a stray chopping knife lying askew on the nearby counter. Reassured by the dull sheen of cold metal against my fingers, I crept silently forwards, flattening a spinach leaf as I edged the freezer door open.

A second, louder shriek drew me into the cold, claustrophobic room and I burst through it, levelling my kitchen knife as I shouted, "Don't move, police."

A furtive, munching figure gaped back at me from one of its chilly corners, a huge spinach leaf hanging from her mouth and a bloody flick-knife in her hand. The woman froze for a moment, and then returned her attention to a terrified chef who was holding a large crate that was filled with vegetables. She held out a hand and demanded, "More!"

He produced a head of broccoli and she grabbed it greedily, shovelling the green florets into her mouth like a lump of candyfloss.

The woman was overweight, dressed in a frumpy suit and had a nest of wiry, grey hair.

"Drop the knife," I ordered calmly.

The woman shook her head and grunted like a Neanderthal, spitting broccoli as she demanded, "More. I want more."

The chef held out a carrot, but she batted it away like poison.

"No, give me broccoli."

"I'm nearly out of broccoli," the chef warbled as she pressed her knife against his neck, and he held out an avocado.

"I hate avocados."

"What's your name?" I cut in.

"Bertha. Find me some spinach then."

The man rummaged through his box and found a small handful of green beans. "How about beans?"

"I can get you spinach, Bertha," I promised, "Just let the man go free."

Where the hell was Max?

The woman's brown eyes were bulging and held wild desperation in them.

I asked, "What vegetable do you like most?"

Her knife hand fell slightly as she said, "Curly kale," and shoved the beans into her mouth.

"I can get tons of curly kale. Really big, juicy leaves, and spinach, masses of it."

"You can?" The woman burped and a green trickle of spit bubbled out of her lips, "Where?"

"There's a vegetable market a few minutes away in Victoria Street, you can eat as much as you want there."

She hesitated.

"Just drop the knife, let the chef go and you can have all the vegetables you want."

The woman dropped the knife, grabbed two large handfuls of beans and pushed the chef away, shovelling the thick green pods into her mouth.

The chef scrabbled backwards and then ran for the door as the woman bent forwards, clutching her stomach.

"Bertha, are you alright?"

Her face spasmed and she screamed.

"Bertha?" I kicked the knife away as Bertha slumped back against the corner.

She grabbed my shirt front and gasped, "I didn't mean to hurt them. I just needed more food."

"I understand, I can help you."

"No. I reached the end."

"You haven't, you can stop this."

"I reached the end and now all I want is curly kale."

Bertha's shirt front bulged and its buttons popped off, arcing like fireworks over her chest.

She dragged me towards her until I was face to face and then huffed with desperate, vegetable breath, "Help me."

"I'm trying, Bertha," I reassured as she shoved her last green bean into her mouth and gagged on it, her hand twisted in my shirt as she swallowed, agony contorting her mouth.

Then her cheeks shook, her skin turned a deep purple and a volcanic eruption forced up through her mouth, releasing a torrent of green mush that hit my face like a projectile fountain.

"I can't..." she choked, "I can't hold it."

Then she became very still as a terrible grumbling, gushing noise built up inside and the volume of her stomach expanded between us, ripping open her shirt. We both looked down at the inflating skin that stretched until it was shining and paper-thin, both wondering how far the balloon could expand until, with a massive bang,

Bertha exploded, her contents bursting out in a fermented, acidic gush of sludge.

I scrabbled back as Bertha slumped, her glazed, dead eyes still holding puzzled agony.

My jacket was coated with her innards and, after scraping off some of the acrid smelling slime, I crawled back to her body, knowing that the damage was horrendous.

Pulling her legs forward to lie Bertha flat, I began pushing on her chest, the glutinous stomach cavity rippling like a marsh swamp with every movement.

My attempts were hopeless and, when I opened her lips to try mouth to mouth, an unending pool of thick green slime made me sit back helplessly.

I wiped a drip from the end of my nose with a mucous covered hand and looked up to see Max standing by the door in his pristine white shirt.

He said irritatingly, "You're obviously coping well without me then."

I pulled off my jacket and flicked a rancid sleeve at him, "We might have saved her if you had arrived earlier."

"I tried."

Max hated the fact that his muscles made him slow and I regretted the comment. "It's alright, she was beyond help. Poor Bertha. What would make a woman eat herself to death?"